"May I come aboard?"

"No! I told you I'm perfectly able." Before Faith could protest further, Connell stepped onto the wagon seat.

To her relief, he didn't try to wrest the lines from her. Still, she ordered, "Get out of my wagon. It's not fitting for you to be here or to talk to me that way."

"If I'd come to court you, Miss Beal, you'd be right. But I have no such intentions. I'm here to speak to you."

He propped one booted foot up near the break and laced his fingers together around his knee. "You're going to hire me."

"*What?* I have no intention of hiring anybody."

"Who's going to spell you along the way? Your sister?"

Faith pulled a face. "You know better."

"You wouldn't be the first traveler to need extra help on the trail. Just feed me and give me a place under the wagon to sleep and we'll call it even."

Faith sat thinking, while the wagon jostled her injured ribs. Finally, she held out her hand. "All right, you're hired."

Books by Valerie Hansen

Love Inspired Historical

Frontier Courtship #4

Love Inspired Suspense

*Her Brother's Keeper #10
The Danger Within #15
*Out of the Depths #35
Deadly Payoff #52
Shadow of Turning #57

*Serenity, Arkansas

Love Inspired

*The Wedding Arbor #84
*The Troublesome Angel #103
*The Perfect Couple #119
*Second Chances #139
*Love One Another #154
*Blessings of the Heart #206
*Samantha's Gift #217
*Everlasting Love #270
The Hamilton Heir #368
A Treasure of the Heart #413

VALERIE HANSEN

was thirty when she awoke to the presence of the Lord in her life and turned to Jesus. In the years that followed she worked with young children, both in church and secular environments. She also raised a family of her own and played foster mother to a wide assortment of furred and feathered critters.

Married to her high school sweetheart since age seventeen, she now lives in an old farmhouse she and her husband renovated with their own hands. She loves to hike the wooded hills behind the house and reflect on the marvelous turn her life has taken. Not only is she privileged to reside among the loving, accepting folks in the breathtakingly beautiful Ozark mountains of Arkansas, she also gets to share her personal faith by telling the stories of her heart for Steeple Hill Books.

Life doesn't get much better than that!

VALERIE HANSEN
Frontier Courtship

Steeple
Hill®

Published by Steeple Hill Books™

STEEPLE HILL BOOKS

Steeple
Hill®

ISBN-13: 978-0-373-82784-8
ISBN-10:   0-373-82784-9

FRONTIER COURTSHIP

Be merciful unto me, O God, be merciful
unto me: for my soul trusteth in thee; yea,
in the shadow of thy wings will I make my refuge,
until these calamities be overpast.
—*Psalms* 57:1

To Joe Roe for helping me understand mules
the way he does. And to my husband, Joe,
for talking me out of buying one and breaking
my fool neck trying to ride it!

Prologue

Ohio, 1850

Clouds boiled black. Threatening. Lightning shot across the sky in endless jagged bursts of fire. A blustery gale swept the hilltop as if bent on clearing it down to the last blade of grass.

Alone, Faith Ann Beal stood her ground in spite of the scattered drops of rain that were beginning to pelt her. She leaned into the wind for balance, determined to withstand the rigors of the early spring storm long enough to place flowers atop her mother's resting place. After the horrible tempest they'd all weathered mere days ago, it was going to take more than a little wind and water to deter her.

Faith kissed her fingertips, bent to touch them to the damp earth, then paused for an unspoken prayer before she said, "I'll keep my vow to you, Mama, no matter where that duty takes me. I promise."

Shivering, yet loath to leave, she straightened and took a shaky breath. Everyone's life had changed in literally seconds when the tornado had mowed a swath through Trumbull

County. It was still hard to believe her own mama was gone to Glory, along with so many of their closest family friends.

There was little left of the farm where nineteen-year-old Faith and her younger sister, Charity, had grown up. The lower part of the chimney still stood behind the iron cookstove, but the rest of the house had been reduced to a pile of useless kindling. The roof had blown clean off the barn Papa had built, too. Most of the livestock that had survived the storm had been rounded up and quickly sold for traveling money.

A hooded bonnet partially sheltered Faith's cold-stung, flushed cheeks and she clasped her black wool cloak tightly to her. Despite that protection, her body still trembled from marrow-deep chill. The sweet, peaceful life she had taken for granted was gone. Over. She felt as if her soul had been trapped and frozen within the numbness that now filled her whole body.

Looking down to where her mother lay beneath the freshly turned earth, she gained comfort by imagining her dear one asleep in the arms of Jesus, instead.

"Oh, Mama, why did you have to leave us?" she lamented. "And why did you make me promise to take Charity and look for Papa? What if I can't find him? What if he's lost forever, like so many of the other men who went to seek their fortunes?"

Bittersweet memories of her father's initial departure, his last hugs and words of encouragement to his family, rushed to soothe Faith's wounded spirit. Would she have reneged on her deathbed promise to her mother if she'd still had a comfortable home in which to wait for her father's return? Perhaps. Perhaps not. It was a pointless question. No choice remained.

"Oh, dear God." Her prayer was as plaintive, as wistful,

as the wind that carried it. "Please, please show me what to do. Spare me this obligation."

No reprieve came. She hadn't truly expected divine intervention to lift her burden. Instead, she found herself remembering how she'd clasped her mother's hand and listened intently as the injured woman had spoken and wept, then had breathed her last with a blissful smile softening her features as she passed on.

"Lord willing, I will come back," Faith vowed, making peace with the past as best she could. In her deepest heart she feared she would never again climb that desolate hill to look down on those verdant valleys and farms of Ohio.

Bending over, the edges of her black cloak flapping wildly in a sudden gust of frigid air, she laid a bouquet of dried forget-me-nots on her mother's grave, turned and walked resolutely away.

Behind her, the storm tore the fragile flowers from their satin ribbon and strewed tattered fragments across the bare ground, destroying their beauty for the moment in order to plant the seeds of future blooms.

Chapter One

Fort Laramie, early summer, 1850

"Look out!" Faith yanked her sixteen-year-old sister to safety, barely in time. Massive wheels of an empty freight wagon ground across the footprints they'd just left in the powdery dust.

True to her nature, Charity gave a shriek. She cowered against the blunt end of a water trough while she worried the strings of her bonnet with fluttering fingers.

Faith caught her breath and waited for her heart to stop galloping. Fort Laramie was not at all what she'd expected. It was more a primitive frontier trading post than a real army garrison. No one seemed to care a fig about proper deportment, either. The rapidly rolling freight wagon that had just cut them off would most likely have run them down without a thought if they hadn't dodged in time!

As it was, she and Charity were both engulfed in a gritty brown cloud of powdered earth, undefined filth and bothersome, ever-present buffalo gnats. The tiny insects had been driving their mules crazy since before they'd reached the lower Platte. Not to mention getting into everything. Even her biscuit dough. She grimaced at the thought.

Waiting for the worst of the blowing dust to clear, Faith spied an opportunity, took hold of her sister's hand and dragged her back out into the fray. "Come on. We can't stand here all day."

"Ouch! You're hurting me." Charity's voice was a childish whine, far less womanly than her budding body suggested it should be.

At that moment, Faith's singular intent was surviving long enough to reach the opposite side of the roadway, whether Charity liked the idea or not. She refused to slow her pace. "Oh, hush. Stop complaining. You'd think I was killing you the way you carry on."

Charity's blue eyes widened. "You might be!" Planting her heels, she brought them to a staggering halt in front of the log-and-adobe-walled trading post. "I don't like it here. It's so…so barbaric. And it stinks."

Faith couldn't argue with that. Between the passage of hundreds of draft animals, plus careless, slovenly local inhabitants and travelers, the place smelled wretched. Though the high adobe walls surrounding the fort were obviously necessary for protection, she couldn't help thinking they'd all be better off if the tightly packed settlement was more open to the cleansing wind and rain of the plains.

Intent on finding the best in their situation, she nodded toward a group of blanketed Indians sitting silently against the front of the trading post. "Look, dear. Isn't all this interesting?"

Charity pressed a lace-edged handkerchief over her mouth and nose. "Not to me, Faith Ann. I think it's awful." She lowered her shrill voice to a whisper, her sidelong gaze darting to the stony-faced Indians. "Do you suppose they understand what we're saying?"

Faith boldly assessed the native women. They were short, like herself, but twice as wide and far more rounded, and seemed to be cautiously avoiding meeting her eyes. Even the smallest children were careful not to look up at the sisters.

"I suspect they may," Faith said, a bit ashamed. "Else why would they act so shy?" Lifting her skirts, she urged Charity up the high step onto the boarded walkway. "We probably hurt their feelings."

The blue eyes grew even wider. "Do you think so? Oh, dear." The fair-haired girl blushed as a tall, manly, cavalry officer in a uniform of blue and gold doffed his hat, bowing graciously as he passed.

Faith's quick mind pounced on the occasion to raise her sister's spirits. "There," she said quietly. "See? Aren't you glad you washed up and put on your best bonnet?"

"Captain Tucker already said I looked lovely, today," Charity countered, blushing demurely and twirling the tails of the bow tied beneath her chin. "I think he's wonderful."

Her sister was appalled. "Handsome is as handsome does, as Grandma Reeder used to say." Faith likened the horrid wagon boss to an unruly billy goat, bad to the bone and just as dangerous a creature to turn your back on. She knew better than to criticize him openly, of course, because he literally held their future in his hands. But that didn't mean she had to pretend to admire him. He was a necessity. Nothing more.

Leading the way into the trading post, Faith took one whiff of hot, stale air and wished she could hold her breath indefinitely. The cloying smells were no improvement over the pungent aromas of the street, they were simply more varied. Spices, coffee beans, vinegar, molasses and salted fish added their own tang to the almost palpable atmosphere.

Judging by the overwhelming odor of sweat and smoke liberally laced with dried buffalo dung, most of the customers had long ago abandoned any notion of bathing, too. Not that Faith blamed them. Now that she and Charity had spent two long months traveling from Independence, Missouri to Fort Laramie in the Territories, they, too, realized how few of their old customs and manners fit the wearying trek.

Glancing around the crowded room for the proprietor, she spied an older woman with a topknot of gray hair. Faith watched her deftly wrap and tie a package, hand it to a matron in a dark wool dress, accept payment, then turn to help the next of the noisy, milling customers.

"Come on." Taking her sister's hand, Faith began to lead her between the piles of flour sacks, kegs of tar and barrels of pickles to wait their turn to order supplies.

They were quite near their goal by the time Faith paid full attention to the tall, broad-shouldered man at the counter ahead of them. He was as rustic as anyone present, yet different. Intriguing. For one thing, he didn't smell as if he never bathed! While his back was turned, she took the opportunity to study him.

Long, sandy-colored hair hung beyond the spread of his shoulders. Worn buckskin covered him from head to toe. When he moved even slightly, he reminded Faith of the sleek, sinewy cougar she'd seen stalking a herd of antelope through the waving prairie grasses along the lower Platte.

Embarrassed to have been so bold, she lowered her focus. The man was speaking and his voice sent unexpected shivers up her spine. Her cheeks flamed as if touched by the summer sun. Surprised by the uncalled-for reaction, Faith nevertheless set aside her ideas of proper etiquette once again and peered up at him, listening shamelessly.

The storekeeper was looking at something cradled in the man's outstretched palm. "Sorry, son. It's been too long. I can't say for certain. Maybe. Maybe not."

Sighing, the man turned to go. With the Beal sisters directly in his path there was little room for polite maneuvering.

For a heart-stopping instant his troubled gaze met Faith's. Held it. His eyes were the color of smoke, of a fog-shrouded mountain meadow at dawn. And his beard, almost the same hue as his buckskins, continued to remind her of a stalking mountain lion. Faith caught her breath.

The man nodded politely, pushing past them toward the door. Charity gave a little squeak of protest and fell back as he passed. Faith stood her ground. She had never felt so tiny in her entire life. Yet she experienced no fear, even though the plainsman was rough-hewn and dusty from the trail.

The gray-haired woman noted Faith's watchful interest. "Feel kinda sorry for him, I do."

Faith frowned. "I beg your pardon?"

"That big fella. He's lookin' for his betrothed. Might as well be lookin' for a will-o'-the-wisp. Got about as much chance a findin' one."

"Oh, dear. I'm so sorry."

Faith saw him pause to show something small to several groups of people, then square his hat on his head and leave the trading post. Thinking of her own home and family, her heart broke for the poor man. She knew all too well what it was like to lose a loved one. As she absently laid her hand over the heart-shaped onyx pendant containing a lock of her mother's hair, she vowed to add the stranger's quest to her nightly prayers.

The shopkeeper shrugged. "Happens a lot out here. Folks windin' up lost, I mean. Now, what can I do for you ladies?"

Focusing on the reason for their visit, Faith took a scrap of paper from her reticule and handed it over. "We'll need these supplies. Do you have them all?"

"Coffee'll cost you dear," the woman said, licking the point of a pencil and beginning to check off items on the list. "The flour's no problem, though. And the bacon. You'll have to go across to the mercantile if you want a paper of pins."

"All right." Faith couldn't help glancing toward the doorway where she'd last glimpsed the intriguing man. Sadly, he'd gone.

"Indians steal pins if I keep 'em here," the shopkeeper went on. "Candy, too. Regular thieves, they are."

Charity grasped her sister's arm in alarm. "You see? I told you we shouldn't have come."

"Oh, nonsense. Surely you don't think there were no thieves at home in Ohio." Faith shook her off.

"You in a hurry?" the proprietress asked. "Otherwise we'll have this packed up and ready to go in an hour or so. Have to send Will out to the smokehouse for another side of bacon. You put aside enough bran to pack it in a barrel real good like?"

"Yes. And there's no hurry," Faith assured her, ignoring Charity's scowl. "Our friend Mr. Ledbetter is at the blacksmith's getting a wagon wheel fixed. No telling when we'll be ready to go back to the train."

"I got lots o' pretty Indian trinkets," the woman urged. "Or you could do what most of the ladies do and go wonder at the dry goods in the mercantile. They got twenty…thirty new bolts o' calico since winter. Been meanin' to go have a look-see myself. Never seem to find time." She wiped her hands on her apron. "Tell 'em Anna Morse sent you."

Faith thanked her for her advice. "We'll be back in a bit, Mrs. Morse. We're the Beal sisters. This is Charity and I'm Faith. We're with the Tucker train."

"Yes," Charity added proudly. "Captain Ramsey Tucker is kindly looking after us."

Faith noticed an immediate change in the woman's countenance. Her gray eyebrows knit, her wrinkles becoming more pronounced as her eyes narrowed in a wary expression. It was somewhat of a relief for Faith to see that she, herself, was not the only one disturbed by references to the captain.

That realization gave her pause. What might Mrs. Morse know about their wagon train? And would she reveal the truth, if asked?

Faith glanced nervously at her sister. Any candid conversation must not take place in front of Charity. The silly girl was too smitten with Tucker to be trusted to hold her tongue, especially if the news was disturbing.

Pondering alternatives, Faith recalled their schedule. They were to lay over in camp the rest of today and tomorrow before pushing on to California. In that length of time she was bound to be able to sneak back into the fort and make some discreet inquiries of Anna Morse. She only hoped she could live with whatever secrets were revealed.

The sun had crested and started toward the west as Faith waited on the plank walkway in front of the trading post. A small bundle from the mercantile, wrapped in brown paper and tied with string, lay at her feet where it had been for the past three hours. The rest of their purchases remained inside.

Shielding her eyes from the afternoon glare, she seemed oblivious to the people pushing past. She fanned her burning cheeks with an embroidered handkerchief while looking left and right in anticipation of the arrival of the Ledbetters' wagon. Repairs to the wheel must be taking a very long time.

Charity tugged at her sister's sleeve. "It's fearful hot and dusty out here. I'm going back into the store." She pulled harder. "Come with me."

"Just a moment more." Faith pushed her slat bonnet off the back of her head, letting it hang down her back by its strings while she dabbed away the drops of perspiration on her forehead.

"No. I'm frightened," Charity insisted. "I told you, Ramsey…Captain Tucker…warned us not to come into town at all. He said he'd take care of buying our supplies for us. He was right. We should have listened to him."

Faith could hardly tell her gullible sister that the nefarious captain was not going to get his hands on any more of their money if she could help it. Not even to run simple errands. She'd paid dearly for their spot with the train because she hadn't known any better. Now, she knew they'd been cheated. She wouldn't play the fool twice.

Instead of arguing she merely said, "We'll be fine."

Cupping one pale hand around her mouth, Charity made a pouting face and leaned closer to whisper. "The Indians get more terrible looking all the time. See them scratching? I hate to think why. Makes me want to dip the hem of my skirt in kerosene to ward off the fleas!"

"You're being a silly goose." Faith took her sister's shoulders, physically turned the girl to face the door to the trading post, shoved the paper-wrapped bundle into her hands and gave her a push. "All right. Go on. Suffer in the stench of those stacks of awful buffalo hides if you want. I'm perfectly happy out here."

Charity turned back. "The captain told us to stay together."

"Captain Tucker is merely our guide," Faith said flatly. "I will not pretend we aren't beholden to him, but neither will I cede to his every command."

"I can't believe you're being so mean. He's a brave and wonderful man."

"That remains to be seen." Faith took a deep breath and made a decision. "Look, I can't abide standing here wasting my time any longer. I have wash to do and food to prepare back in camp. Fixing one loose wagon wheel shouldn't take this long. I'm going to walk to the blacksmith's and see what's delayed Mr. Ledbetter."

Charity gasped. "You can't do that! Not here. Not alone."

"Then you'll come with me?"

The pale girl stepped back quickly, clutching the package to her breast. "I can't. It's not fair to ask me."

That reaction was what Faith had counted on. Two months as her sister's constant companion and chaperone had been an insufferable trial. If the Lord hadn't granted her an extra dose of patience, she'd surely have throttled the girl by now, especially when Charity had claimed she'd accidentally lost both their black dresses while washing them in a flooded river and they'd been forced to cease wearing mourning for their mother far too soon. For Faith, a few minutes respite from her familial duty would be like a breath of cool breeze in the midst of oppressive heat.

She composed herself, then said, "All right, Charity, dear. Then why don't you go inside and check the rest of our order to be certain everything is exactly as it should be?"

"I could do that." The younger woman began to blink and smile sweetly. "The captain would be proud of my efficiency, wouldn't he?"

"Undoubtedly. I'm certain Mr. Ledbetter will tell him you are the picture of virtue. And you needn't worry about me. It's obvious the army has plenty of men here to keep the peace."

"Oh. Well, if you're sure you'll be all right…"

Wheeling quickly, Charity gathered her skirts and darted through the door.

Faith breathed a relieved sigh as she turned away to look down the street. She'd often thought it must be a sin to wish for self-serving favors from heaven, yet there were times she couldn't help hoping some suitable young swain would soon rescue her from her sister's trying foolishness.

Tiny flies continued to buzz around Faith's head. Beads of perspiration gathered on her temples while sweaty rivulets trickled down her back between her shoulder blades. Ignoring the discomfort, she squashed her bonnet back on her head, whipped the ties into a loose bow and started off.

Wide cracks between the rough-sawed boards of the walkway captured the narrow heels of her best shoes, forcing her to either descend into the street or chance taking a bad fall. Since Charity had never learned to handle the mule team, Faith certainly couldn't afford to be incapacitated. Not unless she wanted to be compelled to put up with whatever form of retaliation or retribution the unctuous Captain Tucker decided to arrange.

Since their last set-to over his brutality toward one of her mules that very morning, she'd suspected that the captain would shortly come up with some lame excuse why relief drivers, Ab or Stuart, could no longer be spared to handle her wagon. Well, fine. It would be her pleasure to show Ramsey Tucker that at least one Beal sister was capable of something besides giggling helplessness. If he wouldn't provide the assistance he'd promised when she'd joined the train, Faith would handle the lines herself, just as she had at home in Ohio.

She set her jaw. Tucker had underestimated her for the last time. She'd stood up to him before and she'd do it again. And, oh, was he going to be scalded!

Faith shuddered at the memory of his dark, penetrating eyes, the way he'd stared at her, spitting that disgusting tobacco juice at her feet. He was not a person to be taken lightly. But then, neither was she.

Clouds of choking dust billowed from beneath passing rigs as Faith hurried down the street. Grasping the brim of her bonnet, she pressed it closer to her cheeks. The din around her was so loud, so packed with shouts, curses, strange tongues and the sound of rolling wagons and clanking harness traces that Faith didn't see the danger or hear anyone call out a warning until a melee erupted directly in her path.

A door flew open. Glass shattered. Shutters banged. Three uniformed cavalrymen careened off the walkway and down into the street, tumbling, pushing, swinging and cursing as they went.

Faith jumped aside. One of the men, a thin, filthy fellow who reminded her of a rickety calf, was bleeding from his nose. He wiped the blood on his dirty sleeve, then flung it aside, dotting her skirt with ugly red splotches.

Disgusted, Faith was wiping at the stains in the green calico when a fourth man lurched off the porch. He hit her a jarring blow with his full weight. Breathless, stunned, she went sprawling in the dust.

For an instant she lost track of where she was or what had happened. All too soon, it came back to her. Raising up on her forearms she tasted the gritty substance of the well-traveled street and found her mind forming thoughts quite inappropriate for a lady. Her only clean dress was a grimy mess, her bonnet was askew and, worst of all, no one in the crowd seemed to even notice.

Pausing on her knees, she assessed her pain. Something was very wrong. If she hadn't been in such unexpected misery she would very likely have lectured the careless men on the impropriety of brawling in the streets. As it was, she knew she'd be doing well to merely maneuver out of harm's way.

One of the soldiers had collapsed, gasping and retching,

in a drunken haze beneath the hitching rail. The larger of the two remaining was beating the rickety-calf man to a pulp.

Gathering her soiled skirts, Faith lifted them above her shoe tops with one hand, lurched to her feet and stumbled around a corner. Finding a bare wall, she leaned against it and closed her eyes.

It hurt to move. To breathe. She pressed both palms hard against her aching side. Dear God! As much as she hated to admit it, Charity was right. The streets of Fort Laramie were no place for a stroll.

At the passage of a shadow across her flushed face, Faith's eyes snapped open. The muscled shoulder of an enormous reddish-colored horse was a scant three feet from the tip of her nose. She heard saddle leather creak as its rider leaned forward.

"You should have better sense," he grumbled.

Her blurry vision focused. That beard. That hair. The buckskins. It was him. The man from the trading post who was searching for his lost bride-to-be. She drew a short breath and winced as pain shot from her side to her innards. "Sarcasm is quite uncalled-for, sir."

"Where's your man?"

"I hardly think that is a proper question," Faith shot back, grimacing in spite of herself.

He dismounted beside her, his tone a little more gentle. "You're right. My apologies. Guess I've been alone on the trail too long. Are you badly hurt?"

Suddenly not certain, Faith sagged back against the wall. "I...I don't think so." Taking a deeper breath, she assessed the searing pain that increased every time she moved or dared inhale. "Oh, dear."

"Can you walk?"

"Of course." What a silly question. Why, she'd never had

a sick day in her life, not even when she'd been left to try to cope after Mama had died. Faith bit her lower lip. Today's problems were sufficient for today, as the Good Book said.

The plainsman stood by, waiting, his mere presence lending her added fortitude. She would straighten up, stand tall and prove to him she was fine. The moment she tried, however, agony knifed through her body, bending her double. She bit back a cry.

"Have you got a penny?" he asked, sounding disgusted.

The slim cords of Faith's reticule were still looped around her wrist. Had she been in better command of her faculties, she might have questioned his request. Instead, she raised the drawstring bag to him without speaking.

"Good, because I don't. I'd hate to waste a whole dollar on this."

Although pain was coursing through her like the racing water of a rain-swollen stream, she was still capable of a modicum of indignation. "I beg your pardon?" Her mouth dropped open. What audacity! The man had invaded her reticule to withdraw the asked-for penny.

"This will do." Flipping the oversize copper coin into the air and catching it several times, he whistled at a young boy who was passing. "Son! Over here."

The boy's face lit up when he spied the coin. "Yessir?"

Connell bent low, holding out the penny as inducement. "I want you to fetch that Mrs. Morse from the trading post. You know her?"

"Yes, sir!"

"Tell her a lady is hurt and needs her. Then bring her here and I'll pay you for your trouble."

Young eyes darted from the coin to the pale, disheveled woman leaning against the wall. "Did you hurt her, mister?"

Faith managed to smile. One hand remained pressed tightly to her ribs, but she put out the other and laid it on the buckskin-clad arm of her Good Samaritan. "No," she said. "There was an accident and this gentleman came to my rescue. Now, hurry. Please."

"Yes, ma'am!" The boy was off like a shot.

Breathing shallowly to minimize her pain, Faith peered at the man on whose sturdy arm she was leaning. Soon, she would release her hold on him. Just a few seconds more and she'd feel strong enough to stand alone.

"I do thank you for looking after me," Faith managed. "No one else seemed to even notice."

"They noticed." How delicate she seemed, Connell Mc-Clain thought. Her skin was soft, like the doeskin of his scabbard, only warm and alive. And her eyes. No wonder they had reminded him of a deer's the first time he'd looked into them. They were the most beautiful, rich brown he'd ever seen.

He scowled. Better to keep the woman talking and draw her thoughts away from her injuries. She didn't look well. If she passed out on him before Mrs. Morse arrived, he didn't know what he'd do with her.

"The Indians wouldn't help you because they don't dare touch a white woman," he explained. "And if the soldiers got involved, they'd have to admit they were the cause of your troubles. That could mean the stockade."

"Oh." The woman glanced at the street and seemed to realize passersby were eyeing her with curiosity. "I'll bet I look a fright."

"You have looked better," he said, remembering the strong response he'd had when he'd almost bowled her over in the trading post. Some of the pins had come loose from her hair and it was tumbling down over her shoulders. He hadn't imagined that the coffee-colored tresses under her bonnet would be nearly as comely as they actually were.

Nodding, she folded her arms more tightly around her body in an apparent effort to cope. Between the sweltering heat and the pain she was evidently experiencing, it was little wonder she was struggling so.

"I expect they think I'm your kin, so they're leaving us alone," he offered.

"I'm truly sorry to have inconvenienced you, sir. If I had money to spare, I'd gladly repay you for your kindness. My sister and I are on our way to California. After arranging our passage I'm afraid we have very little left."

A sister? Connell vaguely recalled that there had been another woman with her in the trading post, but for the life of him, he couldn't picture what she'd looked like.

An unexpected twinge caught her unaware and she gasped before she again gained control of herself. Tears gathered in her eyes. He hesitantly cupped her elbow with as light a touch as he could manage and still support her.

"I'm sorry for being such a ninny," she said, with a faint smile. "I'm usually quite brave. Really, I am."

"I'm sure you are, ma'am."

"I can't be seriously injured, you know." She looked east toward the wagon camp. "I may have to drive the team when we leave here." Her voice trailed off. She could tell from the way the man was looking at her that he had already decided she was, indeed, badly hurt. Coming on top of so much throbbing pain, the thought of not being able to function on her own was too much for her.

Darkness pushed at the edges of her vision. Flashes of colored light twinkled like a hundred candles on a festive Christmas tree. Nausea came in waves. She fought to keep her balance, but it was no use. Closing her eyes, she began a slow-motion slide toward the ground.

Connell saw her going out. The doe's eyes glassed over, then rolled back in her head. He cast around for help. Where had that fool boy gotten to?

The plainsman instinctively grabbed Faith's arms, then made the split-second decision to catch her up in spite of his misgivings. Next thing you knew, he'd probably be shot by the woman's jealous husband or brother for trying to help her. They'd bury him on the prairie in an unmarked grave and forget he'd ever lived. Then, who'd be left to find out what had happened to poor Irene?

Connell lifted the unconscious Faith in his arms, trying not to jostle her ribs as he swung her across his chest. She was so tiny. Barely there. He couldn't just walk away and ignore her plight. He wasn't going to leave her until he'd seen to it she was safe and well cared for.

He could only hope that someone, somewhere, was doing the same for his intended bride.

Chapter Two

Connell met the breathless boy halfway to the trading post.

"She die, mister?"

"No. Fainted. Where's Mrs. Morse?"

"She ain't comin'. I told her what you said but she didn't believe me." He trotted alongside, struggling to keep up with Connell's long, purposeful strides. "Kin I have my penny, anyhows?"

Connell muttered under his breath. No telling what had happened to the coin. Chances were he'd dropped it when he'd had to catch the girl.

He glanced down at the eager child. "Look in the dirt, where we were before. If it's not there, follow along and I'll get you another. And bring my horse. His name is Rojo. That's Mexican for red. Call him by name and he won't give you any grief. He's a full-blooded canelo I picked up in California and I'd hate to lose him. I'd never find another one like him out here."

"Aw, shucks. You said…"

Connell was in no mood for argument. "Go, before somebody else finds your money." The boy seemed to see the logic in that suggestion, because he took off like a long-eared jackrabbit running from a pack of coyotes.

Crossing to the trading post, Connell and his frail burden solicited few inquisitive glances. He looked down at the sweet face of the girl. Her cheeks were smudged and her hair nearly undone. The bonnet hung loosely by its ribbons. Her doe eyes were closed, but he could still picture them clearly.

She stirred. Long, dark lashes fluttered against her fair skin like feathers on the breeze. She was so lovely, so innocent looking, lying there, the sight of her made his heart thump worse than the time he'd fought with Fremont against the Mexicans in San Jose in '45.

The quick lurch of his gut took him totally by surprise. He stared down at the girl. She was all-fired young. Much younger than Irene. Couldn't be more than eighteen or nineteen if she was a day. That made her ten or so years younger than he was; about the same distance apart in age as his mother and father had been.

Clenching his jaw, he tried unsuccessfully to set aside the bitter memories of his childhood, the mental image of his mother's funeral and the cruel way his father had behaved afterward. If it hadn't been for Irene and her family taking him in and showing him what a loving home was supposed to be like, no telling what would have become of him back then.

Connell took a deep breath and started across the street, his purpose redefined, his goal once again in focus. It didn't matter how attracted he might be to this woman. Or to any other. It was Irene he had to think about, Irene he had sworn to find. To marry. If he had to spend the rest of his life looking for the truest friend he had ever had, then he would. Without ceasing.

The unconscious girl moaned as Connell mounted the walkway in front of the trading post. Several Indians edged out of his path.

As he made his way into the store, all conversation ceased. He headed straight for the proprietress.

Anna Morse clapped a hand to her chest. "Land sakes! The boy was tellin' the truth."

"Obviously." The plainsman reached her in six quick strides, his tall cavalry boots thumping hollowly on the floor. "Where can I put her?"

"Let's take her upstairs," Anna said. "Her sister's right over…" Pointing, she snorted derisively. Charity had fainted dead away. The girl lay draped across a stack of flour sacks while two other women and a child patted her hands and fanned her cheeks. "Never mind. We'll see to her, later. Bring Miss Faith this way."

Faith. Connell turned that name over in his mind. He'd have guessed she might be called after a flower or some famous woman from the Bible, like Sarah or Esther. Hearing that she was, instead, Faith, gave him pause. Yet it fit. A strong trait, a gift necessary for survival especially when crossing the plains, Faith was appropriate. How was it the scripture went? Something about…"if you have faith as a grain of mustard seed, you can say to a mountain, move, and the mountain will move." This tiny woman was going to need that kind of unwavering faith if she was to survive the many rigors that would face her on the trail.

The upstairs room Anna led him to was small but clean. An absence of personal items led Connell to believe Mrs. Morse probably rented it out whenever she could. Careful not to jostle his limp burden, he lowered Faith gently onto the bed.

As he straightened and slipped his arm from beneath her shoulders, he reached up to gently smooth the damp wisps of hair from her forehead. The act was totally instinctive. Until the older woman cautioned him, he didn't think about how improper his actions must look.

"That'll do, mister. We're beholden to you for totin' her here." Anna wedged between him and the prone figure, which was beginning to stir. "I'll take good care of her."

Connell nodded and touched the brim of his hat. "Yes, ma'am. It doesn't appear the sister'll be much help, that's a fact." Keeping his voice low, he added, "This one got herself knocked down by a bunch of drunken horse soldiers."

"Figures. I swan, this old world has got to be nearin' judgment day."

"Don't know about that, ma'am, but there's four boys in blue who will be when I get ahold of them."

"You ain't plannin' on startin' trouble, are you?"

"No, ma'am." Connell took a few backward steps toward the open bedroom door. "Finishing it."

Anna made a noise of disgust. "Bah! All men are fools. Every bloomin' one of 'em."

At that, the plainsman managed a half smile. "You're probably right." Peering past her, he tried to get another glimpse of Faith. "You think she'll be all right? I reckon her ribs are broke."

"Soon as she comes to, I'll be able to tell for sure."

Turning toward the door, Connell paused. "I'll be back to pay you for whatever the girl needs."

The older woman shook her head. "You ain't her kin. You done enough."

He scowled, his helpful attitude hardening into determination. "I told you why I was here. Whatever I do for Miss Faith, it'll be like I'm doing it for my Irene, too. Understand?"

Anna nodded solemnly. She wiped her hands on her apron. "That, I do. Long as you remember your money buys you no rights to the Beal sisters."

The growing smile lifted Connell's mustache. "Oh, it won't

be my money," he said. "I aim to collect damages due from the sons o'—'scuse me, I mean the *soldiers* who did the hurting."

That seemed to satisfy Anna's sense of decency. "Good for you. Think they'll pay up?"

For Connell, the question was already answered. His decision was firm. It wouldn't take but a few minutes of his time to enforce justice on Faith Beal's behalf. To see to it that she was recompensed. He was certain that was what Irene would want him to do.

"Yes, ma'am, I do," he said flatly. "Those four boys'll be real tickled to help out. You'll see."

Anna shook her head. "I don't want to see any of it. You do what your conscience tells you to do, son, but leave me out of it. You hear?"

Tipping his hat, Connell nodded in affirmation and left her. By the time he'd reached the bottom of the staircase, his anger in respect to Faith's plight was white-hot. How dare those drunken fools abuse a refined, gentle soul like her and then ignore what they'd done without so much as a backward glance or a word of apology?

He left the trading post, jumped down to the street and started off toward the saloon. Very little time had passed since the incident. He had no doubt he'd easily be able to locate the perpetrators.

The door to Maguire's Saloon swung back with a bang as he straight-armed it and headed for the bar. The place wasn't fancy red velvet and sparkling chandeliers like the plush parlors of San Francisco. Nor was it any cleaner than the rest of the fort. At each end of the bar stood gaboons, wooden boxes filled with sawdust, that served as poor men's spittoons. By the look of the floor, no one there took very good aim.

Connell scanned the crowd. Nearly a dozen men were

dressed in the blue of the cavalry but only a few were as filthy and bruised as the guilty parties he was looking for had to be. Bellying up to the bar, the largest of the four was lifting a glass and laughing as another member of the disgusting quartet gave his impression of Faith's shocked facial expression after her fall.

Silent, Connell approached, his jaw set, his fists clenched. The loudmouth had reddish hair and a swollen eye as purple as a ripe plum. When Connell tapped him on the shoulder, he turned, still chuckling, with a sarcastic what-do-you-want? look on his face.

Connell reached up and whipped off the man's hat, turning it over to serve as a collection basket.

"Hey! What the…?"

"For the lady you boys hurt," Connell said. The low, menacing timbre of his voice was as threatening as his words. "Ante up."

The man cursed. "Now wait a…"

Connell had grasped the redhead by the shirtfront and hoisted him high in the air before anyone could interfere. As formidable as the soldier was, he was no match for such ferocious rage and brute strength. The others began to edge away.

"All of you," Connell shouted. "Freeze where you are and fill the kitty." His head cocked toward the hat, which had landed on the bar when he'd grabbed the loudmouth. "Now."

He waited till three soldiers had complied before releasing the fourth. "Your turn."

"I ain't got no money to waste on no stupid settler."

Connell's fist connected hard with the man's jaw, sending his body sliding along the front of the bar where it finally came to rest in a heap near the gaboon. He gestured to the man's friends. "Pick him up."

The smallest of the three shook his head violently and

backed away, his hands in the air. Thin and much shorter than the others, he'd obviously gotten the worst of the brawl. "No way. He wakes up, he'll kill me."

"Judging from what's left of your sorry face, it looks like he nearly did, already." Connell glanced at the remaining two. "You think your friend would be interested in making his fair share of the contribution?" He held out the hat. The few coins it contained chinked together.

"Sure, sure. Ol' Bob, he's a regular fella. He just gets nasty when he's keepin' company with John Barleycorn, is all." The closest one reached into his companion's pockets and came up with a fistful of coins. "This do ya?"

When the soldier dropped the money into the hat, Connell gathered it in his hand, briefly calculated how much there was, then threw the empty hat across the face of its unconscious owner. "He wakes up, you tell him for me that the lady is much obliged."

"Yes, sir. Sure will."

Turning away, Connell stalked out. He was certain neither Miss Faith Beal nor Mrs. Morse would approve of his methods, yet they'd have had to admit they were effective. There was no need to go into detail when he delivered the "donations" to the women. It was enough to know that he'd righted a wrong. An innocent young woman wouldn't have to suffer more hardship because of the yahoos who'd harmed her.

Thinking about Faith's vulnerability, he took a deep breath and exhaled noisily as he reentered the trading post. Near the door, the pale girl with corn-silk hair still sat atop the filled sacks. White flour dusted the back and shoulders of her blue dress, a clear reminder of her fainting spell. An older man and several women were fussing over her. Unsure of whether or not to approach, Connell paused to listen to what they were saying.

"No! I can't stay here. I just can't," the girl whimpered. "Please, take me back to camp with you."

"Now, Miss Charity," the man was cajoling, "you'll be perfectly safe with Mrs. Morse. Your sister might need you."

"No! No, no, no." She stamped her small foot. "It wasn't my idea to come here in the first place and I'll not stay. I demand you deliver me back to Captain Tucker."

One of the matrons patted Charity's hand. "There, there, dear. Of course we'll see that you get to the captain. I'm sure your sister is in good hands."

Shaking his head in disgust, Connell watched them leave before he started for the staircase.

Anna Morse met him halfway up and solidly blocked his path. "Well?"

"The sister left," he said, scowling.

"Figures. What about the fellas what done the hurting? Did you clean their plows for 'em?"

"Enough to get their attention. I never did intend to start another set-to." He transferred the money he'd collected to the proprietress. "If you want more…"

"No need. This'll be plenty. I bandaged her myself. You was right. She's got a few sore ribs."

"You bound her tight?"

"'Course. I did fine and so did she. She's a spunky one, that Faith."

Connell nodded. "That she is."

"Too bad about her ma."

They made their way to the base of the stairs, Connell in the lead. "Her ma?"

"Got kilt by the same twister that wiped out their house and most of their belongings," Anna told him. "That's why she and that worthless sister of hers are on their way to Californy to look for their pa."

"Alone?" Connell couldn't believe how many women tried to cross the plains without proper help or preparation. He didn't fault them for their courage, only for their lack of common sense.

"That's right. Ramsey Tucker's supposed to be lookin' after them. To my thinkin', they'd be better off all by themselves than trustin' him." Heading toward the busy young man who was trying to wait on three families at once, she slipped the coins Connell had collected into her apron pocket. "I'm comin', Will."

Connell followed and asked, "When does the Tucker train pull out?"

"Tomorrow." Anna smiled with understanding. "Don't fret. Our girl'll be able to travel just fine. Now, scoot. I got work to do."

It wasn't till Connell was outside that he remembered what Faith had said about having to drive her own team. Well and whole, she might be able to do it. Hurt the way she was, the pain would be dreadful. Besides, she might make her condition worse. Maybe even puncture a lung.

Muttering and gritting his teeth, Connell argued that Faith wasn't his concern. Irene was. He found his horse where the boy had left it, rechecked the cinch on his saddle, then mounted. It was time to head for Maguire's or some such place. The drink and eats he'd promised himself a whole lot earlier were way overdue.

Standing in the upstairs room in her chemise and drawers, Faith listened at the slightly open door, then quietly eased it closed. Thanks to the tight bindings around her midriff, she'd managed to get out of bed without too much discomfort. She hated corsets. Always had. But she had to admit wearing one might have spared her poor bones.

Placing her forehead and palms against the wood of the door, she closed her eyes for a moment, hoping that somehow, when she opened them again, her current predicament would prove to be no more than a bad dream.

Such was not the case. Breathing shallowly when she really wanted to sigh deeply, she straightened and took a long look at the room. The bed sagged in the middle where the ropes had stretched, but at least it was clean. Mrs. Morse had hung her soiled dress on a peg next to the pine washstand. On the floor in front of it was a small rag rug, just like the ones Grandma Reeder used to make, and laid across the foot of the bed was a plain lawn wrapper.

Barefoot, Faith crossed to the bed and slowly threaded her arms into the wrapper, folding it closed. The process was painful, though not nearly as bad as she suspected trying to put on her dress would be. Pensive, she tied the sash and padded across the cool wooden floor, in search of a breeze from the open window.

The wide, busy street lay below, it's clattering traffic an ongoing performance. Wagons of all shapes and uses were passing, as well as riders and enough foot traffic to more than fill the fondly remembered old streets of Burg Hill. In the midst of all the hubbub sat a man in buckskin astride a giant horse the color of a rusty rose.

With a trembling hand, Faith drew aside the lacy curtains and studied the traveler who had so recently borne her to safety in his arms. It was a kindness she hadn't expected here in this wild country. She fingered her pendant and thought of home. Of family. Oh, how she wished her mother were there to be a companion in her travails, to understand her the way Charity never could.

Well, at least her Good Samaritan had the hope of someday finding his missing betrothed, Faith mused, looking down at him and stifling a tiny twinge of jealousy. She would never again see her dearest ones or the home place she'd loved, no matter how hard she wished or prayed or toiled.

Suddenly realizing she had taken her deliverance for granted, Faith was penitent. Not only had she been spared the fate her poor mother had suffered, she'd been rescued a second time since then. Given the unsympathetic reactions of the other travelers she'd encountered at the fort, it was a wonderment she was not still lying in a heap in the street.

In retrospect, Faith realized she'd drifted in and out of consciousness while being carried to the trading post. She'd felt the rumble of the man's voice beneath his buckskin shirt as he'd told the boy she'd fainted. There was also a vague recollection of a gentle hand on her face as someone touched her to brush back a lock of hair. Could that have been him?

Stepping in front of half of the curtain, she toyed with the loose curls that hung down over her shoulders. Decent, grown women didn't let anyone but their husbands see them with their hair thus, Faith reminded herself. And they certainly didn't stand in a window clad in nothing more than their chemise and a wrapper. Yet she didn't move away, even when the man's head tipped back and he gazed boldly in her direction.

Did he know who he was watching? He must. If not, why stare like that? There was plenty to see in the street below without bothering to peer into a tiny window fifteen feet above the entrance to the trading post.

Faith knew she should step back into the shadows. Displaying herself was indecent. Wanton. Still, there was the remembered touch of a hand on her cheek, the pounding of a strong heart beneath her ear as he bore her away in his arms, and the concern she'd glimpsed in his eyes as mental darkness had overcome her.

One more look, one more thought of intense gratitude

wouldn't hurt. She knew she'd never see the man again. He had a quest of his own—the search for his bride—while she must complete her own journey. That their divergent paths had crossed at all was amazing. She only wished she'd had an opportunity to thank him in person.

Wanting to memorize the image of her rescuer so she could later pay proper homage to his compassion, Faith swayed closer to the thick, white-painted casement. Beneath his beard and mustache, she thought she saw a smile, though it was impossible to be certain at such a great distance. Hopeful, she raised her hand as if bestowing a blessing.

In reply, the man tipped his hat, then squared it on his head, reined his horse hard and rode off.

Faith's heart pounded as she watched him go. Clearly, he'd entered her life to profoundly influence it. No matter how far she traveled or how many more years she lived, she'd never forget him.

Sudden awareness made her breath catch. Of course! The man on the red horse had been the answer to her fervent prayers for deliverance. Accepting that notion tempered her perspective of the ordeal in which she was currently embroiled. Without his amazing intervention she might actually have died, alone and ignored.

And gone to be with Jesus, she countered, certain her lonely soul would approve of the idea, just as it had ever since her mother's fatal accident. This time, however, Faith found she was no longer looking forward to joining Mama in heaven. Yes, she wanted to see all her loved ones again someday, but her earthly tasks weren't complete. Not yet.

By proving she wasn't truly alone in her current trials, a heaven-sent stranger had inadvertently opened her eyes—and her heart—to the possibility of a bright, worthwhile future.

And she didn't even know his name.

Chapter Three

Near evening, the sun turned the adobe walls of Fort Laramie a pale crimson. Myriad cooking fires were burning in the distant wagon camps. Anna brought Faith a bowl of warm gruel with pork trimmings and a cup of broth made with boiled, dried vegetables.

"I'd a fetched you more if I'd figured you could hold it," she said, setting the small pewter tray down on the top of the washstand.

"Whatever you've made is fine." Faith managed a smile and arose with care, her bare feet silent on the wooden floor. Thoughtful, she paused. "I don't know when I'll be able to repay you for all your kindness. If I were going to be here longer I'd offer to work off my bill."

"Ain't necessary. It's been paid."

"But…how? Surely my sister didn't…"

"Not her. Forgive me for sayin' so, but she's about as worthless as a pocket on a pouch."

Blushing, Faith stifled a chuckle. The analogy was funny and most apropos. "Then, how was it paid?" Tempted by the aroma of the hot broth, she raised the cup to sip while Anna spoke.

"Them fellas what busted you up took up a fine collection—with a little prodding."

Faith paused as the liquid trickled down her throat, warming her against the cool of the evening. "Prodding? I don't understand." But in her heart, she did. Unless she missed her guess, her buckskin-clad benefactor had once again come to her rescue. A faint smile began to lift the corners of her mouth.

Anna snickered. "From the look in your eye, I'd say you've got the right idea. Didn't see it happen, myself, but talk is, your Mr. McClain dusted the floor of Maguire's with them boys in blue."

"Oh, dear." Faith pressed her free hand to the base of her throat, over the mourning pendant. It was strange to hear the big man referred to as her Mr. McClain. So, *that* was his name.

"Quite a sight, they say, and I can sure see why. That boy's a big one, all right. Strong as Finnegan's ox."

"He's hardly a boy," Faith observed, sipping more broth to cover her urge to smile at the ridiculous comparison. "Did he say what his given name was?"

Anna raised an eyebrow. "Can't say as he did. Why?"

"I just wondered."

"It's good you've got a friend like him, considering the mess you're in."

Lowering the cup of broth, Faith set it aside before taking advantage of the comment to ask, "When you say mess, are you referring to my injury, or to our business dealings with Ramsey Tucker?"

"Both. Mostly Tucker, I reckon."

Faith reached for the older woman's callused hands, clasping them tightly. "Please. I must know everything you've heard."

"You won't like it."

"Ramsey Tucker has made more than one inappropriate suggestion regarding my lack of a husband or father to care for me and my sister during the crossing. I'd hardly be shocked at anything you'd tell me about his character. He's detestable."

Nodding, Anna led Faith over to the edge of the rope bed and they perched together on the wooden frame. "You're right about him. He's passed through here seven or eight times. I liked him less every time I laid eyes on him."

"But why? I've seen that he's cruel. He's even whipped my poor, innocent mules for no reason except pure meanness. But there must be more. I feel it."

"Maybe so. Not that I have any sworn word on it, mind you, but I hear your captain's been made a new widower on just about every trip." She paused, patting Faith's hands for comfort. "They say he picks out a woman of property, sidles up to her, and before she knows it they're married. Trouble is, his brides don't reach Californy."

Faith's eyes widened. "And he inherits?"

"Every penny. And all his dead wife's possessions, to boot. Makes himself a pretty piece of change, what with sellin' off their rigs and all."

"Oh, dear Lord!" Faith's hands fluttered to her throat again. "He started making up to my sister after I rebuffed him."

"That ain't good. Not good at all."

"I know. But what can I do? We have to get to my father somehow."

"Stay here then. Wait for the next train to come through and join up with them."

"We can't." Ringing her hands, Faith began to pace, oblivious to the pain in her side. "Tucker has most of the money I was able to raise by selling what was left of the farm. We can't afford to pay again. And we might not be able to talk another party into accepting us, even if we could. Not two women alone."

Shrugging, Anna got to her feet. "You're probably right about that." She reached into her apron pocket, came up with a fistful of coins, and placed them in Faith's hands. "Here. Take this. It's not much but it'll help."

"Oh, I couldn't."

"Have to, as I see it," the shopkeeper countered. "It ain't my money. It come from the soldiers I told you about. Way too much for what little your stay here cost."

"Well…"

"Good girl. Take whatever the Good Lord supplies and don't ask questions. That's the way to get by out here."

"Thank you." Faith smiled with gratitude. "Now, what advice can you give me about handling Ramsey Tucker?"

Snorting in derision, Anna shook her head. "That's another kettle of burnt beans, ain't it? As I see it, all you've got to do is keep your little sister locked up tight for the next couple o' thousand miles. Anything so's she don't go gettin' all het up about marryin' that son of perdition—excuse my plain speakin'."

"No pardon necessary. I've thought to call him worse than that myself, once or twice."

"I'll bet many a sensible woman has. It's the foolish ones what get taken in and pay so dearly. I'll be prayin' for you, Faith. I truly will."

"Thank you. Please do. I suspect I'll need all the help I can get before I ever set eyes on the American River."

Dozing in the soft, slightly sagging bed, Faith was nudged into wakefulness just before dawn by the low timbre of a man's voice. Before she was fully aware of what she was doing, she'd donned the wrapper again and tiptoed across the floor to her door, opening it a crack so she could listen.

The voice was unmistakable, both in its inflections and its concern. She knew if she looked out her window to the street below, she'd no doubt see a big red horse waiting at the hitching rail.

The trouble was, she couldn't make out what her self-appointed defender was saying. Nor could she hear Anna's quiet responses. At home in Ohio she never would have ventured out onto the upper landing dressed as she was, but this wasn't Burg Hill. This was the frontier. Her need to know was greater than any false modesty. Nervous, she crept to the railing and looked down.

The plainsman had slicked back his sandy-colored hair and, hat in hand, was speaking with Mrs. Morse at the base of the stairs. One booted foot rested on the bottom step.

"You're sure she'll be all right?"

"Fine," Anna said. "She's a strong one. Stubborn."

"Her ribs?"

"Prob'ly cracked, like we figured. No fever, though. I checked on her twice during the night."

He took a deep breath, releasing it noisily. "Thanks."

Anna merely nodded. "Soon's I get the store ready for today's business I'll take her up some breakfast. The train fixin' to pull out soon?"

"Looks like it. Think she'll be able to travel?"

"Oh, it'll hurt, that's for certain. But she'll do."

Connell muttered an unintelligible curse. "What are idiotic women thinking when they try to make a journey like this practically alone?"

Still poised one floor above him, Faith closed her hands tightly over the banister. She'd heard it all before. Too often.

Who had made the rule that women ought to live their lives according to the rigid rules men set down for them, anyway? It didn't have to be that way.

Her father had left his family to pursue gold. Wealth. Supposed happiness. Waiting behind, her mother had adjusted beautifully to life without a husband to sanction her daily decisions, and Faith had every intention of following that good example. Nobody, least of all a drifter, was going to tell her what she should or shouldn't do. The fact that he'd helped her once didn't give him any right to criticize her personal choices.

The hackles on the back of Connell's neck began to prickle. He'd spent the past eleven years making his way through varying degrees of wilderness. The ongoing experience had honed his natural senses to a keen edge. Either an Indian was about to chuck an arrow his way, a hungry rattlesnake had a bead on his ankle, or Faith Beal had overheard his last comment. For the sake of his hide, he hoped it was the latter.

Raising his eyes, he looked up the stairs, intending only a quick glance. What he saw changed his mind in a blink.

The rising sun was coming through a window behind her, giving her a golden, glowing aura. The plain white wrapper was belted at her waist, its long sleeves gathered at her wrists, the skirt reaching to the floor. And her hair! Soft brown curls framed her face and cascaded in a tousled sheet of silken beauty over her shoulders. Most of the women he'd known, including Irene, had plaited their long hair at night. The wild, untamed look of Faith's tresses took his breath away.

Nodding, he acknowledged her. "Ma'am."

In spite of Anna's sputtered protest, Faith did not withdraw.

"I apologize if I offended you," Connell said, seeing undisguised ire on her face as he spoke.

"Not at all," Faith said. "I'm quite used to men assuming that because I'm a woman I'm about as dumb as an old muley cow."

Connell stifled a chuckle. "Some of those ol' mosseybacks are pretty smart critters. It might be a compliment, ma'am."

"I doubt it. At any rate, my sister and I do thank you for your care and concern, even if it is uncalled-for."

"A pleasure. Can I take a message to your sister for you? I'm headed out that way."

It was a reasonable enough offer, considering. And she did need a way to either get word to Charity or find her own ride to the wagon camp. "Yes, please. Ask for the Beal wagon and have my sister send Mr. Ledbetter back for me, if you please."

With that, Faith stepped away from the railing and disappeared into her room, shutting the door firmly. She was suddenly weak, dizzy. Not that she intended to admit it to anyone but herself.

Pouring fresh water from the ewer into the shallow basin, she splashed her face and breathed as deeply as her ribs would allow until her head cleared some.

Anna had managed to rinse most of the previous day's grime out of her green calico and had returned it to the peg beside the washstand. Though Faith would have preferred to sponge off her whole body before getting dressed, she logically decided against removing the tight bindings and chancing further injury.

Back home, she'd seen Gunther Muller die from a rib that poked into his lungs. It wasn't a pretty sight. He'd lingered for hours while neighbors gathered to pray and offer their support. In the end, he'd died gasping for air. When he'd breathed his last, Hilda had gone out to the corral and put a bullet into the prize bull that had stomped her husband to death.

Faith shivered at the memory. Before she left Fort Laramie she'd be sure to pick up some extra muslin for bandages so Charity could replace her bindings when it became necessary.

Thoughts of the days and weeks ahead before she was fully healed made Faith's heart lodge in her throat. So far, their trip had been fairly easy compared to some of the stories of hardship and loss she'd heard. From now on, however, it was going to be dreadful. Pure and simple.

Not sure she'd have time to eat before the Ledbetters came for her, Faith concentrated first on buying the muslin. Accepting a parcel of fresh biscuits from Anna in lieu of a morning meal, she then waited inside the store, scanning the busy street.

Will had been going in and out, loading goods for a teamster headed up the Platte toward the Black Hills and Deer Creek. He stuck his head back in the door to holler, "Wagon's here for you, Miss Beal."

She rose stiffly from her perch on some sacks of beans and said politely, "Thank you." Approaching Anna, she held out her hand in parting and found herself swiftly swept into a gentle but encompassing hug.

"You take care, you hear?" the older woman warned, her eyes suspiciously moist, her wrinkled forehead creasing even more as she spoke. "Watch your back."

"I will. The Ledbetters are good people. They'll stand by me, I'm sure."

"Still…"

"I know. I'll be careful," Faith vowed. "I promise. If you're ever out Sacramento way…"

Anna stood back. "Doubt I will be, but thank ya."

It was hard to make herself break away and leave the haven of Anna's presence. "Well…"

"Have a safe trip."

"Lord willing."

Turning away, Faith stood tall and walked out the door into the bright morning sun, shading her eyes with her right hand. Her bonnet ribbons, reticule and the string around the small bundle of muslin were looped over her opposite wrist.

Ledbetter's spring wagon was waiting, all right, but Ramsey Tucker was in the driver's seat! The sardonic grin on his face set Faith's teeth on edge.

"What are you doing here? Where's Mr. Ledbetter?"

"He had chores in camp."

"Chores you assigned him?"

Tucker spit tobacco juice over the off side of the wagon. "Maybe. So what? Get in."

She started to place her hands on her hips, realized the motion made her left side hurt worse and lowered her arms. "I'd rather walk, thank you."

"You do and you'll be walkin' from here to Fort Bridger, missy. I'll see to it."

"Don't you dare threaten me."

Tucker cursed. "Come on. Get in. I'm tired o' foolin' with ya." He reached down and grabbed her arm, giving it a mighty tug that lifted Faith's feet off the ground.

She stumbled and swung against the front wheel of the wagon. Searing pain shot through her. Set knives to her spine. Made her cry out.

So far, the package of unbleached muslin had padded her side. It slipped slightly off center when she banged against the wheel rim a second time. If only Tucker would let go of her she'd gladly board! *Anything* to get him to stop jerking on her arm.

Gathering what breath she could muster, Faith struggled to get her feet back under her. She glared up at him. "Stop! That hurts!"

He just laughed. Tucker's meaty hand dwarfed her wrist and her fingers were already turning white from his tight grip. Surely, Charity had told him about her injuries! Therefore, he must be inflicting this horrible pain on purpose.

Suddenly, a buckskin-clad arm shot past her shoulder. A stalwart hand closed like a vise on Tucker's thick wrist, forcing the man to his knees in the wagon bed. The captain let go. His adversary did not.

Faith, clinging to the wheel for needed support, knew instantly who had come to her rescue. The glimmer of fear in Ramsey Tucker's eyes was a truly blessed sight to behold!

The plainsman's voice rumbled. "Are you hurt?"

Rubbing her wrist, she backed away from the wagon. Pure truth could do irreparable damage. Like it or not, without the captain's guidance, she and Charity would never make it all the way to California.

Faith made the necessary choice. "No," she gasped. "I'm fine. There's no problem here. Captain Tucker and I just had a little misunderstanding."

The plainsman regarded Faith, his doubt evident. "You're sure everything is all right?"

"Positive." She labored to make her voice sound stronger, more convincing. "Now, if you'll excuse me, I was just about to get into this wagon and start back to the train. We're pulling out soon."

"Whatever you say."

He released Tucker's wrist, nodded to them both and started away without further debate. Faith could tell he didn't believe her assertion. Not for one minute. And no wonder. The statement, though partially true, had burned on her lips it was such a blatant lie.

She squared her shoulders. With her left arm held tightly

against her waist and side, she faced Tucker. She knew there was loathing in her expression. "Back off and I'll get in."

"You meant what you told him? Well, well." Chuckling with satisfaction, he offered his hand.

Faith gritted her teeth, gathered her skirts, put one foot on the step and managed to boost herself aboard without his help.

"I need a ride and you've come to fetch me. That's all," she said icily, wrapping her skirts around her legs so they wouldn't touch even a smidgen of Tucker's person. "Nothing else has changed between us."

He slapped his knee, guffawing rudely. "Feisty little thing, aren't you? Aw right. If it's a wagon ride you fancy, a wagon ride you'll get." Lowering his voice, he added, "Other kinds of things, you and me'll discuss after you've healed up."

Faith's face flared in anger and embarrassment. Of all the insulting, vulgar… She held her temper, saying nothing. Tucker had the upper hand, for now. Someday, though, she'd best him.

She swore it on her mother's grave.

Chapter Four

Connell stomped down the street, pulling his hat lower over his eyes to shade them from the morning sun. It was going to be another scorcher. Pretty normal for this time of year hereabouts.

A green spring wagon clattered past, stirring up a cloud of dust. Ramsey Tucker rode the driver's seat. Beside him, her back ramrod straight, her bonnet strings blowing behind her, sat Faith Beal. The bad blood between her and the captain was as thick as flies on a dead buffalo, so why had she insisted on letting him have his way?

Connell cursed under his breath. Why should he care? He had enough trouble already. He had to find Irene.

Pushing on the door to the saloon, he paused a moment to let his eyes adjust to the dim light. The place was sure busy. Him, he'd rather have a steak than a slug of whiskey for breakfast. But here was where the drovers from the Tucker train had congregated, so here he'd stay. At least as long as they did.

What few chairs and crude benches the place had to offer were already taken. Connell leaned against the far, canvas-covered wall with some other latecomers and studied the crowd.

A short, slight man with a wary look in his eyes and a Colt revolver stuck through his belt sidled up to him and spoke. "You're not with the Tucker train, are you?"

Connell shook his head. "No. Why?"

"Just wondered. It's a big outfit, but I didn't think I'd seen you before."

"I rode in alone. You?"

"Lookin' for a party going back to Missouri," the thin man said. When he smiled, Connell saw he was missing his front teeth. It didn't look like they'd been gone very long either, judging by his swollen lips and gums.

Noting the focus of Connell's glance, the man closed his mouth as tightly as his injuries would allow. "Saw you face up to the cap'n this mornin'. Wished it'd been more of a fight. He needs to be taken down a peg."

"You know him?"

"Too well." The man rubbed his jaw. "Too blamed well."

Nodding, Connell reached into his pocket for the miniature of Irene and held it out in his palm. "Ever see her before? Last trip, maybe?"

"Your woman?"

"Irene Wellman. My intended."

"Nope. Sorry. You might ask them two by the door. If she was ever with Tucker, they'd know. They been his drovers for years."

"Which ones?"

"Tall, fat fella with the beady eyes in the black vest and beat-up gray hat is Stuart. The shorter, weasely one next to him is Ab. He walks, you'll see he limps a might. Understand he got hurt around St. Jo last trip."

The hair on the back of Connell's neck was bristling.

"What makes you think my Irene might have been with Tucker?"

"It figures. You been payin' a lot of attention to the captain's affairs. If it was me and I was lookin' for my intended, I'd start backtracking. Her trail lead you here, did it?"

Connell took a chance that the man really did have a grudge against the wagon boss. "In a manner of speaking."

"Thought so. Word is, Tucker has a bad reputation with women. No offense, but was your lady the kind to change her mind about waitin' for you and marry up with a fella like him, instead?"

"Marry *him?*" Remembering his recent meeting with the wagon boss, he didn't see how any woman would consider agreeing to such a marriage bond.

"No. Irene isn't like that," Connell said. "We've known each other since we were children. If she'd changed her mind, she'd tell me straight out."

"Well, like I said, if it was me, I'd talk to Ab and Stuart. You never can tell." Pulling his battered brown felt hat lower, he used the floppy brim to partially hide his face. "Just don't let on I sent you, all right?"

Palming the miniature, Connell agreed. He began at the closest end of the bar for his informant's sake, asking after Irene as he worked his way along. By the time he reached the door, the fat man named Stuart was already gone. Ab, the weasel, seemed ready to bolt as well.

Connell touched the brim of his hat. "Morning."

"Mornin'." The shifty-eyed little man glanced toward the open door and shuffled his feet.

"I wonder if you could tell me…?" As Connell lifted the portrait, the man looked the other way, muttered something about being late and darted out the door.

Tucking Irene's image away in an inside pocket with her last letter, Connell followed. He was in time to see the two drovers mount up and ride. For fellows who were just honest, hardworking hands, they were acting awfully suspicious. If they didn't know anything about Irene, why refuse to look at her picture?

He swung easily aboard Rojo and trailed them at a distance. They made a dash straight for the Tucker train, then split up. The shorter man stopped at one of the wagons to help a lone woman harness a mule team. The same woman Connell had rescued twice.

Pondering all he'd learned, he squared himself in the saddle to watch and think. It was starting to look like the key to locating Irene might lie in that wagon train. Her last letter to him had been written while she was at Fort Laramie and she had mentioned a Captain T., without actually spelling out the man's name.

Beyond that clue, Connell had no other leads. Perhaps a kind Providence was trying to tell him something. He had planned to follow the same trail the wagons did, anyway. Why not do it as an actual member of Tucker's train?

Once the wagons were lined out and rolling, Connell figured he'd simply ride along by the Beal rig and offer his services. He already knew the women needed a driver. If he kept his eyes and ears open, someone might inadvertently give him a clue to Irene's whereabouts. And in the meantime, he'd be able to keep a close eye on Miss Faith and her addle-brained sister.

It never occurred to him she might turn down such a sensible offer.

Riding drag for the first hour, Connell figured he'd picked up enough trail dust in his beard to grow potatoes. Shaking it off as he cantered forward, he drew up beside Faith's wagon. There was no sign of her sister.

He tipped his hat. "Morning."

"Good morning." Her glance was cursory. "If you came to judge whether or not I was capable of handling my team, you can plainly see that I am."

"Oxen would be better for a hard crossing like this," Connell said, trying to steer their conversation in another direction. "You could pull a much bigger wagon."

"I grew up with two of these mules, the lead jack, Ben, and one of the jennies. The other two came cheap. A good ox cost more than I could afford. So did a Conestoga." She eyed him curiously. "Now that we've discussed my livestock, why are you really here?"

"Just passing by."

"In the middle of the plains? Really, Mr. McClain."

"Hush. I'd appreciate it if you wouldn't use my name."

"Why not?"

Connell shot a glance at the empty portion of the seat beside her. "Your sister isn't with you?"

"Not at present. You haven't answered my question."

"May I come aboard?"

"No! I told you, I'm perfectly able." She heard him mutter a string of epithets that reminded her of her father's mood just prior to his leaving for the gold fields. Before she could protest further, Connell had urged his horse closer and stepped off onto the wagon seat as easily as if he did it every day.

His presence crowded more than her body. Her senses were full of him: his earthiness, the scent of the soap he'd obviously applied so liberally while at the fort. And his strength! Oh, my! He exuded the power, the controlled force of someone who knew his extraordinary capabilities and took care to harness them as long as he deemed necessary.

To her relief and surprise, he didn't try to wrest the lines from her. Still, she ordered, "Get out of my wagon."

"No."

"It's not fitting for you to be here or to talk to me that way."

He lowered his voice. "If I'd come to court you, Miss Beal, you'd be right. But I have no such intentions. I'm here to speak to you man-to-man…as much as possible. So please keep your voice down and try to look relaxed."

Staring ahead, he propped one booted foot up near the brake and laced his fingers together around his knee. "You're going to hire me."

"I'm *what?*" Faith's voice squeaked. She was still struggling to digest his odd suggestion that they speak man-to-man.

Connell laid a finger across his lips. "Shush. Some of Tucker's people might hear you."

"What if they do? I have no intention of hiring anyone. I already made that quite clear."

"I know, I know. You're a regular mule skinner. Fine. Say that's true. Who's going to spell you along the way? Your sister?"

Faith pulled a face. "You know better."

"Ab or Stuart, then?"

She scowled over at him. "How do you know them?"

"I get around."

"They used to help me out. The last time Tucker beat poor Ben, I stood up to him and caused him to lose face, so now he doesn't want either of them to come near me. This morning, Ab helped me harness up and the captain flogged him across the shoulders for his trouble."

"Nice fella."

Faith couldn't help agreeing with the sarcastic observation. "I wish my sister didn't really believe that."

Taking off his hat, Connell ran his fingers through his thick hair to comb it back. "That's the only part that's got me buffaloed."

"What does?" She was so caught up in their strange conversation she was almost able to forget the shooting pain in her side every time the wagon hit a rut or bounced over a depression.

"Mrs. Morse tells me Tucker's been acting interested in your sister. I can't figure out why. Not that she isn't a pretty little thing."

Faith kept her familiar twinge of sibling rivalry to herself. For as long as she could remember, people had remarked how lovely her younger sister was.

"Charity is comely," she said.

"So's a butterfly, but men don't go around courting them. No. There's got to be something else." He pondered a bit, then shook his head and replaced his hat. "Blamed if I know. From what I've heard about Tucker, he only goes after women of considerable means."

Faith gasped, nearly dropping the reins. "Oh, no! Why didn't I think of that?"

Connell reached over and relieved her of the lines without incurring any protest. "Think of what?"

"The mining claim."

"What claim?"

Faith shifted her body sideways. She wanted to watch her companion's expression while revealing the family secret. "Papa's been gold prospecting. Last we heard, he'd been quite successful. I'll bet Charity told Tucker. She's just foolish enough to have spoken out of turn."

Connell's eyebrows raised. "So that's why you're headed west by way of Sacramento City."

Since they hadn't yet come to the place where either of the

trails to California branched off from the Oregon trail, she was surprised he knew. "Yes, but how…?"

"I've been asking around and keeping my ears open. Same as anybody could do. Chances are, Ramsey Tucker's not the only one who's heard about your papa's good fortune by now, either."

"Oh, dear."

She grasped the wagon seat and held on tight while they jostled across an unusually rough area. The wagon creaked with the stress. Late spring rains and the passage of earlier wagons had left deep, uneven ruts. Now that drier weather had come, the roughness bound the wheel rims and put a twist on the wagon's undercarriage that made it squeal in protest.

"I'll work for *found*," Connell offered, expounding on his original offer. "You won't be the first traveler to need extra help on the trail. Just feed me and give me a place under the wagon to sleep and we'll call it even."

"I couldn't do that," Faith said flatly. "It wouldn't be fair to you. It's been over a year since my father's last letter home. We may not even be able to locate him when we reach California. I couldn't guarantee any pay, even then."

"I never asked for it," he countered gruffly.

Reaching into his pocket, he withdrew the miniature of Irene and held it up. "See this woman? Her name is Irene Wellman. We've been friends since we were children. She disappeared on her way to marry me. I figure, if she was traveling with Tucker on his last trip, she probably mentioned my name plenty. That's why I didn't want you to use McClain. I don't want anybody to get suspicious and shut up before they can spill useful information."

Gently, reverently, Faith took the picture. The woman was young, in her early twenties from the look of it, and pretty in a plain sort of way.

"After my mother died," Connell said, "I lived with Irene's family for a few years and we grew close. She gave me that picture when we parted and we pledged to marry someday. I was sixteen and headed for the mountains to make my fortune trapping. By the time I finally sent for her, she'd decided her bounden duty was to help her father care for her invalid mother, instead."

"What does all this have to do with me?" Faith asked.

"Irene and I kept in touch as best we could. After her parents both died she had no family left, so she finally wrote and agreed to come to California to join me. That was a year ago. Far as I can tell, she never reached Salt Lake. Nobody will admit to knowing what happened to her."

"And you think Tucker may be responsible? Why?"

"Because he's the most likely prospect I've come across, for starters. The only connections I've been able to come up with are the first initial of his last name and the funny way his drovers started acting when I was asking about Irene. I know it isn't much to go on, but it's all I have. I need this job so I'll be in a position to learn more."

Faith gave back the miniature, sighed and turned to face the west where heaven-knows-what awaited her. How awful not to know for sure what had happened to a loved one. Was wondering worse than knowing the worst? She thought it might be.

Her mind made up, Faith held out her hand. "All right. Shake on it," she said. "You're hired."

As soon as there was an easy opportunity to do so, Connell pulled the Beal wagon out of line. Halting the team, he called to Rojo. The gelding responded by obediently trotting up.

"You'll ride him for a while," Connell said, climbing down and holding out his hand for Faith to follow.

"There's no need."

He gritted his teeth. Why did she have to be so proud? "It's not a favor, it's common sense," he argued. "You don't weigh as much as a good-size calf, the horse is making the trip anyway, and your ribs will heal faster if you don't go bouncing around all day on that hard wagon seat." He started to make a token effort to get back into the wagon. "But, if you don't want to…"

"I see your point," she said begrudgingly. When he started to reach up to grasp her by the waist then stopped himself, she reassured him with, "I can manage. My side hurts less when I move without assistance."

Standing by the side of the horse, Connell laced his fingers together to give her a boost up, wincing as he watched the signs of pain flash across her face. You could see from her eyes that she was hurting a lot more than she'd let on. To his surprise, she swung a leg over to ride astride. Her skirt hitched up to her boot tops, showing a bit of white stocking.

Seeing his quizzical expression, Faith adjusted the fabric of her dress and gave him a half smile as she took up the reins. "I was raised riding mules like old Ben without the benefit of a saddle. A body tended to wind up in the brambles if she didn't sit her mount sensibly."

Without comment, Connell climbed back aboard the wagon and called to the team to move out. Nothing Faith Beal did or said should surprise him, yet it kept happening. She was an enigma: a frail-looking beauty with the strength and stubbornness of a mule and more than a few useful skills many men didn't possess.

Connell smiled to himself. Looking at her, he'd never have guessed just how capable she was; nor did he think it wise to tell her what he thought for the present. Something inside him kept suggesting that Faith was the key to finding Irene and he tended to trust his gut feelings. Besides, she made an interesting traveling companion.

He looked over at her astride his horse and sighed. It had taken him months to acclimate himself to life among the Arapaho but he'd eventually adjusted, thanks to the love of Little Rabbit Woman. A Pawnee raid had ended her short life. He hadn't let himself care for a woman that way since. Nor had he wanted to.

Connell cast another sidelong glance at his new boss. No God-fearing Christian woman would submit herself the way Little Rabbit Woman had when they'd been married in the Indian tradition. That was as it should be. So why was he suddenly feeling let down?

Ab and another outrider were the first to notice Faith astride a horse while someone else managed her team. She saw Ab's shocked, nervous expression as the two men wheeled their mounts and rode rapidly away.

Pulling abreast of Connell, she called out, "I think we're about to have trouble."

"I saw. Ab, I recognize. Who's the other man?"

"Calls himself Indiana. That's all I know."

Connell nodded. "When Tucker gets here, let me do the talking."

"In a pig's eye. That's my rig. You work for me, remember?"

With a grin, Connell cocked one eyebrow and pulled his hat lower over his eyes. "Yes, ma'am."

"And you needn't pretend to be subservient, either. We both know you don't feel that way, so stop taunting me."

His resultant laugh was deep and mellow. "You're a hard one to please, Miss Beal. Do you want me to be your equal or your slave? Make up your mind."

Faith had only a few moments in which to send Connell a warning glance before Ramsey Tucker reined his lathered horse up beside the wagon. It made no difference whether or not her new driver had permission to speak for her. As far as Tucker was concerned, she may as well have been invisible.

He glared at Connell. "Who the blazes are you?"

Deferring, Connell nodded toward Faith. "Miss Beal has engaged me as her driver. Seems all her usual assistance is unavailable."

Tucker snorted and spit. "You talk pretty fancy for a drover. Where you from?"

"Around."

"Oh, yeah? Well, you're not welcome here. Get on your horse and scat."

"Nope."

"What'd you say?" Shouting, Tucker was reaching for the coiled bullwhip tied to his saddle by a leather thong.

Connell's eyes met Faith's, their message clear. While Tucker was distracted, she let the canelo fall back a bit, quietly slid the plainsman's heavy Hawken rifle out of its scabbard and held it ready in both hands. At Connell's nod, she tossed it to him.

His left hand closed around the barrel. He swung the long gun around in one fluid motion, laying it across his knees with the business end pointed toward Ramsey Tucker.

"No," Connell repeated. "I'm staying."

Faith saw terrible anger in Tucker's face, vitriol in his eyes. She also sensed raw fear. He'd met his match in the rough-edged stranger and he knew it.

The captain's nervous mount danced beneath him and he jerked hard on its bridle. "What'd you say your name was?"

"Folks call me Hawk," Connell offered. "I rode night hawk for Fremont out in California. The moniker stuck."

"We could use a good hand with the stock." Tucker's voice was filled with false bravado. "You take your turn as a wrangler with the other single men and you can stay."

"Mighty neighborly of you." Connell smiled over at him, his steady regard a warning he'd not be deterred. It wasn't until Tucker had ridden off that the smile became truly genuine.

Faith was grinning broadly. "You'll do."

"I thank you, ma'am."

"And quit with that false politeness, will you? If I'm going to call you Hawk, you'd just as well call me Faith."

"The other respectable ladies would have my hide if I did that, and you know it. Think of all the loose talk that kind of familiarity would cause."

"Let them talk. It's gotten so I don't give a fig what they say." Faith was warming to her subject. "Every one of them has stood by while Ramsey Tucker abused my animals and ordered me around like some worthless chattel. The way I see it, you've earned the right to call me anything you like." She giggled. "Did you see the look on his despicable face when I tossed you that rifle?"

"That, I did." Connell sobered. "I should have thought to strap on my forty-four again once I left town. Did it hurt you to lift the Hawken?"

"Honestly? A bit. But it was worth every twinge to see Tucker running off like a mangy cur with his tail twixt his legs."

"Do you have a pistol of your own?"

"Papa's Colt Walker. Why?"

"Because I intend to drive, eat and sleep with my revolver. I want you to begin wearing yours, too, right out where everybody can see it." With a grin he added, "I assume you have extra cap, ball and powder and know how to shoot."

"Of course I do. What's so funny? Did you figure I couldn't handle a gun?"

"Not at all. I was just marveling at the fact I knew you'd say you could. I assume you're a good shot, too."

"You'd better believe it!"

She nudged her heels against the horse's side to keep him in line with the front of the wagon. Whether Hawk McClain was teasing her or was dead serious, at least he'd quit assuming she was totally helpless. For a man like him, that was pretty good progress, considering they barely knew each other.

"I never shoot animals for sport," she warned. "Only when we need food."

There was genuine admiration in his tone when he said, "You'd make a good Indian. Little Rabbit Woman would have liked you a lot."

"Who?"

"Little Rabbit Woman. She was my Arapaho wife," Connell said quietly. "In another life. She died a long time ago."

Empathy flooded Faith's heart. "I'm so sorry."

"I believe you actually mean that."

"Of course I do. Why wouldn't I?"

"Because she was an Indian and I'm not. Lots of folks would hold that against me."

"Do you think Irene will?"

Connell shook his head, a look of benevolence and calm on his face. "No. Not Irene. We haven't seen each other in years, but I wrote and told her all about my past with the Arapaho before she made the final decision to travel to California to finally marry me."

"I'm glad," Faith said. "That speaks well of her."

"Yes," he said with a lopsided smile that made his eyes sparkle. "It speaks well of you, too, Faith Beal."

Chapter Five

The tight bindings around Faith's midsection were chafing in the heat something fierce by the time the wagons stopped for nooning. Normally, she and Charity shared a cooking fire with the Ledbetters and the Johnsons, but this afternoon the reception she received from the others when she approached was decidedly unfriendly.

In pain and more than a little put out, she returned to the solitude of her wagon.

Connell had finished putting the mules with the other stock being herded out to graze and was about to remove his horse's saddle. The dejected look on Faith's face made him stop what he was doing and go to her.

Gently, he touched her shoulder, then quickly stepped away and apologized for the undue familiarity.

"No need to worry," Faith said with a shrug. "Thanks to the captain's lies, everybody thinks I'm a soiled dove already."

"A sporting woman?" Connell laughed aloud. "You?"

"You think I'm not pretty enough? I don't blame you."

"Hey. Hold your horses. I never meant anything of the

kind. It's simply obvious to me that you're one of the most honest, upright women I've ever met. I can't imagine how anyone would believe such idiotic rumors."

Faith held herself proud in spite of the lingering soreness around her middle. "Thank you."

"You're welcome. Now that we have that settled, what's for dinner? I'm starved."

She sighed and made a disgusted face. "We'll have to kindle our own fire. I'm afraid I'm no longer welcome at the others' camps."

"Their loss," Connell said. He glanced at the calf-hide "possum belly" strung under the wagon to make sure it contained enough kindling and dry buffalo chips for Faith to start a fire without having to go out gathering. "So, what do you fancy? Rabbit, antelope or sage grouse?"

Raising an eyebrow, she began to smile. "You're going hunting? Now?"

"Unless you've figured out a way to get the critters to jump into the pot on their own."

"Very funny. Just bring back whatever you see and I'll cook it, no questions asked."

"That could be dangerous."

She laughed. "Not with you eating out of the same kettle. Now, skedaddle. I'm hungry, too."

Watching him mount up and ride away, she sent a silent prayer of thanks heavenward, adding a postscript plea for his missing bride's safety. If Tucker was truly involved in the woman's disappearance, no telling what had become of her. Faith hoped, for Hawk's sake, that he was wrong about that possibility. Perhaps Irene had simply found herself a husband among the emigrants on her train and gone off to wherever that man was bound.

But what if Tucker had been her choice? Faith thought the

idea quite discomfiting. And what of Charity? If there was even the slightest chance that the captain was guilty of purposeful harm, how was she going to protect someone as innocent and gullible—and stubborn—as her sister?

Faith glanced at the communal fire where Charity was assisting in the preparation of the large noon meal. It was no great surprise to see Ramsey Tucker's horse tied to a nearby wagon.

Angry that she'd been rendered powerless by circumstances beyond her control, Faith began to lay a separate cooking fire. Her mind was whirling and darting like the eddies in a fast-moving mountain stream. Too bad she couldn't really tie Charity up till they reached their destination, the way Anna had jokingly suggested.

Other than doing exactly that, she had no idea how she was going to save her from herself. None at all.

While her new boon companion was away, Faith managed to bake corn bread in the Dutch oven and also boil a pot of beans using side-pork for flavoring. When Connell returned, they added a spit and roasted the hare he'd bagged. All in all, the meal was as tasty as any she'd eaten in a long time, due in part, she was sure, to the good company.

Hoisting the nearly full bean pot by its wire handle, Connell stored it in a box packed with straw in the rear of the Beal wagon. Thus secured, it would ride safely and continue to cook from its own internal heat for some time, making it easy to fix supper after the long day of travel still ahead of them.

When he saw Faith grimace as she bent to clean their dishes, he went to her and crouched down by her side. "Let me do that."

Wide-eyed, she looked at him as if he'd handed her a poke full of gold nuggets. "You? Why?"

"Because it pains you."

"It's woman's work," she said.

"A man learns to do lots of things when he's on his own in the wilderness. Let's make a bargain. You go hunting next time and I'll help with your chores now."

"Don't be silly." She scrubbed harder, her hands flying over the gray surface of the tinware.

"I'm not. You claim you can shoot straight."

"I can, but…"

"But, what?" Taking the dish from her hand, he looked it over carefully. "If you rub this any cleaner, it's liable to end up so shiny it'll start a prairie fire."

Faith wasn't about to admit how much his close presence had dithered her. "Cleanliness is next to godliness."

He drew a hand slowly over his beard, bringing his fingers together at his chin. "While we're speaking of such things, do you happen to have shears and a looking glass I can borrow?"

"In my trunk in the wagon," she said. "I'll get them for you presently." Hawk had fallen into the rhythm of her work and was relieving her of each piece as she finished with it. Since there had been just the two of them for dinner, there wasn't much left to clean up. "I can trim your hair for you, if you like," she offered. "I used to cut Papa's."

He eyed her mischievously. "I trust he had hair to cut?"

"Of course, he did!" Straightening stiffly, she batted him with the corner of her apron, then used it to wipe her hands.

With one eyebrow raised, he warned, "Just a trim, mind you. It's been ten years since I had a city haircut. The back of my neck is real used to the shade." Seeing her heading for the wagon, he followed, reaching out to stop her. "Let me get the shears for you so you don't strain."

Faith halted and wheeled to face him, her hands planted

firmly on her hips. "Look, mister. I don't mean to sound ungrateful, but you're being so solicitous you're driving me crazy. I've been hurt before. I've healed. And I'll do it again, with or without you."

He tried to look chagrined when, in truth, her fortitude pleased him greatly. "Yes, ma'am."

Catching the wry humor in his reply, she hoisted herself into the wagon and looked down at him with a smirk. "You'd best not tease me, sir. Not when you're about to turn your barbering over to me."

"Is that a threat, Miss Beal?"

"Take it as you like," she offered, slipping the scissors, a wide-toothed comb and a small hand mirror into her apron pocket.

Once again, Connell tentatively held out his arms to her. Situated above him as she was, allowing his help in descending was the sensible thing to do. This time, Faith acquiesced.

"Okay. Easy," she said, placing one hand on each of his shoulders and leaning forward.

His hands circled her slim waist, almost fully spanning it, and he lifted gently, slowly and with great care, bringing her closer, then lowering her till he felt her feet brush the toes of his boots.

Breathless at his nearness, Faith was loath to let go. She was remembering how marvelous it was to be cradled against this man's broad chest, to be held the way a loving husband might hold his wife.

Only she and the plainsman weren't husband and wife, nor would they ever be, she reminded herself. Not only was he betrothed to someone else, he was little more than a stranger to her!

Shocked by the wild thoughts racing through her head, Faith decided they must be sinful. She'd always been taught that no good Christian woman desired a man's arms around her, so why did this moment seem so right, so meant to be, as if her whole life had been nothing but preparation for her extraordinary encounter with the plainsman?

Connell knew he should let go of her, yet kept granting himself one more breath of the natural fragrance of her hair, another second to plumb the wondrous depths of her dark, expressive eyes. If they had been alone, he knew he might very well have leaned down and kissed her. Then there'd be a fracas for sure, wouldn't there?

"Did I hurt you?" he finally asked as he released her.

Faith cleared her throat. "Um, no. Not at all."

"Good. Where do you want me?"

For some reason, her brain seemed as befuddled as it had been immediately following her accident at Fort Laramie. "Want you?"

"To sit. For my haircut."

"Oh." She took as deep a breath as her ribs would allow, then gestured toward one of the packing boxes they had used for chairs while they ate. "Over there. Take off your hat."

Connell seated himself, hat in hand.

"You'd better take your shirt off, too," she warned. "Papa always complained I got bits of hair down his neck."

"I'll be fine the way I am."

Faith knew she should let him have his way, especially since his reply had sounded so gruff, yet a perverse part of her nature insisted otherwise. "You act as if I've never seen the top of a man's union suit before," she taunted. "I guess if you're afraid to remove your shirt in my presence we'll just have to make do as is. I won't be responsible, though, if you itch something fierce afterwards."

Casting her a sidelong glance that was more an irate glare than an expression of admiration for her boldness, he reached down, crossed his arms and drew the soft buckskin hunting shirt off over his head. There'd been times when he'd stripped to breechcloth and leggings while stalking buffalo or antelope, but when among those he considered the polite society of his upbringing, he'd always remained fully clothed. Till now.

"Okay. Remember this was your idea," he said.

Hearing muffled gasps from somewhere behind her, Faith clenched her teeth. When Connell tried to swivel his torso to see who was making the fuss, she stopped him with a firm hand on his bare shoulder, a reflexive action that did not go unnoticed by anyone, she was sure.

She bent closer. "You could have mentioned that you weren't wearing a union suit under your buckskins."

"You didn't ask," he grumbled. "I suppose the fat's in the fire now."

"Let it be," she said, rancor in her tone. "All my years I've tried to live a pure, untainted life, just like the Good Book teaches. Soon after Charity and I started this pilgrimage, I realized I'd have to make many concessions in order to survive. The more time that passes, the more certain I am that I'm right."

Taking up the scissors, she handed him the small mirror so he could watch as she began to cut. Instead, he angled it so he could observe her reflection. He thought new maturity had come to Faith in the past few days—maturity and awareness. He saw her glancing openly at the muscles of his bare back and wondered what female notions might be going through her head.

There were certainly plenty of ideas passing through his. In lots of ways, she reminded him of his late Arapaho wife, while in others, her daring spirit far surpassed even his most unrestrained fancy. Knowing she was innocent of any wrong-doing, Faith was willing to stand up to everyone in the entire traveling party to affirm it. Women usually set great store by what their peers thought. Surely, Faith Beal was no exception. She, however, had the backbone to assert her innocence by both word and deed. Such courage was its own reward.

Connell closed his eyes to better enjoy the pleasant sensations of the comb passing through his hair, the slight tug of the shears, the whisper of Faith's apron against his lower back. When she stopped, took up a corner of the apron and began to brush his shoulders off with it, he stood and stepped away, rather than let her see how much her tender ministrations had affected him.

"Thanks, I can do the rest," he said, finishing the job with quick swipes of his hands.

"All right."

She held out shears and comb to him, then watched while he propped the mirror on the side of the wagon and went to work on his beard. It was just as well he'd taken over, she mused. The way her hands had begun to shake, no telling how the rest of his haircut would have turned out if she'd continued.

Suddenly exhausted, she sank onto the packing box Hawk had vacated and tried to regain control of her heightened senses. What was wrong with her? Was it her own unseemly thoughts and actions that were at fault, or was an outside force trying to undermine the purity of her motives and thereby destroy all the good she was attempting to do?

And another thing, her conscience was quick to interject, *look how you're dressed.* Custom dictated that she and her sister should still be in mourning for Mama. Yet, truth to tell, she'd felt a surge of relief when Charity had returned from a trip to the river to do the wash and had reported that their black dresses had been swept away by the current. With so little extra money at their disposal, replacing the somber clothing was out of the question, especially while traveling.

Should she have dyed another of her frocks dingy black no matter what? Faith wondered. She didn't think so. Surely, the Good Lord understood her present predicament. After all, hadn't He sent her a guardian to watch over her?

A brief glance toward the wagon showed just how rough around the edges that so-called guardian was, in spite of his recent tonsorial efforts.

Faith smiled and turned away. Even with an imagination as creative as hers, there was no way she could convince herself the plainsman was actually an emissary from God.

Her smile faded. On the other hand, it wasn't at all hard to envision Ramsey Tucker being a faithful minion of Lucifer, himself, was it?

The afternoon sun was high, the prairie affording no shade except what little could be found under the wagons. Prairie vastness that had once been lush and green was spoiled now. Swaths of bare land miles wide on each side of the emigrant track meant the travelers had to drive their livestock off to find fresh pasture, let them graze, then bring them back so the journey could continue.

Faith knew that. Her heart, however, coveted the presence of her only remaining ally. When Hawk made ready to take his turn as a drover so other men could come into camp and eat, she found herself wishing mightily she could go with him. It wouldn't do to ask, of course, for what good was a protestation of gentility if a body then followed up with such an unacceptable suggestion? Therefore, she'd wait as the other women did and ready the wagon for travel while Charity stayed with the Ledbetters and Hawk rode off to do men's work.

"Take care," she called as he mounted.

Whirling Rojo in a tight circle, he paused and leaned closer. "Watch your back, Faith. Get out the Colt and strap it on like I told you."

"I will."

Connell straightened. "Do it now."

She snapped off a mock salute. "Yes, General."

It was clear from his lack of levity that her jest hadn't pleased him. Well, too bad. As long as she followed orders, why should he care how it was accomplished? Being around him made her feel silly and giddy and altogether unhinged, with an excitement coursing through her that she hadn't even dreamed of before. Daily life was supposed to be mundane. The feelings the plainsman was awakening within her were anything but.

Climbing stiffly into her wagon, Faith let down the flap for privacy before she loosened the bodice of her dress and slipped it off. The muslin bindings had bunched beneath her breasts, their roughness coupling with trail dust to cause an irritation in spite of her soft cotton camisole.

Padding the bandages along the edges with tufts of lamb's wool, she hoped to find enough relief to carry her through till evening when she'd ask Charity to apply clean dressings. At this point, it was hard to decide which hurt worse, her cracked ribs or the cure. Cautiously, she threaded her arms back into the dress sleeves.

Papa's Colt lay beneath the clothing in her trunk. Probing under the piles of folded garments, Faith lifted the holster and heavy pistol. The belt was much too big, as she knew it would be. Preparing to make the necessary adjustments, she seated herself on the ticking she and Charity used for their bed.

The straw-filled softness beckoned, making her admit how

much the trying day had already taken out of her. She'd rest for just a few moments, she thought, lying down on her un-injured side, the Colt beside her, her eyelids so heavy she could barely keep them open.

Camp noises from outside the wagon became a muffled din as sleep overtook her. Drifting in and out of awareness, she only vaguely heard a man say, "I'll kill him before I let him ruin my plans to marry Charity Beal," but that was enough to snap her to wakefulness. She held her breath and listened.

A different voice asked, "Aren't you afraid of him?"

"Naw. I don't care who he really is or who he fought with in California. He'll bleed to death easy as any man."

Faith's eyes were wide, her lethargy gone. There was little doubt who the men were discussing, especially since she rec-ognized the bloodthirsty speaker as Ramsey Tucker and the other as his cohort, Stuart.

"I imagine he'll be shot by renegade Indians real soon," Tucker said, laughing.

"What about Miss Faith?"

Tucker shushed his companion. "Watch your mouth, you lamebrain. She may be about."

Stuart protested that he'd already checked the camp, then began to whisper. Faith could only catch a word here and there. "...trail...problems...accident..."

She yearned to move and press her ear to the canvas but the straw in the ticking would surely rustle if she tried. Once her presence was discovered, there was no telling what might happen next.

Slowly, cautiously, she reached for the Colt. Her fingers closed around the grip and drew it closer till it rested on her stomach. The firearm was heavy, weighing at least four pounds. She held it tightly with both hands, her eyes on the loose flap of canvas covering the rear of the wagon, her thumbs ready to pull back the hammer to cock and fire, if necessary.

It wasn't. Hearing the men walk off, she let out the breath she'd been holding and slowly sat up. Rapid-fire pounding of her heart accentuated her worst fears. Tucker was planning to do serious harm to Hawk McClain, with the help of Stuart and probably others of his henchmen.

And it was all her fault. It wasn't McClain they had started out to best—it was her. By allowing the plainsman to come to work for her, she'd unknowingly placed him in mortal danger!

Maybe it wasn't too late to save him by sending him away, Faith reasoned. Certainly she'd be no worse off than before, and since she now had indisputable proof of Tucker's nefarious character, she'd be doubly on her guard. As long as she carried the Colt and stayed close to the other wagons, she was certain Tucker wouldn't dare harm her, not if he really wanted to win Charity's heart.

The idea of her poor sister in the wagon boss's bed turned Faith's stomach. It didn't matter how much he slicked himself up and minded his manners for courting, the evil shone through. Given time, Charity would see that. She must. Their future depended upon it.

Chapter Six

When the men returned with the sated animals, Faith helped her hired hand harness the mules. They were fastening the trace chains to the hames when she quietly told him, "As of tomorrow, you're fired."

He scowled over at her. "I'm *what?*"

"Fired. It's for your own good."

"What about Irene?"

"Nobody will talk to you anyway, thanks to Tucker. After you've gone and things have settled down, I'll ask around and keep my ears open. If we rendezvous later on at some place like Independence Rock or Fort Bridger, I'll tell you whatever I've learned. I simply can't have you traveling with Charity and me anymore."

Connell ducked under the heads of the lead mules and came closer, his countenance dark. "What's happened?"

"I don't know what you're talking about." Faith turned her face away, afraid the imperative lie would be too plain to miss.

Two strong fingers lifted her chin. "Yes, you do. Something made you change your mind about me while I was gone. What was it?"

She jerked away. "I just decided it would be better for my reputation—and for my sister's—if I didn't encourage any more spurious rumors. That's all."

"And you really want me to go?" His hand had come to rest lightly on her forearm, the contact as necessary for him as was breathing. If she truly did mean to part company, he wanted this brief moment to become seared into his memory the way his idyllic days with Little Rabbit Woman had been.

Connell's heart leaped to his throat at the comparison. *No,* his mind shouted. *No! Not like that. Never again like that.*

To care too much was to invite loss. He should know. He hadn't been able to prevent his mother's death or his father's drunken tirades. And he'd been away hunting when the Pawnees had raided the Arapaho camp and killed his bride. Now, not only was Irene missing, he was beginning to have strong feelings for Faith Beal, as well.

Connell muttered and turned away. Faith was right. The best thing he could do was comply with her wishes. He'd been fooling himself into believing she needed him a lot more than she really did. Without him around to sully her reputation, she'd be free to implore some of the other men for help—men who were more civilized and more to her liking. Besides, nothing said he couldn't keep out of sight and dog the train from a discreet distance without her knowledge.

"All right," he said, rechecking the mule's harnesses while he spoke. "The Sweetwater River passes by Independence Rock. You won't get there by Independence Day, like Fremont did when he named it, but you should arrive sometime in mid-July. I carved my name at the base of the western face in '43. Since you're the only one around here who knows it's McClain, you can watch for me near that mark without causing suspicion."

Faith nodded. "What's your Christian name?"

"Connell," he said quietly, feeling a prickle at the back of his neck as she echoed it ever so softly.

"I like it. It suits you," Faith told him, thinking sadly of their proposed parting. She'd prepare a special meal tonight, something he could also take along on his journey to remember her by.

"How's the pain?" he asked.

"Nearly gone." She hated to lie to him again, but she knew if she told the absolute truth, he'd never leave. And if he stayed, Tucker's men would kill him for sure.

"Good." Scooping her up, he lifted her easily yet gently, set her in the wagon and handed her the lines. "Think you can handle the team from here on out?"

"Yes, but…" She watched him mount Rojo. "Where are you going?"

"No sense waiting till tomorrow to part company," he said flatly. "The longer I stay, the more gossip it'll cause." He gallantly touched the brim of his hat, nodded and said, *"Vaya con Dios."*

Faith had heard that phrase before among the Mexican wranglers. It was a parting benediction.

In her heart she knew she'd done the right thing for Connell McClain. Sending him away was her wordless blessing on his quest.

She only wished there was some way of letting him know the underlying reasons for what she'd done and how much she truly cared about his welfare.

Following parallel, the sun at his back, Connell managed to easily keep the Tucker train in sight. If anyone noticed him, he figured they'd probably think he was just one of the extra drovers, rounding up loose stock, or maybe a lone Indian on a scouting mission. There were sure plenty of those around since the emigrant trains had cut such a wide swath through the plains.

Two days out, he came upon a Cheyenne and Arapaho hunting party in search of buffalo. Seeing members of the two tribes together had become a common sight, especially after the summer council of 1840 had drawn them, plus the Kiowa and the Comanche, to the Arkansas River to make peace amongst themselves.

Ascertaining that he and the hunting party were moving in the same general direction as the Tucker train, Connell spent the next three days riding with the Indians and communicating by means of rudimentary language and sign. To his relief, the hunters treated him like a long-lost relative.

The young men in the party were upset about the presence of so many wagons crossing their hunting grounds, and rightly so, Connell thought. Westward migration of Eastern settlers as well as the influx of Mexicans from the south was unstoppable, and the tribes were only now beginning to realize what all that meant to them.

In the course of the evening meal on the third day, he'd shown them Irene's picture. To his great surprise, Lone Buffalo had nodded solemnly.

"You've seen her?" Connell asked.

Another nod.

"Where?" He had trouble feigning calm in the face of such news, but he knew if he demonstrated much excitement, his cautious companions might choose to tell him no more.

Lone Buffalo pointed north. "Black Kettle camp."

"In the Big Horn Mountains?"

The young Indian recoiled at the use of the settlers' name for such a sacred place, but he nevertheless nodded affirmatively.

None of the others in the hunting party could confirm the

sighting. Still, the lead provided the first glimmer of hope Connell had had in months. Could the woman with Black Kettle really be his Irene? Maybe. And if not, he still had the God-given responsibility to visit the camp and try to rescue whoever was being held captive there. He might not be a Bible-quoting zealot or a churchgoing man, but he was a believer just the same.

Although he'd prayed fervently and long that he'd find Irene in a white man's settlement, he knew she could have done worse than to wind up with the Cheyenne. Of all the Plains tribes, they were the least likely to force her into a quick marriage, since their normal courting rituals took from one year to as long as five. Then again, if she was considered a slave instead of having been adopted into the tribe, those customs wouldn't apply to her.

Connell's jaw clenched. He forced himself to consider various options. If, by tribal custom, she now belonged to one of the Cheyenne families, that relationship could pose a worse problem. It was far easier to purchase a slave than it was to convince a bride's father, adoptive or not, that he'd make a worthy husband.

It would be better to make a formal appeal than to simply grab her and make a run for it, he reasoned. Black Kettle would definitely not take kindly to having one of his band spirited away, no matter what the reason.

What he needed, Connell decided, were twenty good, fast horses as a show of his wealth and importance. Trouble was, he had so little money that, unless he intended to adopt the age-old Indian custom of stealing them, that particular option was out of the question. It was times like these that he wished he hadn't been raised with Christian values. To the Indian, stealing wasn't a sin, it was merely a contest of skill and daring, a besting of one's enemies. Instead of feeling guilt after a raid the way he would have, they celebrated victory.

Bedding down by the communal fire, Connell worked out his next moves in his mind. First, he'd return to Faith, explain what he'd learned, and tell her not to look for him at Independence Rock. Then he'd head for Black Kettle's camp and try to convince the chief that, as Irene's betrothed, he had the right to claim her no matter what her current status. Even if the woman captive turned out to be a stranger, he'd liberate her and see her safely to the nearest fort before he resumed his original search. The plan was simple. All he needed were trade goods, courage and a colossal marvel.

Early the following day, Connell packed the fresh buffalo meat he'd been given for his participation in the hunt, bid his traveling companions goodbye and headed out to intercept the emigrant trail. It was nearly sunset when he finally spied the smoke from the cooking fires of the Tucker train.

Reining in his horse, he paused on a slight rise to watch the activity in the camp and see where Faith's modest rig had wound up when they'd stopped for the night.

As was the routine, each wagon was backed up over the tongue of the one behind, forming a large circle and leaving only a narrow passage from the outside into the enclosure. Stretched across that passage, wheel to wheel, was a heavy chain that formed a gate and kept the loose livestock secure for the night.

Connell spotted the Beal wagon just to the right of the makeshift gate. Inside the circle, oxen milled around with horses, mules and an occasional goat brought along for milk when no freshened cow was available. Attached to the side of several of the wagons were slatted coops containing laying hens, although he imagined they'd wind up in the stew pot before long rather than have precious food and water wasted on them.

Dismounting, he led Rojo behind a hill where they could hunker down against the rising north wind and dropping temperature. No chance to keep a fire going tonight, not with the weather worsening.

He shivered, looking up at the gathering clouds and smelling the moisture in the air. Chances were, he and everything he owned were going to get good and soaked before morning.

"Over my dead body," Ab grumbled as he climbed into the supply wagon.

Stuart snorted in derision. "That can be arranged. I don't make the rules, old man."

"But criminy, Stu, we're gonna freeze out there and get soaked to boot. Why couldn't he pick a dry night?"

"How do I know? Probably figures most folks'll be inside, keepin' out of the storm, so's we won't be so likely to be seen. You ought to thank him." He reached into a burlap sack and pulled out a beaded band of bedraggled feathers and three sorry-looking arrows.

"Don't suppose any of these green settlers will notice that's a Blackfoot headdress and Sioux arrows, do ya?" Ab remarked, stripping off his shirt and sitting down to remove his run-down cavalry boots.

"Naw. Not a chance. To them, an Indian's an Indian. Besides, we'll be in and gone with the girl before most of 'em even wake up."

Ab sighed. "One of these days we're gonna get shot playin' Injun for Tucker."

"Just as long as we don't get separated like last time. You're lucky you were able to handle the Wellman woman alone."

"Yeah." Ab busied himself lacing up the tall tops of his moccasins.

"Tonight, we sneak in together, grab this one and ride. No fancy stuff, you hear? The cap'n said."

"Okay, okay." Ab stood, shivering in the icy dampness that had invaded the supply wagon. "Get the blasted war paint and let's get this over with before I freeze to death."

Stuart soon finished decorating himself and his unwilling companion, picked up the arrows, selected one and put the others back. "We'll have to barter for more of these man-stickers pretty soon if Tucker wants a sign left every time we pull a raid."

Peering first into the darkness to make sure they wouldn't be seen, he led the way out of the wagon and faded into the night. As soon as the rain began in earnest, they'd work their way back to the camp, shove the arrow into the canvas cover over the Beal wagon and make off with Faith, just as the captain had instructed.

That was the easy part. What came next was going to be harder to stomach. He'd kind of taken a liking to the girl. Slitting her throat, scalping her and burying her body in the wild was going to be a lot rougher than most of the other folks he'd killed. He almost hated to do it this time.

Frightened by the lightning and nearly continuous rumble of far-off thunder, the draft animals enclosed by the circle of wagons milled restlessly. A lone dog barked in reply to the distant howls of coyotes.

By the time rain began to pelt the canvas above her pallet, Faith was already up and dressed, preparing to go outside and reassure her mules.

Charity, having made a temporary peace with her sister, was huddled beneath their quilts instead of sleeping in the Ledbetter wagon as she had been of late.

"I don't see why you have to go out there," the younger

girl whined, peeking over the top of the calico fabric, her fair hair in total disarray. "Come back to bed before you hurt yourself again. Captain Tucker will see to our stock for us."

"He won't touch those mules while I still have breath in my body," Faith said flatly. "Go back to sleep."

"How can I when you're running all over the camp like some hoyden? Look what it got you back at the fort."

Faith made a face at her. "You didn't think of that all by yourself. Who's been calling me names?"

"Nobody. Not exactly. Mrs. Ledbetter just says you should remember you're a lady, the way I do."

"Oh, she does, does she? Well, don't waste your time worrying about me. I'll do what I have to do."

Charity's response was to hunker down in the bed and pull the covers up higher.

Faith belted the heavy Colt over her hips beneath an old, oversize India-rubber slicker that had belonged to their father, stuffed her feet into an old pair of shoes she'd walked holes in before they'd reached the valley of the Platte, and tied her slat bonnet on her head. The cotton fabric wouldn't afford much protection against the driving rain, but she needed to wear something familiar so Ben and the other mules would recognize her. Otherwise, she'd have little luck approaching them, especially when they were already so spooked.

Calling to Ben, she threw back the canvas flap and climbed down out of the wagon. Water borne on the unseasonable gale stung her cheeks like freezing sleet, its force whipping at her skirts and making her stagger. Bumping against the sideboards, she was thankful Charity had rewrapped her bruised ribs so tightly.

From where Faith stood, it appeared that few others had left their warm beds to check on their livestock personally. She wasn't surprised, since the makeshift corral did offer considerable protection and there were regular guards posted at the four points of the compass.

Ben quickly responded to her call. His long ears were up and alert and he seemed truly glad to see her as he trotted over and tried to tuck his velvety, graying nose into the front of her slicker.

Stepping behind him for shelter from the wind, Faith hugged his neck and chuckled. "You're spoiled rotten, you know that? Trust me. If I had an apple I'd give it to you. Honest, I would."

She'd been treating the old mule with fresh apples for as long as she could remember, often sneaking into her mother's root cellar to help herself to them after picking season was long past. Undoubtedly, Ben was the reason they'd had fewer winter apple pies than most families she knew.

"Where's Lucy and Lucky?" she asked Ben. "You see them lately? And how about Puck?"

Ben tossed his head and laid his ears back. The rain-slicked hide of his neck and shoulders twitched, his concentration focused beyond the perimeter of wagons.

"What is it, boy? What's wrong?"

Faith turned to scan the darkness in the direction Ben was looking. She soothed him with one hand on his withers while she wiped the cold rain out of her eyes.

"Settle down, Ben. There's nothing out there."

But the mule wouldn't be placated. A clap of thunder set him to dancing and nervously stamping his forefeet.

If she hadn't been so close to their wagon, Faith might have thought Charity needed help and the mule was sensing it. However, she could see the rippling canvas plainly every time the sky flashed bright and all seemed as peaceful as could be expected during such a violent storm.

Stroking the mule's nose, she repeated soothing words of comfort. "Easy, old boy. Easy."

Suddenly, the atmosphere reverberated with a piercing scream. Ben jumped in unison with Faith.

A bolt of lightning split the sky, illuminating the shocking scene before her. Two war-painted figures were exiting her wagon bearing Grandmother Reeder's favorite quilt between them! And the rolled bundle of bedding was writhing and emitting strangled cries.

Faith's heart leaped. Charity! Good Lord in heaven, wild Indians were making off with Charity!

Giving no thought to her own safety, Faith gathered her skirts and dashed forward, her small feet flying across the slippery ground.

Launching herself into the air behind the nearest kidnapper, she grabbed him around the neck and hung on, oblivious to her earlier injury.

He muttered an oath as he spun around. His beefy elbow shot back, clipping her hard in the ribs. With a cry, she doubled up and fell to the muddy ground in a haze of pain.

"Look!" one of the Indians muttered. "We got the wrong one."

Suddenly, Faith felt herself being lifted, dragged, then thrown over the wagon tongue and out onto the soggy prairie. Resting on hands and knees, she shook her head to clear it. Something was dreadfully wrong here! The few Indians she'd heard speaking at Fort Laramie hadn't sounded like they came from some place back east, yet this one certainly did.

As she struggled to regain her footing, she remembered the pistol trapped beneath her slicker. She had to reach it!

Hands dripping with mud and water, she clawed frantically at the copious length of rubberized cloth, finally managing to raise the hem enough to expose the butt of the Colt. Her slick fingers slid off the grip!

Before she could try again to grab onto the revolver,

someone pinned her arms from behind. The man she'd attacked at the outset faced her and drew back his arm. Surely he wasn't going to *hit* her!

Camp lanterns that had been quenched began to flicker to light. Charity was thrashing around in the mud with Grandma's quilt all askew beneath her.

The younger girl screamed for help as she pointed to an arrow sticking out of the canvas of their wagon.

Then, Faith felt a jarring blow to her jaw and everything went black.

Chapter Seven

This storm had Rojo spooked more than usual, Connell thought, watching his fidgeting horse with interest. The strange thing was, he seemed to be feeling the same unexplained nervousness the animal was.

There was bad medicine in the air, as his Arapaho friends would say. He'd already moved down into a draw to avoid being an easy target for lightning. Not that it couldn't strike where it pleased, as many a plainsman had seen. It even took out a buffalo, now and then. He'd never personally witnessed such an event but the stories were numerous. It wasn't a pretty sight. No matter how hungry Indians were, they refused to eat the charred flesh, considering it tainted by evil spirits.

Shivering, Connell arose from his crouched position. He'd donned the oilskin coat he carried and hunkered down beneath the piece of buffalo hide he'd had his meat wrapped in, but it had afforded little shelter. Nothing helped much in the midst of a prairie storm as bad as this one. Soon, the draw he was in would fill with racing water and he'd have to climb to higher ground. If he wasn't already soaked by that time, he soon would be.

He stamped his feet to work the kinks out of his legs and warm himself. This wasn't the first time he'd been caught miles from any decent place to take cover. He'd live. A traveler on horseback couldn't carry his shelter along the way the emigrants did.

Pausing, he listened. The noise of the storm blotted out everything, as far as he could tell, but the canelo seemed to be growing more agitated. He hoped there wasn't a twister brewing!

Connell approached and took up the loose reins. Rojo, ears pricked, was staring toward the distant wagon camp.

"What is it, boy?"

The horse snorted and tossed his head, then went right back to staring into the distance.

Connell peered along the same line of sight to no avail. The rain was falling too hard and fast for him to see much. Yet something had caused the hackles on the back of his neck to prickle. Maybe his nervous horse was spooking him, he argued rationally. And maybe not.

The urge to mount up and ride closer to check the situation was getting too strong to ignore. He'd intended to wait till morning to approach the camp. That way, there'd be lots of activity to cover his arrival and he'd be less likely to be shot by an overeager sentry or one of Tucker's henchmen when he tried to speak to Faith.

Now, however, his instincts insisted on immediate action.

"You're crazy and so am I," Connell told his horse as he lifted the left stirrup to reach under and tighten the cinch before mounting.

Rojo snorted and stamped.

"Yeah. I don't know why, but I think she needs us, too," Connell said, his voice barely audible. He swung into the saddle and nudged the horse into action. "Let's go."

* * *

Closing on the wagon camp, Connell heard a ruckus. Folks were milling about, shouting to each other. A flash of lightning outlined two bent figures sneaking away. His first instinct was to follow them.

Thoughts of Faith gave him pause. Once he'd seen her and talked to her—made sure she was all right—he could go after the suspicious men. Trouble was, in this storm and at night to boot, there wasn't a chance in a thousand of successfully trailing them once they got a head start.

He peered in at the camp. Looked like no one had started to saddle a horse for pursuit. By the time they did, the marauders would be long gone.

A continuing barrage of lightning gave Connell further glimpses of the fleeing men. The taller one was carrying a large, dark object draped over his shoulder while the other walked sideways and backward, apparently watching to see that they weren't being followed. Judging by their headdresses, they'd be Blackfoot, except he'd never seen braves from that tribe so far west or south before.

Connell urged Rojo forward so he could keep his quarry in sight. A pair of horses waited several hundred yards from where he'd first spotted the men. They hoisted their burden, threw it across one saddle, and the smaller man swung up behind it. As soon as his partner had mounted, they whipped their mounts and began to put distance between themselves and the wagon train.

Connell knew now what he must do. Indians sometimes rode saddles of their own making, but he'd never seen a brave yet who could abide a high Spanish cantle.

He spurred the canelo into a gallop, oblivious to the dangers of traveling so fast over prairie-dog-ridden ground. The question was no longer *who* he was tracking but *what*.

One thing was certain. They weren't real Indians.

* * *

"I think she's comin' to," Ab warned, reining up beside Stuart. "And I'm half-froze to death. I don't know why we couldn't wear buffalo robes or at least hunting shirts the way the real Indians do in foul weather."

The heavier man grunted his disapproval. "Shut up, old man. He let us keep our long pants, didn't he? Stop your complaining or I'll shoot you on the spot and leave your sorry carcass for the buzzards when I dump the woman."

"I don't think we should keep doin' this for Tucker," Ab whined. "Trouble comes, you know he ain't goin' to fess up. We'll be stuck payin' for his crimes."

"Not me. I got enough on Tucker to see he rots in some stinkin' prison like the one I seen once in Yuma. Man, it was hot there."

"Don't talk about hot." Ab's teeth were chattering. "It reminds me of Hell, where you and I are probably goin' fer doin' this. How far do we have to ride, anyways?"

"Couple a more miles." He glanced at the slicker-covered bundle across Ab's saddle. "You said she was comin' to. She ain't moving much."

"Quit about as soon as she started. Probably fainted. You know women."

Stuart chortled. "Yeah. If we wasn't on a job here, I'd sure like to see if that one's as good as she looks."

Horrified and dismayed, Faith held her breath, biting her lip to keep from crying out every time Ab's horse took a step. The saddle horn was pressing into her stomach, thank goodness, but her sore ribs got a painful jolt at every stride just the same.

They were going to kill her. That was evident. She'd been a fool to think she was safe simply because she was in the emigrant company. Clearly, a nefarious man like Ramsey Tucker was not above kidnapping her to implement his scheme to get to Charity.

Cautiously, she tried to wiggle her fingers. Ropes held her wrists fast. The same with her ankles. When they'd secured her, they'd apparently looped the rope under the horse's belly because when she tugged the bindings on her wrists, the pressure on her legs increased.

Her mind whirling, Faith tried to reason through the panic that was eating away her ability to think logically. The voices of her captors were all too familiar, yet perhaps that could work to her advantage. From what little she'd heard, it sounded like Ab was the least committed to her demise. Perhaps, if she prayed hard enough, God would make Ab speak up and give her a chance to plead for her life before it was too late.

She held her breath. *Dear Lord!* They were stopping! Tied facedown she couldn't see much, but it was evident the men were dismounting. In seconds she was loosened, pulled from the saddle and released to fall painfully onto the soggy ground. That was the last straw. Unable to keep quiet any longer, she cried out in agony.

"She's awake!" Stuart shouted. "Get your gun on her."

"What gun?" Ab started to laugh like he was crazy in the head. "In case you ain't noticed, there's no room for a holster or a pistol in these danged costumes."

"Then hit her over the head with a rock."

"You hit her," Ab argued. "You're the one who likes that kind of thing."

"I never said that."

"Then why wouldn't you help me save Miss Irene?"

"'Cause Tucker'd a killed me if she'd a got away, that's why."

Ab continued to cackle as if he'd taken leave of his senses. "Then you'd best get ready to meet your maker 'cause that little gal is alive and well."

Stuart shouted a string of curses.

Lying in the mud at his feet, Faith began to give thanks for what she'd just learned. Now, if she could only escape, she could take word to her friend Hawk that his future bride was all right.

It was also a relief to hear that the men were unarmed, since the Colt was still snug in its military holster beneath her black slicker. The trick would be reaching it and using it to defend herself before her kidnappers figured out she had a gun.

She snaked her right arm inside the oilcloth while she tried hard to keep the rest of her body from moving. The dark, rainy night helped mask her cautious movements.

Arguing loudly, her attackers moved off a bit, thereby giving Faith the opportunity she needed. Her cold fingers touched the leather flap over the top of the holster and lifted it out of the way. Under the cover of the slicker she eased the heavy pistol from its sheath and raised it to point toward the two men in case they noticed she was fully awake and getting to her feet.

She need not have worried. Neither man was the least bit interested in her at the moment. Stuart was pushing at his smaller companion's shoulders over and over. Ab was fighting back with angry words.

"I don't care what you say. I done the right thing and I'm not sorry."

"You will be when the cap'n hears."

"Go ahead. Tell him. I ain't goin' back there, anyhows."

"Oh, yes you are."

"No I'm not."

Ruing the added weight of her wet, muddy skirt and petticoat, Faith edged herself partially behind the weary horse she'd been tied to, then pulled the black slicker off the pistol barrel. Having the gun would do no good unless she took careful aim before ordering the drovers to surrender.

Gathering her courage, she shouted, "All right. Hands up, both of you!" How weak and puny her voice sounded in the vastness of the open prairie!

Ab lifted his hands over his head with a wild laugh. "Ha-ha. I see *somebody* remembered to bring a gun!"

"Shut up, old man," Stuart ordered. He began edging away from his companion, making a split in Faith's target.

Not sure which man to continue to point the gun at, she wavered, her eyes blinking fast against the falling rain.

Lightning flashed. For a moment she was blinded. Something told her Stuart was lunging for her, but not wanting to shoot without being certain, she held her fire.

He hit her low, like a cowhand bringing down a steer from the back of a running horse. The blow made her squeeze off one wild shot.

In an instant he'd wrestled her to the ground and torn the pistol from her grasp. The next lightning flash showed him standing over her, the menacing-looking Colt pointed right at her head.

"Nice of you to bring your own gun, Miss Faith. It makes my job much easier."

"I was always good to you." She hugged herself to ease the pain in her side. "Why are you doing this to me?"

Stuart cocked the hammer of the pistol to bring another loaded cylinder into play. "Don't want to," he said. "It's just the way things worked out. No hard feelin's."

His uncaring attitude made Faith boiling mad. He might actually kill her, but she wasn't going to Glory without giving him a piece of her mind no matter how much it hurt to breathe and talk.

"No hard feelings?" she spit out. "You bet there are, mister. I'm going to be mad as a hornet at you if you pull that trigger. Maybe I'll even come back to haunt you. Do you believe in ghosts?"

Ab appeared at Stuart's elbow. "You'd better listen to her. There's talk on the train she's got special powers. Just might be able to do as she says."

"I didn't hear no such talk."

"Well, there was." The thin man raised his trembling right hand. "I swear."

"Bah. Get away from me, you old fool. I got work to do." With that, he raised the pistol higher and took aim.

Connell hadn't been more than a quarter of a mile behind the riders when they and their burden had stopped. He thanked the Good Lord over and over when he recognized Faith's discarded bonnet and realized exactly who he'd been following and what was apparently going on.

He'd dismounted to approach on foot when he heard her shout "Hands up!"

A single gunshot cracked amid the thunder.

Faith cried out.

The sound tied Connell's gut in knots.

It was clear that at least one of the men had doubted she'd really shoot to kill, because Connell had seen a dark, crouching figure run at her and knock her to the ground.

When the man scrambled to his feet, Connell glimpsed the reflection of a shiny object in his hand. Faith's pistol! His heart sank. He'd left Rojo behind in a ravine so he could sneak up on the abductors more easily and his Hawken was still in its scabbard. That left only his .44, a much less accurate weapon than the rifle, even under the best of conditions. Which these were not.

It was dark except for the scattered clusters of lightning flashes. Rain was falling in bursts, as if someone were emptying buckets on him from above.

Connell knew if he chanced a shot and missed, the man with the gun would fire, likely hitting Faith. Yet if he waited until he was within better range, it might be too late. Unless…

Using a trick he'd learned from Little Rabbit Woman's people, he pulled his hunting knife and began to slice off thick bunches of grama grass. The idea was to make his swiftly moving shadow resemble a large, dangerous animal like a mad buffalo.

It would have been much better to use a real animal's hide but he'd left that behind, as well, so a substitute would have to do. The ploy didn't have to fool anyone for long. It was meant only as a delaying tactic and a way to get closer to Faith and the men.

Growling, snorting and making as much animal noise as he could, Connell started off at a dead run toward the three people. He was counting on surprise to keep them from firing at him. He was wrong.

Wheeling, Stuart squeezed off a shot. The bullet whizzed through the grama grass bundles. Connell dropped them, hit the ground, rolled away in the darkness and sprang to his feet with the speed and agility of a pronghorn antelope.

Plunging headlong into the danger ahead, he raced over the wet ground as if he knew every inch of it and with no thought of personal risk. This was the way the Native People felt about the land, about nature, he realized. It had been literally years since he'd sensed such a oneness with a Greater Power and it made him feel almost invincible.

There was no time to pause and draw his .44. Stuart was turning back to Faith and bringing the gun to bear.

With a soul-deep roar of rage, Connell lived up to his

nickname and launched himself into the air with a mighty leap, his arms reaching like a hawk's talons for its prey.

Stuart's scream was cut off by the attack almost before it began. He fell beneath Connell. The Colt flew from his hand to disappear in the mire.

A soggy, muddy mess in spite of the heavy slicker, Faith scrambled to her feet and pushed her limp hair out of her eyes with her hands. The furor died down in mere moments. "I can't believe you found me out here in the middle of nowhere. How did you do it?" she asked, sounding amazed.

Connell shook his head. "It was just a feeling I had. I guess you could say the Good Lord sent me."

"I don't doubt that. I've been asking Jesus to send help ever since these two grabbed me."

"Well, I guess He heard you because here I am." Connell got to his feet and gazed down at the muddy, disheveled woman. "Are you all right?"

"I think so." She managed a smile. "Stuart, I see. What happened to Ab?"

"I'm right here," the weasely man squeaked. His hands were raised high over his head and he was trembling visibly as he edged closer. "D-don't shoot."

It was a natural reflex for Connell to reach for his pistol anyway. Faith stayed his hand. "No. Don't. He tried to help me. Even made up a story that he'd heard I had supernatural powers." She brightened. "And he says he helped your Irene, too."

"What?"

Grabbing him by the upper arms, Connell lifted Ab overhead, gave him a mighty shake and held him there while rain cascaded off him like the headwaters of the Mississippi.

"I did. I helped her," the little man sputtered.

Connell wasn't convinced. "Prove it."

"She's…she's with the Arapaho. I took her there myself, I swear."

"When?"

"Last year, when the wagons came through these here parts. Tucker married up with her, like usual, then told me and Stuart to get rid of her." Ab's thin voice broke. "Only I couldn't do it. She reminded me of my ma."

It wasn't exactly the same story Connell had heard from the Indian hunters, but it was close enough to reaffirm the good news that Irene had survived Tucker's planned destruction.

Angry, Connell thrust Ab aside. "I doubt you had a mother! How could you be a party to such cruelty?"

"It was me or them!"

"All right, all right. Shut up. I believe you," Connell replied. "At first light, you'll take me to Irene. Understand?"

"I…I can try. The camps move around, ya know. Follow the buffalo. Might not be there no more."

"Then we'll keep looking till we locate the right band."

Shivering now that all the excitement was over, Faith tugged at Connell's wet buckskin sleeve. "What about me? And what are we going to do with Stuart? We can't just ride away and leave him here."

"He can rot where he lies for all I care," Connell said. Nevertheless, he gestured at Ab. "Help him up and let's try to get out of this rain before we all take sick."

The thin little man reached for his companion's arm. "I can't lift him."

With a grunt of displeasure, Connell yanked Stuart's limp body to its feet, then hesitated, feeling for a pulse in the man's throat and finding none before releasing him to fall back onto the sodden prairie.

"The Good Lord is wiser than we are," he said flatly. "This man is dead. I think his neck is broken."

"We should bury him." Faith's tone lacked conviction.

"Not if it means we're overtaken by a search party from the wagon train while we dig the grave. Surely they must be out looking for you by now. Tucker has to put on a good show of concern for the benefit of the other folks."

"There's...there's a hole already dug," Ab stammered, pointing. "Over that ridge, I think."

Faith gasped. "It was meant for me, wasn't it?"

Ab said, "Yes," and Faith staggered as if she was going to faint for the second time in her life.

Chapter Eight

The night seemed to drag on forever. Huddled under a rock outcropping with the buffalo hide pulled over them, Faith, Connell and Ab waited impatiently for dawn. Head down, his rear to the wind, Rojo stood quietly nearby.

"I wish you'd let me share this slicker with you two," she said. "It's way too big for me and we could make a fair shelter out of it."

Connell was quick to say, "No," even though Ab was shivering like a quaking aspen in a gale.

Sleep was impossible, given their cramped positions and the continuing noise of the storm. Thankfully, the lightning had moved off to the northeast so at least the danger of being roasted alive had passed.

"We have to go back and get Charity," Faith said.

Both men turned their heads to stare at her. Connell said, "Out of the question."

She wasn't surprised at his attitude. However, she didn't intend to change her mind. "Then I'll go alone."

"You'll do nothing of the kind."

"You have no right to tell me what to do."

"Well, somebody better," he replied. "You aren't thinking smart anymore."

"I can't leave her there!" Faith's voice broke as she fought a strong urge to weep.

Ab interrupted their conversation by saying, "It ain't good for the cap'n to know you're alive, missy. Might rile him up and make him change his plans."

"But…"

Nodding, Connell agreed. "You know what he has in mind, then?"

"I do." The thin man cleared his throat. "He's after the Beal gold mine. Figures it'll set him up for life. Only this time he's got to work it out different. If something happened to Miss Charity before the train reached Californy, her pa wouldn't take kindly to it. That's why I know fer certain he won't hurt her."

"I have to see her again. To reason with her," Faith insisted.

"Well, you sure can't go back to the wagons." Connell sounded gruff. "What do you want me to do, kidnap her and bring her to you?"

"Oh, would you?"

"Absolutely not. What makes you think your sister would listen to you even if you had the chance to speak your mind? You've been arguing with her about Tucker for as long as I've known you and she hasn't learned a thing."

"But this time I can tell her what he tried to do to me," Faith said. "That should open her eyes."

"What if she doesn't believe you?"

"She will. She has to."

Ab cleared his throat. "'Scuse me, missy. I think you're wrong about that. It's my guess she'll be married to the cap'n 'fore the train moves again."

"No! It can't be! What makes you say that?"

"'Cause it's his plan," Ab explained. "Me and Stuart was to pretend to be Indians and do away with you. Then Tucker would move in on Miss Charity and tell her she couldn't travel all alone on his train because she wasn't a married lady. Unless you know of some other young fella she might marry up with, it's my guess it'll be Ramsey Tucker. He's the law out here. He can do anything he wants, even perform his own weddin' if he can't find a rightful preacher."

Faith was glad the darkness beneath the buffalo robe hid her tears as they slid silently down her muddy cheeks. If Charity chose to wed, there was nothing she could do about it. The sanctity of marriage had to be respected.

Given a choice, she would have mounted Stuart's horse and galloped back to the train right then. Trouble was, she had no idea how to find her way back to the wagons without some kind of trail to go by. She had no doubt Connell would not aid her. He was too dead set against her going.

Thinking about asking Ab for help, she decided that wasn't safe, either. Under the present circumstances he seemed innocent enough, but put him back where Tucker's influence could corrupt him again and there was no telling how he would act.

Turning to Connell, she laid her hand gently on his sleeve. "Please, Mr. McClain. I know how badly you want to find your bride. Try to put yourself in my place. What if it were Irene about to marry Captain Tucker and you found out about it in time to stop it. Wouldn't you try?"

He turned away as he mumbled something she couldn't quite decipher. From his tone of voice and attitude, though, Faith decided it was probably just as well she hadn't been able to make out the words. They were most likely not at all genteel.

Rising suddenly, Connell flung off the buffalo robe. "All right. You win. But we do this my way, is that clear?"

"Yes, sir."

Grinning broadly, Faith ducked her head so he couldn't tell how happy she was and therefore change his mind simply because of stubborn pride. She'd learned long ago, by watching her father and mother argue, that men were happiest when they didn't think women had anything to do with their decisions—especially the important ones.

Ab, too, arose. He stood there shivering, pulling the wet, heavy fur robe around his scrawny shoulders. "What about me?"

"You stay," Connell said.

"I'll freeze to death out here!"

"Not before morning. It's my guess this place'll be plenty hot once the sun rises. Usually is."

"At least leave me a horse."

"So you can warn Tucker or ride off to alert the Indians that I'm on my way? Not on your life."

"I won't. I swear!"

Mounting Rojo, Connell rode to where the other horses were hobbled and loosed them to lead. "Stay put. We'll come back for you," he promised Ab.

"What if you get kilt?"

Sobering at the suggestion, Faith stood on a raised, flat rock to climb more easily onto Stuart's mare. "I guess you'd better pray hard that we don't," she said. "I imagine the Lord will even listen to the pleas of a skunk like you, providing you truly repent. I'd give it a try if I were you."

She took up the reins of the extra horse as well as her own and looked to Connell. "I'm ready. Let's go."

Activity started in the wagon camp before dawn. There were animals to harness, food to prepare, goods to stow and no time to waste. Every minute counted when early snows might close the mountain passes or freak storms could make shallow rivers impassable for weeks at a time. Many a man had been lost trying to float his team and wagon across a treacherous river. Broken wood and the bleached bones of oxen lying in rifts on the banks were proof.

Faith wished she'd had more sleep during the long, trying night. Between the shooting pains in her side and a lack of rest, she was thoroughly exhausted. In a way, she wished the remainder of her were as numb from the cold as her feet and legs were.

"We'll dismount here," Connell said, swinging easily to the ground.

When Faith tried to do the same, her knees gave out and she crumpled into a heap next to the horse.

In an instant Connell was beside her. There was no use insisting she was fine when he bent to pick her up. Clearly, she was not. Worse yet, being cradled in his strong arms made her forget Charity and everything else except the two of them and the way his awesome presence was increasingly affecting her.

He tenderly carried her to a hiding place and set her down behind an enormous gray boulder. "You wait here. Take off your boots and rub your feet and ankles to get the circulation back into them. And don't stick your head up. I don't want some overeager meat hunter to mistake you for a drowned prairie dog and take a potshot at you."

"I beg your pardon."

He chuckled. "I forgot. You haven't seen your hair lately. Too bad you lost your bonnet in the storm."

Embarrassed, Faith patted at her head and tried to tuck wisps of mud-matted hair back into the long plait that hung down her back. "I hope Charity recognizes me like this."

"Don't worry about the dirt. It should help prove you're telling the truth," he offered, a softer tone coloring his deep voice.

"I want to go with you."

"No. First of all, I may have to run and you're in no shape to keep up. Secondly, no one knows I'm involved in your troubles anymore, so I can probably ride into camp without arousing much suspicion."

"I suppose you're right," she grumbled.

"You know I am. Sit tight. I'll be back as soon as I can." With that, he mounted Rojo and rode away.

Left alone with her thoughts, Faith used the damp hem of her petticoat to wipe her face and hands as clean as possible. There were some advantages to ladies' abundant garments, weren't there? At least a body had spare rags handy if need be.

Sighing, she contrasted her father with Connell McClain. They both were good men in their own ways. Her father, Emory Beal, had never been as strong or as imposing a figure as the big plainsman was, but she'd loved him in spite of his faults. The hard part was forgiving him for deserting his family to go west to search for gold when he didn't know the first thing about prospecting.

Too bad Papa couldn't have been more capable, like Hawk, she mused, noticing an unexplainable tingle running through her as she visualized her boon companion. Connell McClain was clearly a lot better suited to the rigors of pioneer life than any man she'd ever known.

In the back of her mind she remembered how sure she'd been that she didn't need anyone but the Good Lord to look out for her on the trail. How wrong that notion was. Nobody, man or woman, could hope to stand totally alone. Not out here. Not in these difficult times. And she couldn't think of a single person in whom she would rather place her trust than the big, rugged plainsman.

Clearly, she'd made a mistake when she'd struck out for

California by land instead of trying to scrounge enough money to sail around the Horn. It was one thing to trust God for deliverance, yet quite another to tempt Him by making foolish choices, as she apparently had.

Thinking of Little Rabbit Woman, Faith grew pensive. What was life like in an Arapaho camp? she wondered. What would it be like to live there, the way Irene was, only with someone like Hawk McClain? Her cheeks flamed at the thought. Where had that wild, sinful notion come from? A person would think she was as taken with men as Charity was!

She wasn't, of course, so it surely wouldn't hurt to give her reveries free rein for a moment or two. The man was already spoken for. Therefore, he was not available and could pose no threat to her long-range plans.

Closing her eyes, Faith leaned back against the rock and tried to picture herself as a young squaw, relying on her memories of the women gathered at Fort Laramie to imagine a native costume and wondering which tribe was which. Always, the imposing presence of the plainsman lay in the center of her fancies.

Soon a pleasant euphoria overtook her, pressing fatigue won out, the vision faded and she fell sound asleep.

Connell's arrival at the Tucker camp was just as he'd predicted; he rode slowly among the wagons without attracting more than an occasional "Good morning."

Tipping his hat, he noted that most of the men were as wet and grimy as he was, thanks to their extra duties during the night and the early morning.

As he passed, he listened carefully to anyone who happened to be talking about Miss Charity's close call. Few mentioned the fact that Faith was missing.

The Ledbetter wagon stood directly in front of Faith's.

Through the canvas cover he could hear the voices of at least three women.

"Now, now, dear. We all know you aren't like she was, thank the Lord. Them that live by the sword, die by the sword, I always say. We all saw that horrid pistol she insisted on wearing."

One of the women began to wail loudly while the others offered emotional support. "Here, take this hanky and blow your nose, child. Cryin' won't help a bit. You're a young thing, but you're a woman, just like the rest of us, and you gotta do as your man says."

The wailing abated slightly, then resumed at a high, screeching pitch. Connell didn't doubt for a minute that he'd located Charity Beal.

Which meant she had company in her misery. It wasn't going to be possible to just grab her, throw her across his saddle and cart her away for a meeting with Faith. Emigrant women tended to do everything in a group, from cooking and cleaning to taking care of their personal needs. Catching one of them alone under normal circumstances wasn't easy. Catching Charity by herself on this particular morning was going to be next to hopeless.

Still, he had to try. A promise was a promise whether he liked it or not. Grumbling to himself and wondering how he'd let Faith talk him into doing this, he left Rojo grazing just outside the wagon circle and made his way to the Beal wagon to wait for Charity to come home.

Personal belongings were stacked as low to the ground as possible to help keep the wagon from tipping over in rough terrain. Bedding was usually spread on top of the trunks and boxes at night, then stored away in the morning before travel resumed.

Connell looked inside the wagon and noted that only one

sleeping place remained. It was as if Charity knew Faith was never coming back.

That was when he remembered the old family quilt Faith had mentioned seeing wrapped around her sister the night before. It would be soiled, of course, but perhaps if he could locate it he'd take it to her when he delivered Charity. Poor Faith had precious little else left of the life she'd once lived. Having the quilt would surely give her comfort.

He found the thoroughly soaked coverlet lying discarded on the prairie about twenty-five yards from camp. Picking it up, he squeezed out as much water as he could and took it back to the wagon with him, thinking it might make a good conversation piece when he tried to explain what he was doing there.

Charity was inside her wagon by the time he arrived for the second time. She was fully dressed but still gave a little squeal of fright when he knocked and pushed back the flap. "What do you want?"

In the tight confines of the small wagon he could see she was all by herself. "I came to return this," Connell said, holding up the quilt.

"I don't want it!" Charity's reddened, puffy eyes filled with new tears. "Take it away."

"I heard about what happened to your sister," he went on. "Please accept my condolences."

"We…we shouldn't even be out here in this godforsaken desert," the girl stammered. "Faith insisted we come. Look what her bossy nature got her." She started to sniffle. "I hate this place. All I want to do is go home."

"Lots of folks feel that way, Miss Beal. I could escort you back to Fort Laramie and you could wait there to join up with an east-bound party."

"It's too late for that, I'm afraid. My husband surely wouldn't like it if I rode out of camp with another man."

Connell's fist tightened on the quilt. "You're married? When?"

"Two days ago. Captain Tucker, Ramsey, wanted us to keep it a secret from nearly everyone. He was afraid my sister would pitch a fit and spoil things if she found out." Charity blinked back tears. "When I came back to our wagon last night I was going to explain it all to her, to prove to him he was wrong, but I never could make myself speak the words." She paused to stifle a sob. "How I wish I'd told her the whole truth before…before she…"

"I am sorry," Connell said. "But wherever Faith is, I'm sure she wishes you only the best."

"Will the Indians hurt her?" Charity blurted out. "I couldn't bear that. I just couldn't."

He didn't dare tell her the true details of the fake kidnapping because she might make the mistake of saying something about it to her nefarious husband. If Tucker began to suspect what had really happened, Charity could be in worse danger than she already was. Instead, Hawk tried to comfort her another way.

"The Plains tribes I know are not vicious and cruel the way the dime novels say they are. We don't always understand their ways because they're so different from ours, but they do have loving families. They care about each other the same way white men do…maybe better."

"Truly?"

"Truly," he said. "I can assure you, if your sister is with the local tribes she will be well cared for."

"If she's alive," the girl added.

"I have a strong feeling that she is," he said. "And I promise to keep my eyes and ears open for any word of her."

The hair on the back of his neck prickled a warning. He turned in time to see Ramsey Tucker headed their way.

"I have to go," Connell said. "But first, tell me. Now that you have a husband, do you still plan to meet up with your father in California?"

"Yes, of course." Charity pushed her mussed blond curls back from her pale cheeks. "Looking forward to the day of that blessed reunion is all that keeps me going."

"Then I wish you the best." Quickly tipping his hat, he dodged around the corner of the wagon, leaped into the saddle with the quilt in front of him and spurred his horse out onto the prairie.

Behind him, he could hear the angry curses and shouts of Ramsey Tucker.

Faith awoke to a gentle calling of her name. Sitting bolt upright, she peered up at Connell expectantly, happily, then looked past him right and left. "Is Charity here? Did she come with you?"

"No. I saw her and she's fine, though. A little weary, and you can see she's been crying, but all in all she's the same as always."

"Oh, I'm so thankful."

He hunkered down beside her. "There's more."

Eyeing him curiously, she saw the regret in his expression and realized that the news he was about to deliver was not going to be good. "Tell me."

"Charity says she and Tucker are already married."

"Oh, no!" Faith's hands flew to her throat. "So fast?"

"Apparently it happened shortly before you were kidnapped. Your sister says she tried to tell you everything but couldn't bring herself to do it."

"What can we do? We have to help her."

Connell shook his head. "As I see it, there's not a whole lot to be done for the present. She says they are traveling on to the mining country to meet your father, just as Ab told us they would."

"So?"

"So, that means he was right about her being safe for the time being. As long as we beat Mr. and Mrs. Ramsey Tucker to California and tell your father the whole truth ahead of time, I think we can safely put off doing anything right away."

"We?" Faith's eyes widened in disbelief.

"Did I say that?"

"You certainly did."

"Then I guess I'd better honor it. Get ready to ride."

Praise God! After all that had gone wrong, all the danger she'd already lived through, Faith could hardly believe the amazingly wonderful offer. "You'll take me with you?"

"If you want to go."

The idea of spending more time with Hawk didn't frighten her nearly as much as the nameless joy she found she was feeling in anticipation of the opportunity to travel with him. Still, her strict upbringing insisted she add, "We hardly know each other."

"Yes, we do. We're like family, already. You feel it and so do I, so don't bother to deny it. Besides, did you think I'd ride off and leave you? Just where do you think you could go all alone out here?"

"I—I hadn't thought that far ahead," Faith answered, wondering absently if he had meant family like kin, or family like man and wife.

"Well, I have. I can't send you back to the Tucker train or you'll probably be killed. And I certainly can't abandon you. If the bandits or the hostile Indians didn't get you, starvation or thirst or cholera probably would."

Kin, she decided. Definitely like kin. "That's not a very comforting list of choices."

Smiling, Connell got to his feet. "Glad you realize that. I was hoping you'd be sensible and see this my way. It'll make the next few months much easier on both of us."

Months? Was it really going to take that long? Reeling and confused by all she'd been through, all she'd learned, fantasized about, then dismissed as the ridiculous yearnings of a silly girl, Faith took the hand he offered and let him help her up without objecting.

The bare, moist ground felt cool and soothing beneath her feet, as if she were meant to go barefoot for the sheer pleasure of being in close contact with the earth. Awed, she clung to his warm, steadying hand and tried to explain to him how different she'd begun to feel since coming to the plains.

"I'm not surprised to hear that," he said when she had finished. "I always did sense a trace of the People in you."

"The People?"

"That's what the Indians call themselves. I've never met one who wasn't totally in tune with the wildness of the land and the animals."

Faith followed him to where their horses waited, her shoes and stockings in her hand. She gasped with delight when she noticed the old quilt draped across Rojo's withers in front of the saddle.

"Grandma Reeder's quilt! You found it! Oh, thank you."

"You're welcome. It's pretty muddy, but I think it'll clean up all right." He chuckled. "Hopefully, so will you."

Looking down at the horrid red mud clinging to her skirt she could only imagine what the rest of her must look like. "Is it possible I could have a bath and rinse out my dress before I meet Irene? I'd hate to make a bad impression on her." *Not to mention the impression I must be making on you,* she added to herself.

"Maybe." Connell nodded, thinking. "I don't intend to head straight for Black Kettle's camp without making certain it's necessary. First, I'll take you to meet Little Rabbit Woman's people and try to find out which branch of the Arapaho Ab left her with. I'm pretty sure they'll help us. They may even offer to give you something more appropriate to wear in trade for the clothes you have on."

"These rags? Goodness! Why would they want to dress like me?"

"Their interest in the white man's culture is understandable but worrisome. To them we're as fascinating as a new species of animal. I'm afraid their curiosity about us may eventually be their undoing."

"But, surely they realize we feel the same way in regard to them," she suggested.

"Maybe you and I do, Little Muddy Dove, but you have to admit that particular opinion is not a popular one among most settlers."

Faith giggled at his use of the silly nickname. "Little *What?*"

"Don't blame me. You're the one who came up with it in the first place."

"I hardly meant it to become permanent." She was secretly glad he'd substituted the word "muddy" for "soiled," because of the sinful inference of the latter.

"Why not?" He eyed her up and down. "The muddy part certainly fits you lately. And since I'm the Hawk, I think it's appropriate that my traveling companion be a Dove."

Flattered, Faith thought for a moment, then agreed. "All right. I'll be Little Dove. But you have to leave the muddy part out."

"Little Dove Woman it is, then," he said, adding, "It's customary for all Arapaho squaws to have the identifying word, 'woman,' in their full names."

"Like saying 'missus' or 'miss'?"

"I never thought of it quite that way, but I guess you're

right." He laced his fingers together to make a cradle for her to step into as she mounted Stuart's sorrel horse again. Then he handed the quilt to her for safekeeping.

Faith slung it over her horse's neck the same way he had carried it, smoothing the fabric as best she could and arranging it in loose folds. "Thank you."

"You're quite welcome. Keep turning it like that to help it air out so it doesn't mildew. And don't wrap it up in your slicker till you're sure it's completely dry."

"I know that."

He shrugged and smiled over at her as he climbed aboard Rojo and took up the reins. "Sorry. You look so much like a ten-year-old street urchin it's hard to remember how old you really are." He paused a moment. "How old are you, anyway? I never did ask."

"Nineteen last May," Faith said proudly.

Thoughtful, he drew his hand over his neatly trimmed beard and slowly looked her up and down. "I know you won't take kindly to this notion, but I think it would be best if you didn't try to look or act like a capable, grown woman out here. When the question comes up, which it will, leave the explanations to me, even if others happen to be speaking our language."

"What do you intend to say that I couldn't impart every bit as well as you can?"

"Mostly that you're a little crazy in the head," Connell told her. "Indians fear madness. They think it's catching, like smallpox." As expected, his companion didn't seem to relish his honesty or his sarcasm.

Kicking her horse, she urged it closer to him and flicked the loose ends of the reins to sting him on the arm.

"Ouch! Didn't anybody ever tell you that doves are supposed to be harmless?" Laughing, he dodged her second attack.

"Not this dove," Faith declared. "And don't you ever forget it, mister."

"I'm not likely to," he replied. "Just don't get all het up. What I'm really going to say is that you're my long-lost niece. That way, everyone will honor my decisions about what happens to you."

Was he really old enough to be her uncle? she wondered, doubting he could be much more than thirty now that she'd gotten to know him better. Still, if that was how he wanted to think of her it was probably for the best, especially considering the untoward thoughts she'd been battling whenever he was near. *And* when he wasn't.

"What might happen to me? Just for instance, mind you," Faith finally asked. They had fallen into a comfortable, side-by-side canter and were leading the extra horse as they started back to where they'd left Ab.

"Well, for one thing, I don't intend to let any young brave buy you for one of his wives…unless that's what you want, of course."

Faith coughed and sounded like she was strangling. Connell patted her lightly on the shoulder with the flat of his hand while he laughed out loud at the stricken look on her face.

"Wives?" she finally managed to choke out. "Plural?"

"Actually, you're probably already too old and worn-out for most warriors but we can't rule out an old man maybe wanting you, so it's best to be prepared."

At this point, Faith couldn't tell whether he was teasing her or not. One thing she was certain of, however, was that his suggestion she masquerade as his niece and pretend to be family had touched her deeply. In truth, she already felt more genuine affection for the rough plainsman than she could ever remember having had for any man except her father.

As for the rest of the unsettling feelings she was struggling to understand, perhaps they were better forgotten as much as possible, at least until all their other problems were solved.

And there was no time like the present to begin acting the part Hawk had chosen for her. "I'd be pleased to consider you family," she said with genuine affection. "And I promise I will try to comport myself well and make you proud of me, Uncle."

"I already am proud of you," Connell told her.

Faith was so touched by the honestly spoken praise she didn't bother to ask why he felt that way. Having his complete acceptance was enough.

Chapter Nine

Ab was in better spirits by the time they returned to fetch him. At sunup he had managed to locate the shallow grave intended for Faith, drag Stuart's body into it and bury him, but not before stripping the other man of every stitch of clothing and keeping it for himself.

Consequently, the skinny little man was no longer freezing, which helped lift his dour mood considerably even if he did look strange with Stuart's trousers draped over his shoulders like a soggy shawl.

"How far to the Arapaho camp?" Faith asked as she rode along beside Connell with Ab bringing up the rear.

"Not far. Which reminds me, you'd better let me carry your Colt from here on out."

"I thought you wanted me armed all the time."

"That was only to impress Tucker. Where we're going, most women aren't warlike."

"Neither am I," she said, unbuckling the belt and handing the holstered pistol to Connell. "You sure I won't need to protect myself from the Indians?"

He huffed. "If you did, one gun sure wouldn't be enough."

"I suppose that's true." Faith shifted in the saddle. "I'm not used to riding so long. Can't we stop and rest?"

"In an hour or so you'll get all the rest you want." He was scanning the horizon. "We should start seeing the Coyote Men pretty soon."

"The what?"

"They're a guard society of the Arapaho. They dress in white buffalo robes and paint their faces white, too, then stand sentry duty outside the main camps."

"Oh, like in the army."

Connell glared over his shoulder at Ab when the old man snorted in derision. "Not exactly like that. In the cavalry a different man takes over the post every few hours. Coyote Men do their jobs for years. They live in the hills, build no shelter no matter what the weather, and remain totally alone for as long as they continue to hold the office."

"You mean *totally* alone?" She blushed and averted her gaze.

"Yes," Connell said. "They have no families, most especially no wives. Women are considered far too much of a distraction."

Faith was flabbergasted. "I've never known anyone that dedicated to their job."

"It's more than a job to the Arapaho," he explained. "It's an honor. When one Coyote Man decides he's finished, he takes his decorated rifle or war club and personally passes it to the man he has chosen to be his successor."

"Goodness. There is a lot to learn about red men, isn't there?"

Ab was chuckling and trying to stifle the noise by covering his half-toothless mouth with his hand.

"That's another myth," Connell said. "Indians aren't red by nature, they paint themselves that color for certain ceremonies. For instance, when a family member dies, there will be a year or more afterward when mourners who have cut off their long braids for the burial will not try to improve their appearance in any way. Then, when the mourning time is over, an elder will paint their faces and hair with red clay. That signals that they're free to dress and act like everyone else and resume normal life."

"They aren't born red?" Faith continued to be astonished. "But I've read lots of novels that said they were."

"Written by men who had never been west of the Mississippi, I'll wager," Connell said with disdain. "Some of them have darker skin and distinctive features, but that's all that sets them apart. That, and their primitive culture. Many's the time I've thought their ways made a lot more sense than ours."

While he'd been explaining Indian custom, Faith had been studying his strong profile and wondering what he might look like without a beard. There were tiny wrinkles in the outer corners of his eyes, caused undoubtedly by his prolonged exposure to the elements, but she was willing to bet he was a lot younger man than he let on.

"I have an idea," she ventured, hoping to change the subject enough that he at least quit scowling. "Instead of pretending to be my uncle, why don't you be my brother?"

From the rear, Ab piped up, "I vote for that one, mister."

A half smile lifted the corner of Hawk's mouth as he nodded in agreement. "Sounds good to me, too. Only there's something you should know first, Miss Faith."

"What now? Will you be painting me red, too? I know I should still be in mourning for Mama."

"Oh, no, nothing quite so easy to bear, I'm afraid. You see, from puberty on, Arapaho brothers and sisters are not permitted to speak to one another. As my sister, you would be expected to keep totally silent in my presence and not dare to even look at me, no matter what."

"Oh, dear."

Connell's smile grew. "Something told me you wouldn't cotton to those rules. Of course, if you want me as a big brother instead of an uncle I have no objections."

Faith knew he was having fun at her expense, a conclusion that bruised her pride. Granted, she talked a lot but what did he expect under the circumstances? She needed to learn as much as she could before reaching the Indian camp or she might break some obscure Native taboo and inadvertently get them all into terrible trouble.

As for her habit of staring at Connell so much of the time, well, she couldn't help that. Not really. She'd tried to keep from gawking and had succeeded in subduing her yearning only enough to limit it to the instances when she didn't think he'd notice the undue attention. Obviously, she had not been nearly as surreptitious as she'd fancied.

And now, both he and Ab were laughing at her. Well, let them. For the present she had little choice about anything, including her traveling companions, and it was of no consequence whether or not she was happy about the trying situation. Later, when they had rescued Irene and put Tucker in his place, she'd speak her mind. Until then she intended to play the acquiescent compatriot even if it galled her something awful to do so.

Faith never saw any guards outside the Arapaho camp, which, of course, didn't mean there had been none. The thing that did astound her was the noise of so many barking dogs and the shouts coming from the horde of people who flocked out of the teepees and gathered around them as soon as they entered the camp circle.

Looking down from atop her mount at the hundreds of stern-looking Indians pushing in on them, she found herself much more breathlessly frightened than she had imagined she would be.

As if reading her mind, Connell reached over and patted her hands, taking the reins of her horse from her without protest to lead her farther into the fray.

Faith felt a bent old crone tugging on her skirt and forced a brief smile of greeting, only to be met with a toothless sneer. Most of the men, as well as the children, were nearly naked. For the most part the people were thin and muscular, with the men being taller than those few old women she could see.

In the distance, younger women watched in relative silence, some balancing babies on their hips or packing them in cradle-boards decorated with brightly dyed porcupine quill designs. The designs looked the same as the ones on the beautiful doeskin rifle scabbard Connell treasured so.

"We should have brought gifts," he called back to Faith. "Too bad there wasn't time to at least hunt on our way here."

Her reply was thin, quavering, in spite of her brave front. "I just hope you know what you're doing."

Without comment, Connell swung down off his horse and began to make hand signals to an impressive-looking man.

Faith took him to be the chief, due to the deference everyone else was paying him and to the larger-sized teepee from which he had emerged.

The entire group of Arapaho stepped back abruptly, leaving Connell and the Indian standing alone inside a tightly packed outer circle of taciturn braves.

Faith was intensely glad she had not insisted she play the part of Connell's sister, because she couldn't have taken her eyes off him at that moment if their lives had depended upon it. He was magnificent! Standing tall and strong, he faced the Arapaho leader as an equal, showing no fear, while he made sign language with his hands.

The surrounding din was such that she couldn't hear whether he was also speaking aloud, although she assumed he must be. The bits and snatches of language she could hear in the background were foreign sounding. Some had a lilting quality that fascinated her, making the hair at the back of her neck prickle in primitive warning at the same time.

The chief finally shook Connell's hand, nodded, then made a sweeping signal with his arm. To her amazement the mob on that side of the camp divided into two halves as obediently as she imagined the Red Sea must have parted for Moses!

Connell made some apparently corresponding motions then returned to stand beside her horse and speak briefly. "Irene was here, like Ab said, but the hunters I talked to were right about her being with Black Kettle now. His camp is over that ridge to the west. We'll have to hurry. All the tribes are getting ready to start their move toward winter quarters."

Faith nodded. Connell's demeanor remained cautious and rather stilted as he mounted Rojo, adding to her already considerable nervousness. He obviously knew the chief to whom he had been talking, yet it seemed as though their relationship was not an overly friendly one in spite of his earlier references to his late wife's people.

She fell into line behind him, with Ab closely following, and they rode through the legion of braves. Waiting till they had cleared the camp, she finally gathered the courage to ask, "Is everything all right?"

"Yes," Connell said quietly aside.

"What about gifts? Don't we need to get some to ransom Irene? And what are we going to do with Ab, drag him along all the way?"

"I should have made you my sister," he muttered.

Faith was not subdued enough by his obviously disapproving tone to give up completely. "I just wondered."

Connell relented. "Ab will be staying with Black Kettle as a willing slave, if the chief will have him—by his own choice, I might add."

She frowned. "Who was that noble Indian we just left? He acted awfully important."

"He is. Chief Bull Bear was my wife's second cousin," Hawk explained, glancing back over his shoulder at the circle of teepees behind them. He was speaking softly, as if the wind might carry his words back to the chief's ears even at that great distance.

"You're considered related to him, right?" The assumption made her feel a lot safer in their present circumstances.

"I was, yes. No one was pleased when Little Rabbit Woman married a white man, but I made enough gifts to the family after our marriage to atone for her supposed sins and they ultimately accepted me as one of their own."

"Then why are you acting so uneasy?"

"Now that my wife is dead, I don't have as secure a place in the tribe as I once did."

"There's more, isn't there?" Faith asked, nudging the sorrel in the flanks to keep up.

"Yes," he said. "Bull Bear knew all about my family history. I had never mentioned having a brother, let alone a niece, so he suspects I lied about you. He's willing to overlook it for now, but there's no telling what he might do to save face if he learned the entire truth about your past, especially regarding Tucker. He hates emigrants. Wagon trains carried cholera to the plains last year. Many tribes saw half their members die of the white man's sickness."

"Oh, dear."

"My sentiments, exactly. Now, if you're through asking questions, let's make tracks."

Trembling, she reined her horse and fell in behind him, praying silently for God's guidance and strength in the trials yet to come.

Faith seldom took her eyes off Hawk's broad back until they were within sight of the second camp.

Hundreds of teepees stood in an enormous circle, their outer walls shimmering and pale beneath the blazing sun as wisps of gray smoke rose through the openings at the peaks.

Off to one side, a group of women had pegged buffalo hides to the ground and were kneeling next to them, removing the last remnants of fat with handheld scrapers of bone and antler. Nearby, little girls were pretending to be busy at the same task as they mimicked their mothers.

Faith looked over at them and smiled, remembering her own childhood and the way she'd wanted to be exactly like her mother in every way. Oh, how she wished she were a carefree child again, at home with her parents, instead of being led through hostile territory into goodness knows what kind of awful danger.

That sobering thought was enough to destroy the brief camaraderie she'd been feeling in regard to the other women and girls and make her once again assess the Indian camp with a critical eye. Many Cheyenne had lifted and tied up the skins lining the lower several feet of their teepees, apparently to take advantage of any cooling breezes. That was certainly sensible, given the weather of late.

Faith sighed. The flat, nearly treeless prairie radiated heat like an iron skillet. Without her slat bonnet or a hat of any kind, she was a helpless victim of the sun. She yearned to raise her hand, to shade her eyes so she could better observe the details of the village, but hesitated sensibly. Any untoward movement, especially one which could be construed as fear or aggression, would be very foolish. She wasn't about to do anything that might trigger an attack response. She and her companions were obviously in enough hot water already.

Ahead, Connell rode slowly into the circle of teepees, his back ramrod straight, and she followed. It was clear that their imminent arrival had been expected. Faith assumed Bull Bear must have sent word to his Cheyenne cohorts, because their little threesome was not creating nearly the furor it had in the other camp, although a few little boys did stop their stick horses and lower their play bows and arrows to watch the unusual party pass by.

Dogs of all sizes and descriptions set up an awful din, some even darting out to nip at her horse's heels, but other than that, very few Cheyenne ceased their daily labors. Nor did fierce-looking warriors seem to be gathering in the numbers she had seen in the Arapaho village.

Maybe Connell had been worried about their situation for nothing, Faith mused, trying to convince herself more than anything. Perhaps he had borrowed trouble simply because he'd felt so uncomfortable facing his former Arapaho relatives.

And maybe the reverse was true, she added with dismay as her thoughts came full circle. Given Hawk's Indian background and his awareness of her stubborn temperament, perhaps he was minimizing their danger merely to keep her from worrying or trying to help. If he felt he had a choice, would he tell her about the inherent dangers of their journey or would he hide them from her?

She knew the answer to those unsettling questions as well as she knew her own name. Hawk McClain would not have told her any details about their shared peril if he had felt there was an alternative way to govern her thoughts, words and actions.

Consequently, they were no doubt muddled in a far bigger predicament than she'd so far imagined and she wished mightily that she had not been quite so quick to figure out the truth.

The question now was, how personally risky was the trouble they were about to face? And what could she hope to do about it, unarmed as she now was—thanks to him—other than pray more fervently than she had before?

Prayer, she concluded, was a *very* good idea.

Chapter Ten

"Black Kettle is generally not warlike, but don't expect him to be as genial to us as Bull Bear," Connell warned aside, preparing Faith for their upcoming encounter.

"You're certain this is where we'll find Irene?"

"I hope so. Black Kettle bought her from the Arapaho. If he didn't turn around and sell her to another chief, she'll be here."

Faith could tell from the set of his jaw and the way his chin jutted out that he was anything but pleased to hear that his future wife had been traded like a prized horse or a bundle of bright cloth. Still, she was alive. There was that to be thankful for.

"What else did you find out?"

"Not much more," Connell said. "I do know she's unmarried, which is a surprise. Apparently she's been living with an old Arapaho medicine man. They say he's the only one who's not afraid of her magic, so Black Kettle bought them as a pair."

"Magic? What magic?"

"Your guess is as good as mine. All Bull Bear would say

was that she can make the heavens sing and the earth tremble whenever she wants."

"Dear me."

"I expect I'll be invited to sit and smoke with the Cheyenne," Connell explained, reining in his horse and leaning closer to speak with her more privately. "I plan to refuse to leave you behind with Ab, but there are some rules you'll need to observe no matter what happens."

"Go on."

Her tone was so compliant, so cooperative, Connell raised one eyebrow and studied her expression for a few moments before continuing. "If Black Kettle doesn't come out to greet us in person, that means we'll be taken into the lodge to see him. Just follow my lead and you'll do fine."

Faith was trembling. "What if we're separated?"

"That's not going to happen."

"But what if it does? How will I know what to do, how to act around the Indians?"

"I can't possibly tell you everything you'd need to know in the few minutes we have left."

"Well, try," she insisted. "You'd be surprised how clear my mind is when I'm scared to death!"

Connell smiled slightly as he dismounted and circled the big gelding, patting the faithful horse's rump as he went. Approaching Faith's horse, he gathered up the reins of both mounts and handed them over to Ab for temporary safekeeping before helping her dismount.

He paused a moment to make sure she was steady on her feet before letting go, then whispered, "All right. There are a few details which might help. Remember to always turn to the right when entering a lodge."

"Why?"

He gave her a stern look. "Do you want instruction, or not?"

"I do, I do. Go ahead. What else?"

"Once you're inside, pause and wait to be invited farther, then do whatever your host indicates. In my case, Black Kettle will probably ask me to sit on the left, which is an honor because it's the family side of the teepee. You stay to the right unless you're told otherwise."

She nodded gravely. "I understand. Go on."

"If you're moving around in there for any reason, never walk between your host and the fire, or between the fire and anyone else, for that matter. Go behind them, even if there's precious little room to pass. They'll lean forward for you."

"Okay. What else?"

He sighed, yet graced her with an amiable smile. "That's enough etiquette for now. Get that much right and you'll impress them plenty, believe me."

Directly ahead lay the largest teepee of the scores Faith could see. Its skin flap of a door was propped open by means of two straight sticks, but the outer walls were let all the way down to ground level. A tall, stalwart brave armed with a feather-bedecked lance and a round, leather shield was standing guard.

Connell received the invitation he had expected and took Faith's hand to pull her along behind him, leaving Ab outside to mind the horses and fend for himself.

Daunted, she walked softly, cautiously, recalling her brief instructions on proper comportment and wondering what other details she should know that Connell hadn't had time or inclination to impart. Why, oh why, hadn't he used their time traveling between the Indian camps to educate her?

As her vision adjusted to the dim light she saw a dozen pairs of shadowy, narrowed eyes trained on her. In the gentile society from which she'd come, such undue attention might have made Faith embarrassed at her unkempt appearance but it wouldn't have frightened her. Here, it unhinged her almost to the point of wanting to yank free of her partner's hold and try to flee.

Connell must have sensed her distress because he said something to the gathered savages that made them laugh, then physically plunked her down on the ground near the door before proceeding to greet the chief and take a seat beside him by direct request.

Faith tucked her legs beneath her to mimic the posture and demeanor of the other women and tried to keep her ever-widening eyes demurely averted. It was impossible. Finally she gave up fighting her curiosity and settled for feigning submission while she peeked from beneath lowered lashes.

Black Kettle, Connell and several other men began to smoke a long-shanked pipe that they passed around the semi-circle with great ceremony. The bowl nearly touched the ground and the long stem pointed to the sky every time a different smoker took a turn.

Far younger than she'd expected him to be, the chief was wearing a leather shirt ornamented with beads and small hanks of hair. Swallowing hard, she shuddered to think where the latter decoration might have come from!

Except for quill and bead adornments, the other braves were bare from the waist up. In spite of their inherent ferocity they were truly magnificent specimens of humanity, Faith thought, blushing, although not one was nearly as appealing looking as Hawk had been when she'd convinced him to strip off his shirt while she cut his hair.

Immediately penitent, she wondered what her prim, godly mother would say if she happened to be looking down from heaven and was able to read her elder daughter's decidedly scandalous thoughts!

The heat inside the tent was stifling compared to the

outdoor temperature, not to mention the strong odors of cooking and goodness knows what all else that filled the air. Clouds of worrisome gnats buzzed around Faith's head. If the others had been paying the slightest attention to the pesky insects, she would have shooed them away. As it was, however, she was loath to move a muscle, so she sat and endured the itching, tickling flies, praying, above all, that the tiny bugs would not scoot up her nose and make her sneeze!

One of the Indian women across the tent suddenly arose and began to fill a wooden bowl with bits of roast meat from a skewer. The sight made Faith's mouth water. Food! She was so hungry she knew she could eat almost anything and be truly thankful for it.

With a respectful bow, the squaw offered the bowl to the chief, who took four small pieces of meat and raised them in his clasped hands in what Faith took to be a spiritual blessing akin to her family's habit of saying grace over a meal. The bowl was then passed to Connell and proceeded around the circle of men.

Faith waited. The food bowl never came her way. Instead, everyone was acting as if she were invisible.

Correction, she thought glumly. Not invisible. Of no importance. There was a big difference. Not that she cared one whit about the Indians' personal opinions of her. She just wished they'd feed her something—anything—before the noisy growling of her stomach disturbed the entire gathering.

Connell noticed his erstwhile niece's fidgeting and quieted her with a stern look. The woman who had offered the meat had returned to her place across the tent while a younger and much prettier squaw had been summoned and was bowing before the chief. In moments, that girl ducked out the door and disappeared.

Instinct told Faith a momentous event was about to take

place. Her pulse quickened. She couldn't tell much from looking at the faces of the Indians, but Connell's expression clearly held promise. Every muscle in his body was tense.

Long minutes passed. Faith had been so intent on watching Hawk she flinched noticeably when a skinny, bent, old man limped into the teepee. He was leaning on a crutch that was nearly as gnarled as he was and in his opposite hand he carried a small leather pouch.

The old man stopped. A hush fell over the crowd. Everyone turned to look at the doorway.

There stood the most elegant woman Faith had ever seen. Her dress was of softly pliant deerskin adorned with porcupine quills and beaded fringe. The left shoulder of the short gown was loosely draped while the woman's right arm was encased in a sleeve that reached her elbow. Below the calf-length skirt, her legs were hidden by leggings and the tops of her moccasins.

The woman glided forward with the utmost grace, making no noise as she approached Connell. Faith could see from his expression that he was deeply moved. Could this regal Indian possibly be his lost love?

In moments Faith had decided that the newcomer was, indeed, Irene Wellman. The woman's native garb had confused the issue at first, as had the fact that her long, dark hair had been braided and elaborately decorated with beadwork, then wound into coils against the sides of her head, one coil over each ear.

There was little time for Faith to speculate further. The man who had preceded Irene into the teepee handed her the leather bag and stepped aside with a low bow.

Seated where she was, Faith couldn't see everything that was transpiring, but her observations of the Cheyenne told her plenty. They were clearly in awe. Some even looked frightened, although they hid the emotion well.

Irene opened the beaded pouch and reached inside. Someone coughed nervously. Caught up in the mood of the moment, Faith held her breath like everyone else. She believed in the kind of miracles that were mentioned in the Bible but not in magic. What could possibly be in that little bag that could have bamboozled so many Indians so thoroughly?

Irene raised a small, shiny object aloft in her upturned palms and murmured words that sounded a lot like a civilized, Christian prayer. The only other sound was raspy communal breathing.

Heart pounding, Faith clasped her hands together tightly and kept them in her lap, waiting along with the rest of the company for whatever was about to happen.

Suddenly, the silver object Irene held began to whir and jingle, the cacophony of sound heightened by the close confines of the teepee. Every Cheyenne present gasped, some even ducking and cowering against the tent.

The breath went out of Faith's bursting lungs in a loud whoosh of relief the moment she recognized what she was hearing. Papa had once owned a pocket watch with an alarm bell just like that! He had often delighted his daughters by setting it to go off at odd times. Until now, it had never occurred to Faith that anyone might be frightened of the pleasantly interesting sound, yet these people obviously were.

Her eyes bright, her soul comforted, Faith chanced a smile at Connell and was rewarded by the most threatening look he had ever bestowed upon her.

Immediately repentant, she lowered her glance and struggled to control her outward glee. How foolish! Of course she must not show any sign of relief or amusement. To do so might destroy the Indians' confidence in Irene's supposedly supernatural abilities and undermine her position of importance within the tribe.

Cautiously subdued, Faith peeked up at the priestess of the pocket watch long enough to ascertain that the gathered worshippers had not noticed the untoward reaction from their uninvited guest. Good. At least she hadn't jeopardized Connell's plans, whatever they might be.

Sighing, Faith noticed for the first time that she had a splitting headache, which was not at all surprising considering the fact that she hadn't eaten in longer than she could recall. Not that she would really have welcomed dinner from the communal pot the others had shared. She'd heard stories about some tribes' fondness for dog meat and she wasn't all that sure that the Cheyenne didn't partake of such atrocities. Give her a delicious rabbit stew any day.

The ridiculousness of that thought was not lost on Faith. As a child she'd made pets of all the farm animals, much to her parents' regret, and had often refused to consume nourishing food simply because she had known the main course too personally.

Customs being different for various societies, she supposed she had no real right to be shocked by anything the Indians did, any more than they would be expected to understand that the mechanical workings of a fancy pocket watch did not qualify it for deification.

Irene was lowering her arms and bowing before Black Kettle. If she had acknowledged recognizing Connell she had done it in a guileful manner hidden from Faith.

Hawk got to his feet, as did the chief. Black Kettle led the way to the door, followed by Connell, then Irene and her stooped companion.

Faith hadn't been instructed what to do next. She'd not been able to catch Connell's eye for direction either. If she hadn't seen one of his fingers crook slightly as he passed, she'd have been at a loss. Hopefully, it had been his signal to follow rather than a nervous twitch!

Her decision to bolt wasn't a hard one to make. The Cheyenne men had all filed out, but the few women remaining were staring at her as if she were the most repulsive person they had ever seen. The last thing Faith wanted was to remain there with them.

Struggling to her feet, she straightened her clothing and brushed off her skirt as if it had been clean to start with. No one spoke or stepped forward to stop her. She took a tentative step toward the door. *So far, so good.*

If she'd been visiting in the home of one of her friends back in Burg Hill she'd have known the proper way to behave. Here, she could only guess. Surely, some pleasant parting word was in order, if only to make herself feel more normal.

With a slight smile and a nod to the other women she said, "So nice of you to invite me. Sorry I can't stay and chat. Maybe next time."

Their bewildered looks widened her smile. Obviously, they hadn't expected her amiable tone of voice or polite leave-taking.

She proceeded to the door, then paused and turned. "I know you don't understand a word I'm saying, but I am grateful. I doubt anyone I know back home would have welcomed you the way you've welcomed me." The corners of her mouth lifted once again. "I just wish you smiled a little more."

To her surprise, the Cheyenne women not only smiled, they began to giggle.

Connell hoped Faith had seen his signal and was trailing along behind, as was the custom. He hadn't dared speak to her as he passed or break stride while accompanying Black Kettle on through the camp. To do so could have caused him to lose face, setting him back a long way in his negotiations to free Irene.

He'd figured from the start that he'd have to either buy her or convince the chief she was already his wife and therefore belonged to him. Now that he'd seen how important her so-called skill was to the Cheyenne, however, he suspected he'd have to rethink his plan.

If Irene had been adopted into that Cheyenne band, his task would have been much easier. As chief, Black Kettle was supposed to set an example of benevolence for his subjects, which meant he would take no personal revenge if Irene decided to run off. Moreover, the chief was wearing a scalp shirt, indicating that he bore an even bigger burden to live in peace with tribal members. Both of those elements could work to Connell's advantage as long as he didn't push his demands too far.

Above all, it was critical he find a way to be alone with Irene and learn her exact situation. Then they could work together to secure her freedom. In theory, that sounded easy. In truth, the problem was far from simple. And speaking of solving insurmountable problems, he still had Faith to worry about, too.

Connell altered his even strides just enough for a quick glance back. The sight that greeted him was so comical he nearly burst out laughing.

Black Kettle noticed and paused to look back, too. The men's eyes met in shared good humor.

"She is brave," Black Kettle said.

Nodding, Connell chuckled. "Sometimes too brave."

"The little ones like her."

"True." The plainsman laughed, incredulous. "I hope they don't tear her to shreds proving it."

As he watched, Faith struggled to make forward progress while surrounded by a gaggle of excited children, some barely big enough to walk. He could tell she was speaking to them because she kept bending down, first one way, then another, in response to a tug on her skirt or a tap on her arm. One little girl of about five was holding up a miniature cradle-board with a doll made of deer hide tucked inside.

Faith barely had time to properly admire the doll when another girl thrust a tiny brown puppy into her arms. She held it the same way the child had, like a baby, and rocked it, much to all the children's delight. When the pup started to wiggle then lunged up to lick Faith's face, the entire group burst into riotous laughter.

Eyes twinkling, smile bright, Faith's gaze met Connell's and he was struck by the fact he'd never before seen her look so happy. She was like a child, herself, a carefree girl enjoying an amusing time with friends. Had she been that lighthearted before her mother had died and she'd been forced to take charge of her foolhardy sister? he wondered. Or had she always been the serious, overly conscientious person he'd helped at Fort Laramie?

Whichever it was, he was glad to see her smiling now. Very glad.

Chapter Eleven

Though Irene and the medicine man went on ahead, Connell and the chief waited until Faith and her playful entourage drew nearer. When the little ones stopped in deference to Black Kettle's authority, Faith did, too.

She was still holding the squirming puppy in her arms and grinning. "Sorry you had to wait," she told Connell. "I would have been here sooner but somebody made me designated babysitter and I have no idea how to quit the job!"

"They're just curious about you," Connell said. "And little wonder. They probably think you sprouted from the earth like a stalk of corn."

"Why would they think that?" His cursory glance at her muddy clothing answered the question. "Never mind. I get the idea. Do you suppose I—?" She'd been about to say *Irene,* and stopped herself in the nick of time. "I mean, would it be possible for me to clean up while we're here? I'd love to be able to wash."

"How about your ribs?" the plainsman asked. "Don't you need them wrapped again?"

"I told you before. They're fine."

"Humph. I didn't believe you the first time you gave me that story and I certainly don't believe it now. Not after the manhandling you got from Stuart."

"I'll be okay," she insisted.

Sobering, Connell turned to Black Kettle and they began to converse in Cheyenne.

When he again faced Faith he said, "We'll be given a lodge for the next two days. After that, everybody will break camp and move north to follow the buffalo for better hunting."

He waited, watching her face until he saw the full portent of his statement register. The moment she opened her mouth, he interrupted. "That's right. One lodge. Don't look so shocked. It's the custom in all the tribes. Families live and work together. In *harmony*."

"But…"

"As my niece, you will be expected to cook and clean and care for the teepee while I go out hunting with the braves." He smiled benevolently. "Actually, it's not all that different from the arrangement we had before."

"You didn't bunk in my wagon!"

"We have no choice."

"Well, I have a choice. I'm not sleeping with you!"

Standing off to one side, Black Kettle began to chuckle, then said in perfect English, "I am glad she is your kinsman, Pale Hawk. Forget what I said about making a trade. I would not have such a prickly pear if you gave her to me with a hundred fine horses."

The lodge they were assigned was on the outskirts of the village. Connell entered first and Faith followed. In the center, directly below the vent hole at the top, a small fire smoldered. Buffalo robes lay at one end of the room, hair-side down, and folded leather parfleches filled with dried fruit and meat hung like decorated saddlebags from the slanting rafters. The only worn or soiled things in the room were the sparse trappings they'd had with them while traveling, including Connell's rifle scabbard and Grandmother Reeder's quilt.

"This place looks brand-new," Faith marveled.

"It is." He closed the door flap for more privacy. "It belongs to a newly married couple. They'll stay with relatives until we're gone."

"How unfair! We can't let them give up their home."

"We can't refuse. It would be disrespectful. The fact that we were offered this lodge shows we're highly valued guests."

"Oh." She walked slowly around the perimeter and assessed the fine handwork on the parfleches as well as the embroidery on the tent lining. "This is beautiful. Did the bride make all this?"

"Probably none of it," Connell explained. "It's customary for her mother to prepare the lodge and pitch it near her own, then furnish it just as you see it and present it as a gift. Sometimes other relatives contribute things, too, but it's the bride's mother who's in charge."

"Won't she be resentful of us? Most women would be."

"If she is she won't show it," Connell said. "One of the things the white man doesn't understand about the Indian is his sacrifices for the common good. Even though tribes make war with each other, there's very little dissension within the bands. If a man is poor or sick, the others take care of his family's needs without hesitation."

"We do the same back home," Faith argued.

"Really? After the tornado blew your house away, how many of your neighbors offered you another house, or even a bed?"

"They would have if they could have. They'd been hit hard, too. Everybody suffered terrible losses."

"I understand that," Connell said. "But out here another branch of the tribe would have brought all they owned, if necessary, and given it to you with no strings attached. In return, all you'd have been expected to do was try to get back on your feet and someday do the same for another needy neighbor."

"That's like the scripture, 'Do unto others'!"

"Exactly."

"How wonderful."

"Yes, it is. But that isn't all there is to this culture. Rules are strict. Customs can seem harsh. Even cruel. Justice is swift and deadly. Tribal life is not for the fainthearted." He looked at her tellingly. "Or a good place for a lone, unprotected woman."

"I know what you mean. So, how are we going to save Irene?"

Connell snorted. "That's a good question. One I've been asking myself ever since I saw how important she's become to the Cheyenne. I need to know more details, which is why you won't have to worry about me getting in your way tonight, Little Muddy Dove Woman."

She ignored the jest. "Why not? Where will you be?"

"Standing under a blanket in front of Irene's lodge and waiting to properly court my future bride," he said flatly. "If she plays by the rules and comes out, she'll join me under the blanket and we can huddle together to talk privately—all night, if necessary—as long as we stay in the public view."

"What if she doesn't come out?"

"Then I may have to abduct her."

Faith couldn't help the catch in her breath. "Isn't that dangerous?"

"Not for Irene and me. Even if Black Kettle weren't the

chief, he's wearing a scalp shirt. Both dictate his code of conduct. If he came after us he'd be breaking a taboo and proving he's not worthy to remain chief." The plainsman's brow furrowed. "But that doesn't prevent him from getting even another way. You and Ab might have to pay dearly if I left you behind."

"You wouldn't!" she blurted, immediately penitent when she saw the hurt in his eyes. Her voice gentled. "No, of course you wouldn't. I know that. And I'll do whatever I can to help you free your beloved Irene. I promise."

Without a word, Connell nodded, turned and walked out.

In minutes, a girl of about fifteen arrived bringing food, water and a soft, pale deerskin shift. Faith had never been so thrilled to receive new clothes in her entire life. She slipped out of her dress, unwound the chafing muslin strips that circled her torso, and gladly donned the native attire over her bloomers.

The girl showed her how to wrap and tie the leggings she'd brought, then lace moccasins over them. The completed outfit was comfortable beyond belief. Faith stepped back and twirled to show off the dress.

"Oh, thank you! I love this."

Her words were heartfelt and simple, yet clearly not understood, so she smiled and patted the teenager's hand in a motherly fashion.

Acting shy, the girl held up a small rope.

Faith took it and looked down at her garb. Nothing seemed to be missing. "What's this for?" She chuckled at her own silliness. "Never mind. Of course you can't tell me." Holding it out, she asked, "Show me?"

The Indian girl gestured to her waist, then made a tying motion, so Faith knotted the rope around her dress like a belt, much to her companion's muted glee.

Shaking her head and covering her smile, the girl went to work on Faith's hair with a wide-toothed comb, eventually making long braids, leaving them loose instead of rolling them as Irene's had been. She then led her to the food she'd brought and presented it proudly, using hand signals to urge her to eat.

Faith was so intent on devouring the dried fruit and stringy meat she didn't even bother to protest when the Indian girl gathered her ruined calico into a bundle and ran from the lodge with it.

At dusk, Connell waited patiently outside the door to Irene's teepee. A blanket was draped across his shoulders in spite of the continuing heat.

To his consternation, he wasn't her only suitor. A muscular brave who looked to be about twenty-five, had come to stand beside him. The enmity in the Indian's eyes was as sharp as an arrow point and as menacing as the fangs of a prairie rattlesnake.

Connell's only advantage was that he had arrived before the brave and was therefore closest to the teepee door. If Irene stuck to Cheyenne custom, she would speak to him first, perhaps ignoring the other man entirely. In that case, Connell knew he'd best not turn his back on his rival unless he wanted his hair parted with a war club.

He could hear Irene inside the lodge. She was talking to the old medicine man in a mixture of Cheyenne and Arapaho. Pleased at the sound of her familiar voice, Connell listened. It seemed strange to hear her speaking languages other than English, but he was proud that she'd become so accomplished. Some prisoners never even tried to understand their captors, let alone learned from them.

Neither man moved a muscle when the old Arapaho appeared at the teepee door, paused to tell Irene he was going off for a quiet smoke, then limped away.

Tense, Connell waited for her to come out. Seconds seemed to tick by very slowly. *Like a pocket watch in need of winding,* he reflected. His heart swelled with gratitude that Irene had had her amazing watch with her when she'd been kidnapped, and that she'd had the intelligence to use it to such good advantage.

He could only think of one other woman who would have done as well, and that woman was Faith Beal. Except that Faith would probably have talked too much or acted stubborn and gotten herself into a worse pickle, Connell thought, smiling to himself. She was quite a woman. Unique. With a heart as big as the prairie and courage that would put many a man to shame.

His musings came full circle and his gut gave a twist. Irene was his betrothed, not Faith. Irene should be first in his heart even if they were both merely honoring an old promise rather than being madly in love, so why did he keep thinking of Faith with so much affection? And why had no other woman ever stirred such fervor within him? *Not even Little Rabbit Woman.*

As if summoned by his turbulent thoughts, Irene Wellman left the confines of her lodge to face her suitors.

Connell lifted the front edge of his blanket. So did the brave standing close by.

She hesitated, looking from man to man, and raised her hand toward Connell, palm out, as if urging patience. To his total astonishment, she then stepped into the arms of the Cheyenne brave!

Connell froze. Had his worst fears been confirmed? Was he going to have to resort to the same kind of warlike tactics that had put her in the Indian camp in the first place? He strained to hear what she and the brave were saying, but their words were muffled beneath the wrapped-around blanket. All he could hope at this point was that she'd give him a chance to talk to her, too.

A tug on his buckskin distracted him momentarily. He looked down to see who had had the audacity to break into a courtship ritual. The most unlikely Indian he'd ever seen was grinning up at him.

"Thank goodness I finally found you," Faith said.

Connell scowled. "I should have known. What are you doing here?"

"Looking for you, mostly." She pivoted to display her dress for him. "A sweet girl brought me this. Isn't it wonderful? And so comfortable. Even my sore ribs feel better. She fixed my hair and fed me, too."

He was eyeing her costume. "Who dressed you?"

"The same girl. She didn't understand a word I said and I didn't understand her, either, but we managed just fine."

One corner of his mouth twitched in a repressed smile. "Not entirely."

"What do you mean?"

"Irene can explain it to you," he said, cocking his head toward the blanket where the two still stood, wrapped together from the waist up. "When she's done with him."

Faith lowered her voice. "That's her? Under there?"

He nodded. "Why don't you go into her lodge and wait for us. There's nobody else home right now so it's perfectly safe."

"Are you sure?"

"Positive." He allowed his smile to spread. "I'm sure glad I already warned the tribal council you were crazy in the head."

"Why?"

"Never mind. Just get inside, out of sight, and wait for me."

Faith faced him, hands fisted on her hips, and pressed her

lips into a stubborn line. "No. I'm not going anywhere till you tell me what's so funny."

"You won't like it."

"Try me."

"Let's just say, as your *uncle,* I'm disappointed in your up-bringing and leave it at that."

"Oh, no," she said, shaking her head. "Talking in riddles won't get you off. I intend to know what's going on around here or else—even if I can't speak the language."

"Okay," Connell drawled, "but remember, I didn't want to do this. You asked for it."

Pausing for effect, he smiled and added, "Little Dove Woman, I regret to inform you…you've tied your chastity belt on the outside of your clothes."

Mortified, Faith had immediately wheeled and run for the privacy of Irene's teepee, fumbling to untie the rope as she went.

Although she'd now had hours to examine the knotted cords more closely, she still couldn't visualize how they were supposed to be applied or what good they'd do.

Her cheeks flamed. No wonder the Indian girl had giggled and looked so embarrassed when she'd mistaken the rigging for a sash!

In retrospect, she felt slightly vindicated, however. Never in all her reading or listening to tales of fellow pilgrims had she heard even a whisper about Indian women wearing such things. On the contrary, more than one emigrant had sworn that promiscuity was the norm for the tribes of the plains.

Was it? Were the Cheyenne that different from all the rest? If so, they must have a terrible time adjusting to living and working beside other groups. No wonder so many of them fought amongst themselves as well as against white men.

With neither pockets nor a reticule in which to hide her humiliating error, Faith wadded the string girdle into a ball and stuffed it beneath the edge of a buffalo robe, then sat down on the robe to wait for Irene and Connell.

The soft background hum of the camp blended into a slumberous blur. Weariness encroached on her mind, urging much-needed rest. She gave in only enough to lie back on the soft skins, fully intending to remain awake. Her lids grew heavy, her aching body finding the respite it so desperately craved.

The next thing she knew, the rumble of Connell's voice was pulling her back from a dreamless sleep.

"She's game," he said.

A woman answered. "Young."

"Yes. And all alone, thanks to Ramsey Tucker."

"We must take her with us."

"I was hoping you'd say that. I've already promised to escort her to California."

Connell came across the room and stopped. Faith could sense him standing over her. She tried to keep totally still, but a flutter of her lashes gave her away.

"I think she's awake," the woman said.

"Yes, I am." Faith opened her eyes and sat up with a yawn and a languid stretch. "Sorry. I didn't mean to doze. It's been a long day." She smiled up at her companions. "Actually, the last couple of months seem like a lifetime."

The woman smiled sweetly. "It is easy to lose track of time out here, even if you have a pocket watch." She offered her hand. "I'm Irene Wellman. Connell tells me your name is Faith Beal."

"Yes. It's an honor to meet you, Miss Wellman. I've heard a lot about you."

"Please, call me Irene." Grasping Faith's outstretched

hand, the older woman pulled her to her feet. "How would you like to sleep here with me, tonight?"

A terrible weight lifted from Faith's conscience. "Oh, could I? I don't know all the rules and I'm so afraid I'll make another dreadful mistake if I don't have a woman to ask for advice."

Irene looked puzzled. "Advice about what?"

"Everything!" she interjected, hoping and praying that Connell would be gentleman enough to refrain from explaining her most recent cause for embarrassment. It was bad enough that he'd noticed the belt in the first place. Bringing it to her attention in public like that was an inexcusable breach of etiquette.

Faith's cheeks burned as if she'd just spent another week under the scorching sun without her bonnet. Yes, she knew she'd pressed him, even threatened him, but that didn't mean he'd had to *listen* to her.

"I think I'd better be going," Connell said with a low chuckle, "and let you ladies talk privately."

"What about the old man? Where's he?" Faith asked.

"Walks With Tree is going to stay in Connell's lodge. It's all been arranged. You and I will have this one all to ourselves."

"Praise the Lord!"

Irene laid a hand lightly on Faith's arm. "It would be best if you didn't mention our God quite so loudly. The Cheyenne are tolerant of other people's beliefs, but this teepee is considered sacred because I keep the watch in here most of the time. I have to be very careful."

"Sorry." Faith pulled a face. "That's what I mean. I need advice. *Lots* of it."

"My pleasure."

In the background, Connell huffed with derision. "I hope

she takes directions from you better than she has from me. Little Muddy Dove Woman can be as hardheaded as a bull buffalo."

Laughing, Irene repeated the Indian name, then asked Connell, "What made you call her that?"

Faith answered instead, rather than give him the chance to explain that her ruined reputation on the wagon train had been the initial reason for the nickname. "And mud seems to follow me wherever I go. I washed up, but I'm afraid my hair is far from clean."

"I'll help you work on that."

"Oh, would you! That's wonderful."

Irene glanced at Connell. "Weren't you leaving?"

"I sure was. When two women start to sound off like a gaggle of geese I'd just as soon skedaddle."

Raising his hands, he ceremoniously folded his arms across his chest, each fist coming to rest at the point of the opposite shoulder. All teasing ended, he bowed slightly and said, "Good night," before ducking out the door.

Faith's breath caught. No one had to tell her that the sign he had made in parting was one of affection. Its meaning had been evident, both from his manner and his expression when he'd looked at Irene.

I was right here, too, Faith's pride insisted. *He could have meant it for me, as well.*

She would have loved to convince herself of that but she knew she was only making believe, just like the Indian children who had pretended that darling puppy was a real baby. Connell belonged to Irene and Irene belonged to Connell. End of story. Except…

Faith looked over at her doeskin-clad hostess. "Can I ask you a personal question?"

"Of course. You and I should have no secrets."

She steeled herself for the disavowal she was certain would come. "Who was that man out there under the blanket with you?"

"Ah. That was Red Deer." Irene's eyes misted. She sighed. "I will miss him terribly. He and I were planning to be married as soon as the first snow fell. He loves me—in spite of the fact that I'm almost seven years his senior."

Faith could hardly believe her ears. "Married? What about your promise to Connell?"

"I'd been assured he was dead. I thought I'd never see him again," Irene said sadly. "Ramsey lied to me about that, too."

"Perfidy seems to be his keenest skill."

"So I've learned." She mellowed noticeably. "Connell is amazing, isn't he? Imagine him locating me after all that's happened. When my so-called husband tried to do away with me, I should have presumed Connell was still alive and would keep searching till he found me. He was always very tenacious, even as a boy."

"How long have you known him?"

The older woman signed. "Forever. Our families were neighbors when we were children. After Connell's mother died, he and his father argued all the time. His father used to get drunk and beat him terribly. He ran away several times and came to our house for refuge. I think he was about thirteen and I was nearly seventeen when we pledged our troth."

"That's a long, long time ago," Faith offered innocently.

Irene smiled. "Not *that* long."

"I'm sorry. I didn't mean to imply you were old. It's just that when I think about my life when Mama was alive, it seems like years and years have passed."

"How long have you been on your own?"

"About three months. I've kind of lost track since I left the wagon train."

"Connell says your sister is still with the Tucker train."

Faith made a sour face. "Unfortunately. She told Connell she'd married the captain. There's nothing I can do for her as long as she insists on believing Ramsey Tucker's lies instead of listening to her own kin."

"How about you? Is there no special boy waiting back home for you?"

"I shall never marry," Faith insisted, thrusting out her chin for emphasis.

Irene merely laughed. "We'll see about that, Little Dove Woman. I hear there are many lonesome men in California yearning for a good wife."

"Well, it won't be me. I've learned plenty since I left Ohio. Men can be nasty and cruel. Look at Tucker. And Ab. And Stuart. Mr. Ledbetter was nice, but I couldn't even count on him for help when I needed it. I want nothing to do with the likes of any of them."

"Not all men are so unfeeling," Irene cautioned. "For instance, I happen to know that Connell admires you greatly."

"He does?" Faith's heart leaped like a frightened jackrabbit and landed in her throat.

"Yes. And I'm sure that if you can't find your father, Connell will be happy to take his place and make sure you get a good, honest, hardworking husband."

Faith's jaw dropped. If she could have thought of anything to say in reply that didn't sound unkind or ungrateful, she would have spoken. Unfortunately, assailed by such conflicting emotions, she had no adequate words to express her consternation.

Instead, she bit her tongue and prayed silently for God's forgiveness for the thoughts whirling wildly through her mind. It wasn't Irene's fault that they were all victims of such a complicated dilemma. Blame lay at Ramsey Tucker's door. Faith knew that.

She was also positive that whatever Connell's eventual place in her life became, she would never be able to see him as anything like a father figure. Never.

Chapter Twelve

Morning in the Cheyenne camp came early. It seemed as if Faith had barely closed her eyes when she heard Connell in conversation outside Irene's teepee. He was probably speaking in Cheyenne, although it could just as easily have been Arapaho or any of the other odd languages she'd heard of late and she'd not have known the difference.

The timbre of his voice sent shivers dancing over her skin and skittering up her spine to tickle the fine hairs at the back of her neck. After the conversation she and Irene had had the previous night, she was even more confused. Faith didn't know exactly what she wanted Connell McClain to be to her, now or in the future, but she was certain she didn't need another daddy. Or an uncle, for that matter.

Then what? she asked herself. What was he? Rescuer? Friend? Cohort? Boon companion? Her guardian in buckskins? He had been all that…and more. When she looked at him her heart raced. The sound of his voice made her tremble. Mere thoughts of his gentle touch stole her breath away and left her yearning to seek him out, to be near him once again.

"Foolish, foolish, foolish," Faith muttered, disgusted with

the flight of fancy her imagination had taken. It was one thing to appreciate the big plainsman as a heaven-sent blessing, yet quite another to let her thoughts imbue him with characteristics beyond the norm. He was simply a man.

Ah, she mused, *but he is so much more!*

"And I am crazy," she grumbled as she got to her feet. *"Lock me up in the woodshed and hide the ax crazy."*

From the doorway Connell said pleasantly, "If you say so."

Faith jumped. "Oh! You startled me."

"Sorry. I heard you talking and I was afraid Walks With Tree had sneaked past me."

She quickly scanned the empty lodge. "No. I'm alone. I was having an argument with myself."

"Oh? Who won?" he teased.

"I did, of course." Faith couldn't help grinning at him. "I couldn't hardly lose, given the lack of an intelligent adversary."

That candid observation made Connell laugh aloud and shake his head. "Has anybody ever told you how naturally funny you are?"

"Not as a compliment."

"Well, consider this to be one. If I wasn't so worried about our current situation you'd have me in stitches all the time."

"Thanks. I think."

"You're quite welcome." He stepped back while holding open the door flap. "Come on. We're having a powwow in my lodge. I'd like you to be there."

Faith followed his orders without hesitation and fell into step beside him. "Will Irene be there, too?"

"Of course. She's waiting for us. We'll need her help if we expect to get out of this mess and keep our hair."

Scurrying to keep pace with his much longer strides, she made a sour face. "That sounds awful."

"Sorry. I didn't think. I'll try not to be so blunt."

"No, no," she said, laying a hand lightly on his arm. "I don't want to be coddled. I'm a part of all this and I need to know everything, just like the rest of you do."

"You're sure?"

"Positive. In spite of what everybody seems to think, I'm not a child. I'm a grown woman."

The muscles of his arm flexed beneath her fingers as he said, "I'm more than aware of that, believe me."

"All I have to contribute is Rojo," Connell told the group, "but if I have to give him up, I will. Black Kettle had never seen a canelo before. I know he fancies the red color."

Faith had folded her grandmother's quilt into a small bundle and was sitting on it instead of the buffalo robe. "I wish I still had the money Anna Morse gave me so I could donate something," she said, "but it's with Charity in our wagon."

Both Connell and Ab shook their heads. The plainsman explained. "Out here, the best currency is on the hoof. A swift, sure-footed horse can carry a hunter after buffalo or a warrior after his enemies. It's worth its weight in gold."

"That's right," Irene said. "Horses are used as a dowry, or payment of a debt, or as a reward for heroism…lots of things. A husband even has to give one to his mother-in-law if he wants to talk to her face-to-face. She can't even go visit her daughter unless she's sure her son-in-law is not at home."

Connell smirked, "Now that's a habit a lot of men would like to see spread to every culture."

"Very funny," Faith countered, making a face. "That rule was obviously made by men."

"Perhaps," Irene said. "But in many ways our women have more rights than you do. For instance, the horses given to a bride's father by her husband-to-be become her property and the whole herd stays with her even if the marriage breaks up. She also remains within her own tribe and he joins that one, instead of the other way around."

"Oh, my." Faith was surprised to hear the older woman seem to identify so closely with the Indians, but since no one else had noticed that Irene had referred to the Indians as "our" women, she made no comment. *Poor Irene.* It was getting easier and easier for Faith to push aside any niggling envy and feel sorry for her. After all, the woman had loved Connell and believed he was dead, then married a skunk like Tucker and almost lost her life because of it.

Being sold into slavery to the Arapaho or traded to the Cheyenne sounded like solace after having endured all that other grief.

Except what about Red Deer? Faith added, keeping her thoughts to herself while the others continued to discuss various options relating to barter with Black Kettle. How sad it was that Irene had found true love, only to be forced to abandon it. Still, she had been reunited with her betrothed. Some women never had even one chance at happiness, yet here was Irene, so blessed with men who loved her that her heart was torn between them!

I will not be jealous, Faith insisted. *I will not covet her good fortune.*

Furious at the difficulty she was having living up to those noble declarations, she felt like stamping her foot and shouting, *I won't, I won't, I won't.*

How adult. How ladylike. How stupid, she told herself wisely. The others were never going to accept her as their equal unless she took control of her emotions. It was high time to stop thinking with her heart and start relying upon her wits again.

It would also help her mature image if she quit running around with her Cheyenne garb tied around her waist, she added, blushing. Now that Irene had explained how the knotted cord was supposed to be tied and that its presence was more symbolic than functional, it was easy to see what the Indian girl had been trying to explain with her confusing hand signals.

Lost in thought, Faith worried a loose thread in the quilt hem with nervous fingers. Every time she recalled her encounter with Connell from the previous evening she was mortified all over again. If she lived to be a hundred years old, she didn't think she'd *ever* be more embarrassed than she had been the moment she'd fully comprehended her openly scandalous error.

No one asked Faith's opinion during the impromptu powwow so she offered none. When the group broke up and Connell left to meet with Black Kettle, she was the only one who chose to remain in the teepee to wait for him.

Upon his return his countenance was grim. She managed to allow him a few moments of peace before her curiosity and impatience got the better of her and she blurted out the questions that had been nagging her.

"Well? Did you make the trade? Can we leave soon?"

"Yes, I've arranged for Irene's freedom. And, no, we can't leave right away."

"Why not?" Faith's imagination immediately saw many possible scenarios—all of them bad.

"Because Black Kettle wants to hold a special feast in our honor."

Her breath left in a whoosh of relief. "Oh, is that all? When?"

"Tonight. That's when the exchange will take place and Irene will confer her supposed spiritual powers on Walks With Tree."

"Can he be trusted?"

"As long as he sees an advantage for himself, yes."

"What if he pretends to go along with your plan, then changes his mind and tells Black Kettle the truth?"

Connell regarded her with concern. "He won't."

"But what if he does?"

"Let's worry about the things we can control and leave the other stuff to the Good Lord, okay?" He stopped looking so somber and smiled encouragingly. "If you want to help, I suggest you spend the afternoon praying that our plan works and that nobody gets hurt in the process."

She pulled a disgusted face. "Maybe you should do the praying for both of us. I'm afraid God isn't very happy with me right now."

"Oh no? What terrible sin have you committed, Little Dove Woman?"

"I keep breaking a commandment and I can't help myself."

"I find that hard to believe." There was growing mirth in his eyes, in the lopsided quirk of his mouth.

"Don't make fun of me."

When he came closer and laid his hands lightly on her shoulders, Faith felt his controlled strength, the warmth of his palms, and imagined that he caressed the strip of bare skin where her Cheyenne dress had left the curve of one shoulder exposed.

Surely, he couldn't have done so. Connell loved Irene. They were still promised to each other. Faith looked up into his smoky-colored eyes and saw them glistening.

"I would never make fun of you," he said earnestly, quietly. "Never."

At that moment, if he had asked her what sin she was battling, she could not have kept from confessing her covet-ousness. To her relief, he didn't press for an explanation.

Instead, he said, "I'm sure God understands what's in your heart, Faith. You want do the right thing. But you're human. We all make mistakes. God's grace and forgiveness take care of that."

"Only if we repent and stop doing the same thing over and over," she said in a hushed voice.

Connell drew her into his embrace. "It'll be all right. You'll see. You'll feel much better when you're back with Charity and we find your father."

The moment he'd pulled her close, Faith's arms had slipped around his waist as naturally as if they'd done the same thing a thousand times.

Clinging to Connell, drawing on his strength, she listened to his heart pound in unison with her own racing pulse. Truth to tell, if he hadn't brought up her estranged family she wouldn't have thought of them at all. Not now. Now when she was so dizzy with excitement, so taken with his nearness, that there was no room in her consciousness for anybody or anything but him.

Could she *love* him? she wondered in awe. Was that what these turbulent feelings were?

Why not? her conscience answered. Of course she cared for Hawk. It was perfectly normal to be grateful for all he'd done and all he'd promised to do when they finally got to California. She'd be lost without him, both literally and figuratively, and when the time eventually came to part, she was going to miss him terribly. The thought of never seeing him again brought unshed tears.

Long minutes passed in silence. When he finally did ease his hold on her, Faith was reluctant to let go.

Connell once again grasped her shoulders, but this time it was to put her away from himself and say, "I'm sorry. I shouldn't have done that."

"I didn't mind. Really."

"Still, it was wrong. It won't happen again."

The fact that he was obviously determined to keep that vow was underscored by the squaring of his shoulders, the jut of his chin.

Faith's pride reared up and took control of her tongue before she could stop it. "Fine. Don't touch me. Don't even act like my friend if it pains you so. Just get me out of this horrible camp, point me toward California and forget about me. I can look after myself."

Taken aback, Connell scowled down at her. "Who put the burr under your saddle?"

To her utter dismay her lower lip began to quiver. "Nobody. Go away. Leave me alone."

Instead, he reached out and gently cupped her cheek. "I won't desert you, even if you try to get rid of me. Don't cry."

"I'm not crying," she insisted.

His large thumb intercepted a tear on her cheek and whisked it away. Then, with a hoarse groan he once again pulled her close. Holding her as if he never intended to let go, he laid his cheek against her hair and murmured, "I'll keep you safe, Little Dove. I swear it."

Touched by his sincerity and warmed all the way to her soul, Faith was about to answer when he whispered one more thing just before he broke away and strode quickly from the lodge.

She couldn't be certain, but she thought he'd said, "Even from myself."

Chapter Thirteen

Faith didn't see Connell again until evening. The day had seemed endless. Bored, lonely and growing more fidgety by the hour, she'd thought of offering to help the Cheyenne women with their chores. If they'd seemed more amiable when she'd approached them she might have tried.

Some of the young warriors, however, were a different story. They'd acted much *too* friendly when she'd left the meeting lodge and started to walk back across the encampment toward Irene's teepee. Rather than stir up more trouble, Faith had decided to be discreet and had reversed direction, determined to stay out of sight until Connell called for her.

Several shy little girls had peeked in at her by getting down on their knees and peering under the raised outer edges of the teepee. Then they'd run away giggling when Faith had tried to talk to them. Other than that, and the occasional passage of a rangy dog, she'd remained totally isolated for the rest of the day.

Shadows lengthened. A cooling breeze wafted beneath the vented skirts of the teepee, bringing Faith welcome respite from the stifling heat. Outside, the camp was coming alive.

People called to each other, women sang, children shouted, and somewhere not far-off somebody was playing a flute.

The sound of passing hoofbeats drew her to the door. She moved the edge of the flap just enough to see out. Several mounted Cheyenne were driving fresh horses into the circle and exchanging them for ones that had been staked in front of various teepees during the day. The men rode in such harmony with their horses it was as if they and the animal were a single entity. Little wonder the U.S. Cavalry had found the Plains Indians to be such formidable foes.

Though weary from relentless pacing, Faith couldn't force herself to rest. She'd been almost ready to throw caution to the winds and make a mad dash for Irene's when Connell finally appeared. He ducked inside and let the door flap fall closed.

"Oh, thank goodness! I thought everyone had forgotten me," she said, hurrying toward him.

His raised hand stopped her. "Simmer down. I just came to check on you and tell you to stay put. I'll send for you later. When it's safe."

"Safe? Here? How can any of us be safe in this camp? You should have seen the way those Indians leered at me when I tried to go find Irene!"

"You went out? By yourself?" He muttered an unintelligible expletive. "No wonder."

Faith was sorry he was upset, but she wasn't willing to accept the blame for his foul mood. "You never told me to stay inside," she argued. "As a matter of fact, you didn't bother to tell me anything before you went off and left me. What was I supposed to do? Sit here and twiddle my thumbs all day?"

"It would have been preferable to attracting attention. Have you looked outside our door lately?"

"I watched a herd of horses go by about half an hour ago," she said with a scowl and a glance past his shoulder. "Why? What's out there now?"

"A Cheyenne with a flute. Didn't you hear him playing?"

"I heard some unusual music. Is that important?"

"To him it is. The flute and the special tune come from a medicine man. Hearing it is supposed to make you fall in love with whoever plays it."

"Me?" Eyes wide, she gaped at Connell. "That Indian expects me to fall in love with him?"

"He sure does."

"Oh, dear. What should I do?"

"Well, for starters, don't get close enough for him to throw his blanket over you. If you do, he'll take it as a sign you're willing to be courted."

"You mean like Red Deer and Irene?" The moment the words were out of her mouth, Faith rued them, wished she could call them back, but the damage had been done.

She saw Connell's jaw clench, his spine grow rigid. "No," he said. "Like Red Deer and Singing Sun Woman."

"Who's that?"

"That's the name the Arapaho gave Irene. After tonight she'll become Irene Wellman again and Singing Sun Woman will cease to exist."

Faith wasn't so sure. It seemed inconceivable that Irene could just forget the past year and go back to being the same person she'd been before coming to live with the Indians. A lot more had changed than just her name. And speaking of her name…

"I can see why they'd think the watch was singing, but how did they come up with the sun part?" Faith asked.

"The pocket watch has a gold case. Maybe it looked like the sun to them."

"That makes sense." Puzzled, she thought of the few descriptive Indian names she knew. "What about Walks With Tree? Did they call him that because he was born crippled and needed a wooden crutch?"

"Probably not. Children aren't given permanent names when they're little. Sometimes they do something special to earn their adult name. Other times they'll be presented a name as a gift. An older warrior may admire a younger man and give away his own good name as a kind of blessing."

"Wouldn't that get confusing? Two people would have the same name?"

"It doesn't work like that. Once a name is given away it's treated like any other gift. The one who had the name before chooses a different new one for himself."

"Gracious. I'd be totally befuddled."

"Not if you were used to it."

"I will never get used to all this," she said, sweeping her arm in an arc that took in the whole teepee. "How much longer must we stay here?"

"We'll leave tomorrow," he said. Then he smiled slightly and added, "Unless you go wandering again and get yourself engaged to be married before morning."

When the same girl who had brought her clothes and food the previous evening returned, Faith was so glad to see a familiar face she felt like hugging her. How she wished the young woman spoke English so she could properly thank her for her kindness. Still, she reasoned, there were some emotions that lent themselves well to pantomime, graciousness being one of them.

Faith grinned as she reached for the girl's hand and said, "I'm so glad to see you again." Genuine tears of thanksgiving misted her vision. "I'm going to be leaving soon. I want to thank you for letting me wear your beautiful dress."

The girl tried to pull away. Faith resisted. "Don't be frightened. I want to be your friend." A barely perceptible hesitation on the girl's part encouraged her. "That's right. Friend," Faith repeated.

She let go to use both hands for gesturing, sweeping her hands from herself to the other and back again while continuing to nod and smile. "Friends. You and me. Good friends. Yes?"

The girl finally nodded.

Faith was thrilled to have spanned their language barrier, however minimally. She pointed to her own chest and said, "Little Dove Woman," then gestured toward her companion, eyebrows raised questioningly.

The Cheyenne said something in her own language, then translated it. In English it became, "Spotted Fawn Woman."

Feeling like a teacher who had just broken through to a difficult student, Faith could tell her companion was as proud of their progress as she was. Encouraged, she caught up folds of her soft deerskin dress as if about to curtsy and tried again to make herself understood. "My dress? Where is my dress?"

Spotted Fawn shook her head and took a cautious step backward.

"It's okay," Faith cajoled. "Don't go. You can give it to me later."

Again came the shake of the girl's head, this time a lot more insistently and accompanied by a wave of her hands.

Faith frowned. "What's wrong? I don't know what you're trying to tell me."

Whirling, the young Cheyenne made a dash for the door, only to be stopped by running into Connell's broad chest with a dull thump.

He caught her neatly. Held her fast. His gaze shot to where Faith stood. "What's going on?"

"I don't know. I thought we were becoming friends, then she suddenly got upset and tried to run away."

He spoke calmly to the girl. Her answer made him smile. "She thinks you want your old dress back."

"I do." Faith continued to scowl. "I'll need it to wear when we leave here."

"That's not how this works," he explained carefully. "Spotted Fawn Woman offered you the best she had. When you accepted it, you agreed to a trade."

"She wants my old calico? It's a mess."

"Is it the best you had?"

"It's *all* I had," Faith said.

"Then she's happy with it. If you insist on trading back you'll be insulting her skill. She made what you're wearing with her own hands. It probably took months of her spare time just to do the beadwork."

"Tell her it's the most beautiful thing I've ever owned and I wouldn't dream of parting with it." Faith spoke to Connell, but her tender regard rested on the Indian girl. "I'll treasure it always. And please say I wish I had something better, something prettier to give to her besides my old dress."

Watching closely, Faith could tell when he'd conveyed the full message because Spotted Fawn's expression softened and her winning smile returned.

"You do have one other thing," Connell reminded her. "The quilt."

For an instant Faith's heart rebelled. Then she got control of her selfish desire to keep her grandmother's handiwork and nodded at Connell. "You're right. That will be perfect. I'll get it."

Lovingly displaying the quilt in her outstretched arms, Faith presented it to the younger woman. "Tell her I want her to have it," she said sincerely. "To go with the dress."

He spoke, then said, "She wants to give you something else in return."

"No. This outfit is already an unfair trade. We don't know what's ahead for us. Anything could happen. I'd like to know my grandmother's quilt is safe and treasured, as it should be."

Tears sprang to Spotted Fawn's eyes when Connell translated the presentation of the gift. That emotional reaction was all the thanks, all the confirmation, Faith wanted or needed.

It was wonderful to be so positive she was doing the right thing for a change. She knew there was a time, not long ago, when she would have clung to her last possession, seeing it as the most important element in her life. Yet, now that she'd been stripped of every concrete tie to her past, she felt liberated.

Faith's eyes also filled with unshed tears when the girl accepted the quilt and clasped it close to her heart as if it were the most precious gift she'd ever received. Giving it was certainly the most rewarding thing Faith had ever done.

Being able to part with the quilt and be truly glad to have given it away felt like a direct answer to her prayers for deliverance from covetousness. Seeing how happy she'd made the girl doubled Faith's blessing and she silently thanked the Lord that she'd been allowed to atone for her sins so perfectly. So conclusively.

This is going to be the first of many more selfless decisions I make, she told herself proudly, *beginning with not being jealous of Connell's relationship with Irene anymore.*

To her consternation, that thought doused her jubilance like a bucket of water poured over a roaring campfire. Though a remnant of joy remained, it was overshadowed by a sense of loss that was just like the way Faith had felt when she'd realized she was going to have to put aside her own desires and leave the place she loved in order to keep the promise she'd made to her mother.

This recent promise to eschew jealousy was even more binding, she realized with chagrin. It had been part of a prayer, so it was a vow directly to God.

Faith was still scuffling with her inner self over that judicious reasoning when Connell said, "That was a real nice thing to do. I'm proud of you, Little Dove Woman."

She huffed in self-deprecation. "You'd best keep calling me a dirty dove for a while longer. I haven't quite got the hang of keeping my thoughts pure yet."

The surprised look on his face was bad enough. Watching him erupt into laughter a few moments later was worse.

"I think you'll do just as you are," he said when he finally stopped chuckling enough to speak.

"Ha!" Faith made a face, said aside, "I hope the Good Lord agrees with you. Somehow, I doubt it."

Before she left the lodge, Spotted Fawn Woman carefully combed and braided Faith's thick, dark hair once again, this time also rolling the plaits into spirals, one on each side of her head, and fastening them there with leather thongs trimmed in beads and small, colored feathers. It wasn't until the girl was leaving with the quilt that Faith realized she had stripped the decorations she'd used from her own hair.

Standing alone in the center of the teepee, every nerve in her body taut, Faith listened. She could only imagine what was going on outside. Most of the individual calling and conversing had died down. Chanting and the syncopated beating of drums had taken their place. Everything vibrated in unison, as if the camp itself contained a living, throbbing, human heart.

Instead of the noises lulling her, as before, this cacophony raised gooseflesh. Where was Connell? He'd promised to return for her as soon as he could. Suppose something awful had happened to him? Suppose he'd been hurt? Attacked? Even killed! That notion was enough to spur her into action.

"If he's not back by the time I count to a thousand I'm going to find him," she muttered. "One, two, three…"

The tent flap swung back. Faith gasped, then took a ragged breath of relief. It was Connell.

"Thank heavens! Where have you been?"

"Busy," he said. His glance traveled over her from head to toe and back again. "I wish you didn't look quite so pretty tonight."

"Thanks, I think. Would you like me to rub some mud on my face again?"

"Too late for that." Turning, he started through the door. "Follow me. And don't say a word. Is that clear?"

"Of course, but—"

He stopped only long enough to scowl down at her and say, "Hush. If you don't do one other thing I tell you the rest of the way to California, do *this*. Understand?"

Faith nodded solemnly, lowered her eyes and fell into place behind him like the subservient person she was supposed to be.

It was not his plea for silence that made her comply, it was the glitter of warning in his stare, the threat of menace underlying his tone.

She didn't think for a minute that Connell would harm her if she disobeyed.

But what the Cheyenne might do if they discovered Irene's subterfuge in displaying the so-called magic of the watch was quite another matter. One Faith didn't even want to consider.

Chapter Fourteen

Flames from the communal fire in the center of the camp bathed the gathered throng in a shimmering aura. The aroma of roasted meat mingled with more earthy odors, swirling toward the heavens in smoky eddies that both tantalized and repulsed Faith.

Connell must have sensed her uneasiness, because he glanced back to tell her, "You're doing fine. We're almost there."

In passing, Faith was able to pick out Spotted Fawn among the dancers primarily because the girl had the familiar quilt draped over her shoulders. Trancelike, the Cheyenne followed one another around the fire with a shuffling, bobbing gait, paying no heed to anything but the drums and their own repetitive steps and chants.

No wonder Connell had wanted her to stay inside the lodge! Getting too close to this ceremony could undoubtedly be dangerous as well as foolhardy, especially for someone who knew almost nothing about tribal lore. Clearly, her experiences with Spotted Fawn Woman, although fascinating and rewarding, had imparted a sense of security where none existed.

Faith shivered imperceptibly. She might be dressed as a Cheyenne, but she was still an outsider. It would behoove her to remember that, especially if she didn't want a hank of her own hair added to Black Kettle's scalp shirt!

She chanced a brief look at the chief. There he was, big as life, wearing the proof of people he'd killed like so many war trophies.

Which was exactly what they were, she reasoned. Those scalps were his medals of valor. They might be more grisly than the ribbons or stripes the soldiers at Fort Laramie wore, but they stood for exactly the same thing. What a sobering thought!

Studying Black Kettle from a distance, Faith was struck by his departure from the amiable nature he had displayed before. Here and now, he was the unquestionable ruler of all he surveyed; a force not to be trifled with. Everything about him, from his proud posture to his defiant expression, insisted that he be obeyed.

In Faith's eyes, the only person more formidable looking was Connell McClain. Praying silently for his deliverance, she watched him stride forcefully toward the chief and the tribal council. He never faltered, not slowing until he stood eye to eye with Black Kettle.

Frenzied chanting and drumming ceased. Even the dogs seemed to sense a momentous event in the offing, because they stopped yapping.

Faith was sure anyone standing near her could hear the wild thumps of her heart. *She* certainly could. She held her breath as Connell began to speak. Though she couldn't understand what he was saying, his voice came across strong, his confidence in himself and his cause evident. Irene couldn't have asked for a better champion.

And speaking of Irene, where was she? Faith wondered, scanning the crowd.

That question was answered quickly. Connell swept his arm in a grandiose arc and pointed. Irene was approaching on foot, accompanied by Walks With Tree. Between them they led a magnificent horse. Bunches of feathers and beads were tied in the horse's mane; a blanket was draped across his back and he was decorated with war paint. That was why it took Faith a few seconds to realize she was looking at Connell's horse, Rojo!

Overwrought on behalf of the plainsman, she had to clamp her hand over her mouth to keep from protesting.

The assembled Cheyenne closed ranks behind the little procession and pressed in on their chief and his captive medicine woman.

Faith edged closer, too, wanting to keep Connell and Irene in sight, but she was far too short to see over the heads of those in front of her. Determined to follow the drama, she circled around to the opposite side of the campfire where a group of wide-eyed youngsters had gathered to watch the show. Their smiles of remembrance warmed her heart. One little girl even reached up and took her hand.

"Hello again," Faith whispered.

The child tugged her to sit beside her on the ground.

"Okay." How Faith wished she could educate this dear child, could tell her the truth about the so-called magical watch without risking everyone else's life. She didn't dare, of course. Too much was at stake. Yet it seemed so unfair to let the impressionable girl go on thinking a mere pocket watch held spiritual significance. Perhaps someday, after they'd rescued Charity and found Papa, she'd be able to return to the Cheyenne as a teacher or a missionary or both and set things right.

That notion took her totally by surprise. Before she could pursue it further, however, Irene held up the watch. On cue, the alarm sounded.

Children gasped. So did many of the adults. The little girl who had befriended Faith ducked beneath her arm to hide.

Faith pulled her closer and leaned down to offer quiet reassurance. "It's okay, honey. Don't be afraid. It won't hurt you. I promise."

She thought she'd spoken cautiously enough to keep from being overheard, yet in seconds two sinewy warriors appeared in front of her, grabbed her by the wrists and yanked her to her feet as easily as if she weighed less than one of the children she'd been sitting with.

Shock overrode any modicum of remaining restraint. "No!" she screeched. "Let go of me. I haven't done anything!"

They ignored her protests and dragged her through the assembled throng while she writhed and kicked like a rabbit caught in a snare. The child left behind began to wail.

Faces passed in a blur. Angry faces. Hostile faces. Shouting faces. The braves delivered Faith to the chief and dropped her in a heap at his feet, then shoved her facedown into the dirt.

Spitting and struggling, she tried to right herself but was immediately forced prostrate once again. They pushed her so violently this time she could hardly catch her breath.

Over the sounds of the surrounding melee she heard Connell shout something in Cheyenne. His voice held so much pathos she needed no translation to know he was pleading on her behalf. She covered her face with her hands and lay very still, too shocked to think straight let alone pray rationally.

More nearby voices joined in expressions of rage. Faith's head was spinning. This was all wrong! She was innocent of any crime. If only she could explain and apologize, surely they'd see she'd simply been trying to comfort a frightened child and had meant no harm to anyone.

She suddenly remembered that Black Kettle spoke English. He'd understand what she was trying to convey.

She pulled her knees under her, preparing to rise, but before she could even look up, Connell gave a guttural shout and threw himself over her as a human shield, knocking her back down and keeping her there.

His mouth was inches from her ear when he rasped, "Don't move."

"I—"

"And don't say another word."

Faith bit her lip so hard she tasted blood mixed with the gritty dust in her mouth. Poor Connell! What had she done? She clamped her hands over her ears and squeezed her eyes shut tight. So much shouting was going on all around them it would have been impossible to tell who was saying what even if everyone had been speaking English. At this point, all Faith was certain of was her own precarious position—in more ways than one.

A lance tip had cut through Connell's shirt to pierce his back near his left shoulder blade. He knew the quick thrust had been meant to warn, not to kill. Yet.

Every muscle in his body readied for defense while his mind insisted that such resistance was futile. What could one man do against hundreds of armed braves? More importantly, how could he hope to save Faith Beal when so many were now calling for her execution?

Reality hit him squarely. The truth was, he couldn't save anyone. Especially not now. He'd shown his true allegiance when he'd thrown himself between Faith and the warriors' weapons, thereby sealing his own fate. It was going to take a lot bigger influence than Irene's watch could provide to get any of them out of this predicament alive. It was going to take genuine Divine intervention. The kind that came from only one source.

Connell hadn't consciously, purposely, talked to his God since Little Rabbit Woman's death. To pray now, when he was about to join her, seemed sacrilegious.

A surprising calm descended upon the plainsman. If he must die, he would face that fate with honor. With courage. With few regrets except his inability to deliver on all his well-intentioned promises.

Hunched over beneath Connell, Faith sensed a change in him that gave her hope. As soon as she figured out what he planned to do, she'd gladly cooperate and they'd all get out of this mess in one piece. Together. Just as originally planned. In the meantime, she wished somebody would say something in English so she'd have a little idea of what was going on.

As if in direct answer, Connell again warned, "Don't move," and began to slowly lift his upper body off her while remaining on his knees before Black Kettle.

Faith almost disobeyed his command when she heard his muffled groan of pain. It was only with the utmost effort that she kept her eyes covered, her posture submissive.

Head already bowed, eyes closed, she turned to silent prayer. *Dear Lord, please help Connell. Help us all. I know You sent him to help me and I disobeyed You when I didn't listen to his advice. I'm so sorry. Please, please forgive me. And tell me what to do now, Father.*

Above her, she heard courage in the plainsman's voice as he said, "Black Kettle is a wise chief. A brave warrior. Will he make war on a crazy woman who knows nothing of the ways of the Cheyenne? Will his ancestors honor him for her death? If he must have another scalp, let him take one from a brave fighter who has proved himself in battle. Let him take mine."

Faith's heart leaped to her throat and choked off her breath. Was she doomed simply because she'd spoken out of turn? It seemed impossible. Yet Connell obviously thought so or he wouldn't have offered himself in her place.

No, God! No! her soul screamed. *There must be another way. There must be. Please!*

A hush fell over the crowd. Tempted almost beyond her strength to resist, Faith yearned to rise and somehow defend her champion.

Reason prevailed. That was exactly the kind of rash behavior that had thrust them into this fiery furnace of wrath in the first place, she reminded herself, contrasting her current dilemma with the biblical deliverance of Shadrach, Meshach and Abednego.

I trust God like they did. I do, she insisted. *So where is God now? Where's the answer to my prayer for deliverance?*

Had God forsaken her because she'd been unable to overcome her jealousy even after she'd recognized it as a sin? Or was He expecting her to bravely declare her Christian faith and become a martyr? It wasn't hard to admit that that particular prospect didn't appeal to her one bit. It had been a lot easier to think of God as master of her destiny when she hadn't been facing the final precious moments of life. Yet what better time for total commitment?

Faith took a deep breath as she raised her head and looked straight at Black Kettle. Their gazes locked. A barely perceptible tilt of the chief's head was all the warriors needed to tell them to move Connell off her and keep him out of the way.

No longer encumbered, Faith got to her feet, spread her hands wide and bowed before the Cheyenne chief to say,

"The child was afraid. I comforted her because I have the heart of a woman, of a mother. If I must die for showing a woman's kindness, then I am ready."

She straightened, proud and unwavering, her shoulders back, her chin raised. She didn't know if Black Kettle was surprised at her unusual boldness and reasoning or not, but *she* was certainly shocked by the wisdom that had just popped out of her mouth! Moreover, she had absolutely no idea where those erudite thoughts had originated. They certainly hadn't been rehearsed, nor had she planned to do anything but apologize profusely when she'd gotten to her feet in front of the chief.

Silence reigned. Any other time, Faith would have continued to babble, to try to add to her appeal, but absolutely nothing else came to mind. It was as if any connection between her brain and her lips had been severed.

Finally, Black Kettle spoke. "You have the courage of a warrior, Little Dove Woman. If your tongue did not wag all day and all night like the tail of a hungry dog I would buy you from your uncle and make you my fourth wife." He chuckled to himself and waved her off. "Go with Pale Hawk and Singing Sun Woman and leave us in peace."

"Yes, sir!" Faith's grin was so wide her cheeks hurt.

Backing away, she glanced over her shoulder to locate Connell. The braves had released him, too, and he was standing near Irene. Walks With Tree now held the precious alarm watch and was hunched over it, muttering.

Faith skirted the old medicine man and went directly to Connell. She yearned to ask him if he was all right but decided that query could wait. The only serious question she had at present was in regard to their future mode of transportation since he'd obviously given his horse away. Surely, he didn't intend to walk the rest of the way to California!

Sidling up to him, she waited for him to pay her heed. When he continued to ignore her she gave a light tug on his sleeve, expecting him to lean down so she could whisper to him privately.

Connell slipped an arm around her shoulders. Instead of bending an ear, however, he crooked his arm just so and placed his large hand directly over her mouth! Holding her thus, he nodded to the chief who laughed heartily.

Faith struggled in vain to dislodge the plainsman's firm grip. It was no use. She couldn't even pry his fingers loose by using both hands. Disgusted, she stopped trying.

Leaving her hands clamped over Connell's, she watched the tableau unfolding by the fire. If Walks With Tree intended to impress everyone with his skill as guardian of the magic watch, he was going to have to hurry because the crowd was beginning to stir impatiently.

The old man held the watch aloft just as Irene had. Nothing happened. He lowered it, held it to his ear, then nodded sagely before speaking aside to Black Kettle.

Listening, the chief began to frown. Was Irene going to have to stay behind after all? Faith wondered. Worse, if the old man couldn't make the watch work, were they going to be made the scapegoats for his failure? Irene must have explained the alarm to him. Could he be too uncivilized to understand how to set and then secretly trigger it?

When Black Kettle stared at Connell with skepticism, Faith felt the plainsman's arm muscles clench. Whatever was going on, Connell was jittery about it. She held very still, hardly breathing, and watched the parade of emotions on the chief's face. Finally, he shook his head and barked an order to his guards. Two saddled horses and a laden pack animal were immediately led into the circle.

Connell boosted Faith aboard one saddle and helped Irene

mount the other while Walks With Tree began a vigorous chant over the watch. Still, it remained silent.

Then Rojo was brought forward. Black Kettle took the horse's reins and handed them ceremoniously to Connell. Everyone paused, waiting and listening expectantly. Mere seconds dragged by like hours.

Faith's stomach was knotted, her heart racing. The mount beneath her sensed her apprehension and shifted its feet, uneasy.

Patience had never been one of her virtues and she was about to come to the end of what little she had left when the bell inside the watch suddenly began its noisy clamor.

The shock jolted everyone, including the horses. Faith's jittery mount probably would have unseated her if Connell hadn't still had hold of its bridle. Even steady Rojo flinched and snorted.

Connell mounted quickly and wheeled the big gelding to lead the way out of the camp. It wasn't until they'd passed the final perimeter lodges and sentries that he hesitated long enough to pass the reins of their horses to the women.

Faith had been about to burst. "You've been hurt. There's blood on the back of your shoulder!"

"I know. It burns like fire," he replied, "but we can't stop now. Not yet. Irene can take care of it when we camp for the night."

Irene. Faith had to bite her lip to keep from commenting adversely. Of course Irene should take care of it. After all, he was planning to marry her. And she had been living with the old medicine man, Faith added, so she probably did know a lot about wounds and such. Still, the idea galled. It shouldn't have, but it did.

"What happened? When did you get hurt?" Faith pressed.

The older woman spoke up. "He took the spear thrust meant for you."

"Oh, no. Oh, Connell, I'm so sorry."

"You'd be a lot sorrier if he hadn't shielded you the way he did," Irene said harshly. "You two almost ruined our whole plan. Walks With Tree kept his head or we'd be in deep trouble right now."

"What happened?" Faith asked. "About the horses, I mean. When I saw Rojo all decked out in feathers and paint I was sure Black Kettle was going to keep him."

"He was," Connell answered, "until Walks With Tree convinced him the magic wouldn't work unless he released us and our horses, too."

"How clever. And how nice of him."

Irene snorted. "Don't give the old fox too much credit for altruism. He's no fool. He knew the less we left behind, the stronger his own position would be."

"And he wanted to make sure we put plenty of distance between us and him as soon as possible," Connell added. "That's the only way he could be sure the Cheyenne would continue to see him as indispensable. To do that, we needed good horses."

"I'm glad you got your beautiful red horse back," Faith said. "He really is magnificent." She sighed audibly. "I just wish I'd been able to rescue Ben from Tucker."

"Who's Ben?" Irene asked. "I thought your only relative on the train was a younger sister."

"Yes. My sister, Charity," Faith said with a wistful smile. "Many's the time I'd have gladly considered trading her for another faithful friend like Ben. Not that I'd actually do it, mind you, but the thought certainly has appealed to me from time to time."

Connell laughed quietly to himself, then explained to Irene. "Ben's a mule. One of those big Missouri ones that can pull all day without giving out."

"Mercy sakes," Irene said. "The way you were talking about him I figured he was a person."

"He almost is. He's been my dearest friend for most of my life," Faith said solemnly. "I'd trust him a lot longer than I'd trust most people, especially lately. It was poor Ben who first showed me the rotten side of Captain Tucker."

Irene was clearly interested. "How? What did he do?"

"Well, he didn't want the captain to get near me, for starters. Kept stepping between us whenever he could. Then I caught Tucker beating him one night and that was the last straw. I didn't even think about what I was doing or how dangerous it might be. I just grabbed the first whip I could lay my hands on and lashed at Tucker the way he'd been whipping Ben."

"You didn't!"

"Oh, yes, I did. And the captain backed off. But he'd been shamed in front of the other men. After that he never missed a chance to make my life miserable." Her shoulders slumped. "And now he's not only got my sister in his clutches, there's no one left to defend Ben."

"Then we'll steal him for you," Irene said brightly.

Connell coughed. "We'll *what?*"

"Steal him. It won't be hard. All we have to do is locate the train and watch till the drovers take the stock out to graze. Then you and I can create a diversion to distract the guards and Faith can creep in to fetch her mule. We do it all the time."

"We?" Connell's eyebrows arched quizzically.

"I mean the Cheyenne do it," Irene said, blushing slightly. "Besides, the mule truly does belong to Faith. All we have to worry about is hiding the fact that she's still alive. It'll be simple." She grinned over at the younger woman. "Even her sister wouldn't recognize her in that getup."

"She wouldn't, would she!" Faith was caught up in the

plan. "I might even be able to sneak close enough to get a look at her myself. I've been so worried. Charity was always the baby of the family. I don't know how she's managing to cope after all that's happened to her. She's never been strong, like me."

Connell laughed cynically. "We agree on that. I doubt there's one woman in a hundred who would have the courage to stand up to a war chief the way you did, Little Dove Woman. Maybe not one in a thousand."

"Thanks." Gratified by such high praise, Faith glanced over at Irene, expecting her to concur, and found her scowling. She quickly added, "Don't forget what Irene did. It must have taken great heroism to fool so many savages for such a long time."

Instead of the appreciation she'd anticipated, Faith was taken aback when Irene said, "The Cheyenne are far less savage than many whites I've met. When a warrior makes a vow he keeps it, no matter what it may cost him to do so."

"I meant no offense," Faith told her.

Irene nodded. "Nor did I. I simply speak the truth. If a liar like Ramsey Tucker were a Cheyenne he'd have been thrown out of the tribe or executed for his crimes long ago instead of having so many chances to repeat them and hurt more people."

Tears of frustration clouded Faith's vision as she visualized that kind of swift, sure justice. "I wish…" she began before her voice trailed off, leaving the unacceptable thought unspoken.

Connell finished it for her. "You wish that were the case right now, but you feel guilty because your Christian upbringing argues that it's wrong to take personal revenge. I can understand that. Just remember, wanting to even the score is a normal human reaction to injustice."

"Murder is a sin, no matter what the reason," Faith said. "'Vengeance is Mine, I will repay, sayeth the Lord.'" She looked from him to Irene and back again while struggling to gain control of her whirling emotions.

"What about your sister?" the older woman asked. "Wouldn't you like to see her freed from that awful man?"

"Of course I would! But killing him isn't the answer. Think. There are only three of us against fifty or more armed men on that wagon train. As long as they all believe Tucker's lies, we wouldn't stand a chance of escaping. All we'd do if we went after Tucker is get ourselves shot. Then who would be left to bring him to justice?"

"White man's justice is too slow." Irene's eyes were sparking with hatred.

Faith laid a hand of consolation on her arm. "Try to be patient. With your help I know we can prove his guilt and see that he's held properly accountable when we reach California. It's the right thing to do. This is hard for me, too, you know. Very hard." She managed a slight smile. "Be patient? Please?"

"Faith's right," Connell said. "Even if we did manage to do away with Tucker we'd be hard-pressed to get Charity away from the others. Plus, we'd be draining their precious resources. They'll need every ounce of fortitude they have left to make it across the desert. Innocent folks will die if they waste their energy chasing after us."

Watching Irene's face, Faith saw eventual signs of resignation. What she didn't see was compassion for the emigrants who were about to embark on such a difficult leg of their long, arduous journey.

Chapter Fifteen

Connell had serious misgivings about bothering with the mule. He could have thwarted the plan by simply pretending he couldn't locate the Tucker train. That idea had occurred to him—more than once. Trouble was, the emigrant track across the high plains was spread so wide, its path of desolation so evident, a child could have easily found and followed it by day.

Not only had the passing wagons left behind deep ruts and trampled vegetation, there were so many household items discarded along the trail it looked like a parade of drummers had passed by dropping off samples of their goods. Had those travelers who came later not been in the same dire straits as their predecessors, they could easily have provisioned themselves many times over—with anything but food and water.

Connell knew that choosing between heirlooms or survival became easier and easier as the westward migration progressed. The first things to go were usually those special niceties the women had insisted on bringing along, such as mirrors and pianos or trunks crammed with fancy frocks.

By the time the overland trail reached the Sierra Nevada,

travelers were more than ready to let go of the last vestiges
of their past lives in the hope of enduring long enough to see
a future. Any future.

Connell held up his hand to bring his little party to a halt
on the crest of a ridge. Irene rode up on his right. Faith took
the opposite side. The trail lay in the barren valley below, accentuated by a long, snaking column of dust that partially
obscured a wagon train.

"Is that them?" Faith asked. She strained to see. "I can't
tell from here."

"I think so. The timing is about right," Connell said. "The
wagon boss will call a rest near here so the stock can gather
strength and the men can load extra fodder and water to get
them across the desert. When he does, I'll ride closer and see
if I can spot Tucker or some of the others we know."

"It looks to me like they're already in a desert," Faith said,
worried.

"It gets a lot worse west of here." He pointed. "There's a
good forty-mile stretch of nothing but dry sand between the
Humboldt Sink, where the river disappears underground, and
Carson Pass, when the trail starts up over the Sierras."

"Oh, dear." She shaded her eyes, stood in her stirrups. "I
don't think I see my wagon. Maybe this is the wrong train."

"Wagons break down, draft animals give out and families
have to combine their resources," Connell reminded her. "I
wouldn't be surprised if Charity isn't back with the Ledbetters so Tucker doesn't have to bother with her."

"Oh, do you think she could be? That would be wonderful! I've been so afraid…." Faith's voice trailed off again. She
couldn't bear to think or speak of her naive sister sharing that
horrible man's bed.

"If she kept on wailing the way she was the last time I
talked to her, it's certainly possible. Tucker needs her alive

and well when they meet up with your father, so we know he'll make sure she's well cared for. I just can't see a man like him putting up with her hysterics for very long. Not when he could farm her out and let someone else deal with the buckets of tears instead."

"And she can't cook a lick," Faith offered, spirits rising. "Never tended to the animals, either." She grinned over at him. "She's useless! Isn't that wonderful?"

Her enthusiasm made Connell chuckle. "In Charity's case, it may be." Reining the canelo around, he started down the back side of the ridge, away from the wagon train. "Come on. We need to find a good place to make camp before dark. Somewhere far enough away that the smoke from our fire won't be spotted. I'll come back later and do some more scouting."

Irene followed obediently.

Faith held her horse back with a jerk on the reins. "Whoa. Wait! We can't leave yet. We're not even sure that's the Tucker train. What if you're wrong? What if it isn't? What then?" She noticed Irene's disdainful smile, arching brows and the way her eyes darted to Connell to assess his reaction.

Instead of answering Faith, he smiled at Irene. "Do you think it's too late to go back and sell her to Black Kettle after all?"

Irene huffed. "I'm afraid you'd have to pay him to take her, not the other way 'round."

"Oh, well in that case," he said with a chuckle, "I guess we'll have to keep her. I doubt there are enough good horses in the territories to make Black Kettle change his mind."

"Very funny," Faith grumbled.

The ensuing mutual laughter of her companions didn't amuse her one bit. Gritting her teeth, she watched them ride away for a few dozen heartbeats, then kicked her horse in the sides and followed reluctantly.

For once, she actually missed having another woman like her sister to talk to. Charity might be self-centered but at least she thought and acted in ways Faith was used to. Irene, on the other hand, was a lot more like an Indian than Faith had imagined she'd be.

As she rode behind her companions, she was able to observe them without blatantly staring. Connell sat his horse straight and strong in spite of his injured shoulder and Irene rode beside him as naturally as if they'd been a couple all their lives. Perhaps they had.

All the more reason to believe they were ideally suited to each other, Faith reasoned. If she were truly honest with herself she'd have to admit that the best thing she could do for Connell McClain was to drop out of his life for good. As soon as possible. That notion stuck in her throat and burned like a dose of Grandma Reeder's homemade spring tonic.

Alone with Irene after Connell left on his scouting mission, Faith tried several times to breach the gap between her life and the other woman's by making small talk. Her efforts were to no avail. When Irene did deign to speak, her conversation was terse and strictly to the point instead of chatty as Faith had hoped.

By the time Connell returned, she was about ready to start talking to clumps of inanimate sagebrush.

"Well?" she blurted as he dismounted and started to loosen the canelo's saddle girth before reporting. "What did you learn?"

He paused, turned to give her a patient look. "Your wagon broke an axle about fifty miles back. After that, the Ledbetters and the Johnsons took what they could carry of Charity's stuff and left the rest behind, wagon and all."

"Then we did find the right train!"

"Yes. And a more demoralized bunch of folks I've never seen. A quarter of their party split off back at Fort Bridger. The rest are complaining about all the hardships of Sublette's Cutoff, even if it did save them a week of travel. If they think that was bad, this next patch of rough country is going to really wake them up."

"Is Charity okay? Did you see her? Talk to her?"

"I saw her. From a distance. Didn't see any reason to stir things up by bothering her. She's a little the worse for wear but otherwise fine. Looks like she's had to learn to do chores since you left. She was tending a cooking fire while a couple of other women fussed at her."

"Thank heavens." Faith sighed with relief. "But what about Ben? If we don't have a wagon anymore, what are they using my mules for?"

"Nothing, at the moment," Connell said. "I spotted Ben and one of your other mules. They're a little gaunt but not sickly or broken down like some of the horses. That's a good sign. If we can liberate the old boy before he's driven across the desert with the rest of the herd he'll have a better chance."

"Then let's do it! What're we waiting for?"

Irene shook her head, clearly concerned. "Is she always this enthusiastic?"

"Most always," Connell answered. "She goes off half-cocked more often than a worn-out flintlock."

Faith faced them, hands fisted on her hips. "I do not. I just want to get my mule and be on our way, that's all. I keep expecting to see a bunch of Indians riding after us."

"She has a point there," Irene said. "Walks With Tree is an old man. If something happened to him, Black Kettle might decide he wants me back again."

Not to mention what Red Deer wants, Faith thought. The virile Cheyenne brave had stared daggers at Connell as their party had ridden out of camp and she wouldn't have been a bit surprised to see him sneaking through the brush, readying an arrow. There had definitely been times lately when she'd felt as if someone or something was watching them, following them. It wasn't the same kind of sensation a person got from knowing they were being looked after by a benevolent Providence, either. It was more like what she imagined an antelope might feel at its first glimpse of a mountain lion lying in ambush. A shiver followed the conclusion that their invisible nemesis might indeed be a lion or other dangerous denizen of the wilderness.

"All right," Connell said, breaking into Faith's thoughts. "We'll use Irene's diversion idea since I haven't been able to come up with a better one. She and I will cause a stir so you can sneak into the herd to get Ben." He scowled at Faith. "Just Ben, mind you. If other mules follow him we'll have to take them, too, but I'd rather not. The less fuss the better."

"Right." She unfastened her braids to let them hang free. In answer to Connell's questioning look she said, "Since I don't have my bonnet and Ben's not used to these clothes either, I want him to know it's me. He's smart. Too smart. There's no way I can catch him if he doesn't want to be caught."

"Take one of the horses," Connell ordered. "Ride him close enough to spot Ben, then decide whether or not to approach on foot. We'll leave that up to you. Just get in and out as fast as you can. If nobody spots you and gives chase, come back here to camp. If you're followed, head west. We'll find you."

Faith pulled a face. "Ha! The way you two have been talking about getting rid of me I'm not very comfortable being separated."

Chuckling, Connell patted her on the top of the head.

"Don't worry. I imagine by now you're a regular legend in the Cheyenne camps. If they did pick you up again you'd be treated well as long as you kept your mouth shut and minded your own business."

"Yes-sir-ee," Faith drawled cynically. "I'm about the quietest, most harmless little dove there ever was. Have to live up to my Indian name, don't I?"

"I should have named you Babbling Brook or Squeaking Wheel Woman," he countered, amused though also worried about her participation in their mule-theft plan. "If there was any other way to be sure we'd be able to get to Ben without being noticed, I'd leave you behind."

"You can't. You need me," Faith said flatly. "We all agree on that. So, are you going to stand around jawing all evening or are we going to go after my mule?"

"We're going to go after your mule," he said. "If you can't sneak close enough to safely nab him tonight, we'll wait till daybreak and try again when they drive the livestock to water."

"I'll get him tonight," Faith vowed. "I'm not giving Ramsey Tucker any more chances to hurt him. I just wish there was some good way to make off with my sister, too."

"We've already been over all that. You said it yourself. The men would form a posse and hunt us down if we kidnapped her."

"I know, I know. And they won't miss Ben the way they would Charity. Especially since he's not being worked. I understand that. I was just wishing things could be different, that's all."

Irene nodded sagely, soberly, and surprised Faith by saying, "I know *exactly* how you feel."

The country was open. Flat. Faith couldn't very well show herself to the emigrants while still clad as an Indian, so she dismounted, left her horse behind and crouched low to approach the weary herd.

The closer she got, the worse the livestock looked. Innumerable flies buzzed around oxen's eyes and dotted their backs, especially where the yokes had rubbed their hide raw. The poor beasts were so exhausted they barely flinched from the biting insects.

Their suffering touched Faith's heart. If only she had some of her homemade tansy-and-sulfur ointment to put on those wounds. But that precious tin of salve, as well as personal belongings like the mourning pendant she'd worn in memory of her mother, had probably been abandoned when her wagon was left behind.

An enormous brown and white ox lifted its head to glance at her as she came closer, then went back to wrapping its tongue around tufts of coarse grass and yanking it out by the mouthful.

Faith laid a steadying hand on its withers and kept the large animal between herself and the wagon train so she wouldn't be visible if anyone chanced to look her way.

Speaking calmly, she soothed her four-legged concealment. "Hello, old boy. That's it. Keep eating. I hear you're going to need every bite."

There had been a time, early in their journey, when even the most placid ox or mule would have resisted the touch of anyone who might place it back in harness before it was sated. Now, however, the animals were too tired, too sore-footed, to fight any longer. They seemed as resigned to their fate as their human owners.

With barely an occasional twinge left to remind her of the injury to her ribs back at Fort Laramie, Faith felt guilty to be enjoying renewed well-being when there was so much suffering, man and beast, all around her.

Well, better to help one poor traveler than none at all, she reasoned. She hadn't come to rescue the wagon train from the harrowing trek. Only God could do that. Her task was to locate her faithful mule and spirit him away undetected.

That was plenty, considering the size of the herd and the waning daylight. Men would soon return to gather the draft animals and drive them inside the corral formed by the circled wagons. If she didn't get to Ben before then, they would have to wait till morning, as Connell had warned.

She crept closer and closer, hoping to catch a glimpse of Charity while continuing her search for Ben. Sound carried well over the tranquil prairie, but she was unable to pick out her sister's voice above the general hum of the camp. Still, that much background noise would help to mask her summons if she shouted to Ben. With time growing short, she decided it was a chance worth taking.

"Ho, Ben," she called, beginning softly as a test.

Peeking over the oxen's broad back, she stood on tiptoe to see if Ben—or anyone else—had heard. To her amazement, she was now the only two-legged creature remaining on that side of the wagon circle!

On the opposite side, however, a hue and cry was rising. People were running to and fro, waving rifles and pointing at two mounted figures silhouetted by the glow of the setting sun.

Faith smiled to herself. Clever Connell. He'd put himself and Irene directly in front of the sun so no details about them were discernible. All they had to do was sit there like Indian scouts and wait to be spotted. The imaginations of settlers who had already faced more than one raiding party since leaving St. Jo would do the rest.

Freed of remaining inhibitions, Faith stepped out from behind the ox, cupped her hands and started working her way through the herd shouting, "Ben! Here I am, Ben. Ben," over and over.

Darkness was falling. She was just about to give up and sneak back to where she'd left her horse when a soft snort at her elbow startled her. Her old friend had come!

She wheeled, grinning, and opened her arms to hug his neck the way she always had. "Good boy!"

Unsure, the mule tossed his head to escape her grasp then went back to sniffing her Cheyenne outfit.

Faith settled for scratching the bridge of his nose and spoke to calm him. "That's right. It's me, boy. Sorry I don't have any apples for you."

She hadn't thought to bring a lead rope either. Thankfully, she didn't need one. All she had to do was turn and start off with a quiet, "Come on. Let's go, Ben," and the mule followed her through the herd like an oversize, obedient pup.

They were almost in the clear when a distant shout went up. "Indians! Quick, boys. Mount up. They're after the horses!"

Faith's initial reaction was to freeze and look around her for the threat. In another instant she realized that *she* was the Indian they were hollering about!

If the emigrants caught her, Tucker would find out she was alive. Then there'd be no escape for sure! But how was she going to elude capture? She'd left her riding horse ground-hitched at least a half mile away, maybe farther. Making a run for it and reaching it without being overtaken was not feasible. But what other choice did she have?

Think. Don't panic. There must be a way!

If she were astride Ben, escape might be possible, she reasoned. The trouble was, she was short and he was sixteen hands at the shoulder. That put his back far above her leaping ability.

Lacking stirrups for a quick boost she cast frantically about for something to stand on. A rock or a stump would do. Anything. As a child at home she'd always led Ben over to the edge of the back porch where he'd stood patiently and waited for her to clamber aboard. Unfortunately, there weren't any handy porches in the middle of the prairie!

If only she could vault from the ground onto his back without aid the way she'd seen the Indians do it. Then again, they'd had their horses' long manes to grab hold of while Ben's had been roached short and bristly, leaving nothing except one little lock of longer hair right at the base by his withers.

The old mule sensed her fright and tossed his head. "Easy, boy. Come on, Ben," she pleaded. "We've got to stick together till we find something for me to stand on."

She broke into a trot, dodging sagebrush and trying to keep the clumps of long grass that the herds had not yet decimated between her and her pursuers. Here and there, the bones of long-dead animals lay scattered, cleaned by scavengers and sun bleached. The largest of the lot was the skull of a bull buffalo. Maybe it would be enough.

Faith stopped and motioned to Ben. "Here, boy. Over here," she gasped. "That's it." She knew that if he didn't trust her implicitly, the sense of death surrounding the bones would keep him away.

Head down, treading cautiously and blowing through his nostrils, he came.

Thrilled, Faith could hardly contain her nervous energy long enough to let him step into proper position. She grabbed hold of the lock of mane before she jumped onto the skull and began her leap of faith. It was now or never.

Momentum carried her in a forward arc toward the mule's side. His big head came around fast, almost as if he wanted to help. That additional swinging movement gave her just enough boost to manage to plant the inside of her right foot and ankle on his backbone!

Thanks to her leather moccasins, her foot didn't slip back off. Inching along and finally hoisting herself the rest of the way to sit astride was easy compared to making that initial leap.

The moment she straightened, a rifle shot cracked. Faith ducked to lie closer to the mule's back and pressed her cheek against the side of his neck, then urged him forward with a prod from her heels and a familiar, "Let's go, Ben."

She was certain the settlers wouldn't want to risk hitting valuable animals by firing too low so she figured as long as she kept her head down and Ben kept moving she'd be safe enough.

Logic quickly countered by reminding her that anyone who came after her on horseback might manage to get a clear shot. Worse yet, one of the undisciplined drovers might decide to sacrifice the mule in order to down a real Indian.

That sobering possibility was enough to spur her to more drastic action. Tightening her knees against the mule's sides and holding on for dear life, she kicked him as hard as she could and let out a war whoop that would have made Black Kettle proud!

All around her, animals shied and scattered. Only Ben remained steady. Without a single buck or lunge, he changed gaits and gained speed until he was covering the ground at a gallop faster than most horses could equal.

It had been years since Faith had ridden the mule without a saddle, let alone raced him. At that moment she cared less about where he took her than she did about keeping her tenuous balance. Later, she'd worry about where they were. Right now all she wanted to do was escape in one piece, together with Ben.

Thankfully, she and the old mule seemed of the same mind.

Chapter Sixteen

From his vantage point on the ridge opposite all the commotion, Connell saw what was happening. He wheeled his horse and raced after Faith without pausing to explain anything to Irene.

After reaching the flatlands, he skirted the milling herd, staying in their dust to hide his passing. He needn't have bothered. No one was paying the slightest attention to him. All they wanted was to catch the so-called Indian they thought was making off with one of their mules.

Frightened oxen were lining out and starting to run in spite of their fatigue. Connell saw his chance to solve everyone's problems at once. Riding straight at the advancing animals, he waved and shouted, turning them back. Others followed the leaders, creating a whirlpool of stampeding, panting, wild-eyed livestock.

Trapped in the midst of it were the mounted settlers who had started in pursuit of Faith and Ben. Tucker was among them. Spurring his horse mercilessly, the wagon boss worked his way out to where Connell was patrolling the perimeter on Rojo, preventing breakouts.

"What the blazes do you think you're doing?" Tucker shouted.

"Saving your bacon," Connell yelled back. "You almost had a stampede."

"Bah! Nothing me and my boys couldn't handle." He stood in his stirrups to scan the distance. "I should hang you fer lettin' that Injun get away like that."

"What Indian? All I saw was a bunch of dumb critters fixin' to run themselves to death. That what you wanted, Captain?"

"'Course not. You tryin' to tell me you didn't see nobody out here stealin' horses?"

"Not one single brave," Connell said. He was proud of avoiding a blatant lie and wondered if Faith was going to appreciate his effort at veracity. She might, especially if he made a joke out of it when he told her about putting one over on Tucker.

"You was pro'bly in cahoots with 'em." He started to swing his rifle barrel toward the plainsman.

Connell reached out and tore the weapon from his hand, then reversed it and pointed it back at its owner. "I'd watch my mouth if I were you, mister. There's plenty of folks sick to death of your meanness. Bet they wouldn't mind a bit if my finger slipped and I accidentally pulled this trigger."

"You wouldn't."

"You're right," Connell said, sizing up his adversary, "I wouldn't. But not because I'm so forgiving. You've made this trip before. You're the only guide these folks have, sorry as you may be. They need you. I won't take that away from them."

Ramsey Tucker obviously wasn't a man who understood altruism. "Ha! Wouldn't surprise me if you wanted my job."

"If I thought I could get these wagons through better than

you can, I'd take your place gladly," Connell said. "Let me put everybody on horseback instead of in wagons and I might try it. But I don't know enough about managing settlers and all their gear, especially through the Sierras. That's rough country up ahead."

"Well, stopping a few cows from running off won't get you another job on my train," Tucker said, gesturing at the herd. "The Beal wagon is long gone and so is Miss Faith. We've got no place for you here anymore."

"Pity." Connell touched the brim of his hat. "In that case, I guess I'd better ride."

"Where you headed?"

The plainsman smiled. "California. Same as you." His grin spread. "Maybe we'll run into each other out there."

"Not likely," Tucker countered, eyeing his rifle. "You ain't gonna ride off with my gun, are ya? I need it for protection."

"I'll leave it on down the trail a ways. If nobody steals it before you get there, it'll be waiting."

"What about the Injuns?" Tucker sounded incredulous.

"You'd better hope I'm right and there aren't any Indians hereabouts. If you were imagining them, your rifle will be right where I put it. If not, well, there's nothing I can do about that."

"You could hand it over right now."

"And give you a chance to shoot me in the back when I ride away? Not hardly."

"You don't trust me? Why not? What did I ever do to you?"

Connell wasn't about to let himself be drawn into a conversation that might make him so angry he'd accidentally reveal too much and thereby put others in more danger.

He turned Rojo quickly and rode away as additional men joined the wagon boss.

It vexed Connell to have to travel the emigrant trail to dispose of Tucker's gun. He'd chosen that route simply because Faith had headed in the opposite direction. The longer he kept Tucker and the settlers distracted, the better her chances of escape.

The last time Connell had seen her she'd been clinging to that mule's back as if she was part of it, going like the wind. Since she wasn't using a bridle, he hoped she'd have enough control to keep her mount from instinctively circling back to rejoin the familiar herd.

If the rider in question had been anyone but Faith Beal he'd have doubted that feat was possible. In her case, however, he'd learned never to underrate her capabilities. If anybody could convince an old mule to behave, using nothing more than voice commands and a few firm nudges, Faith could.

It was a sight he wished he could stick around to see for himself instead of having to hightail it west on account of Tucker. Oh, well, Irene could tell him all about it when he rejoined her.

Irene!

Taken aback, Connell realized he hadn't even remembered to bid his future bride goodbye when he'd ridden off so abruptly. All his thoughts, then and since, had been of Faith. All his concern had been only for her.

His gut twisted with remorse, yet he couldn't help feeling continued apprehension for the young woman whose bravery, wit and compassion had earned her a special place in his heart.

There was no way to make amends until he went back to camp, either. Fortunately Irene was a mature, sensible woman. Surely she'd understand his actions, if not his motives.

Did he understand those motives? Did he want to? That was an excellent question, one he was not ready to consider, let alone answer too honestly.

He slowed his horse, tossed Tucker's rifle to the ground and sped away. There was no time to waste. Wherever Faith was, she needed help. His help. He'd rescued her before and he'd keep doing it as long as necessary. It was impossible to imagine himself not caring, not looking after her, no matter where she went or what she did.

That thought plunged into his consciousness like raindrops splashing onto the surface of a river to instantly become part of the flow. How could he and Irene marry as they had promised when they were little more than children, while he continued to shepherd Faith through life's trials? Even the most tolerant wife would wonder why her husband took such an inordinate interest in another woman.

And she wouldn't be the only one wondering, Connell told himself. He'd been pondering the same question lately.

His life, his thoughts, his heart, had become so entwined in Faith Beal's dilemma he couldn't imagine ever breaking free. The question was, did he even want to try?

Fingers cramped, muscles throbbing, Faith didn't know how much longer she'd be able to hang on…or how many more miles Ben was going to travel. Though he'd slowed to a stiff trot as he picked his way through the unfamiliar landscape, he was still making good time. She could hear him snorting, feel his sides heaving with every breath.

By listening carefully she decided no one was pursuing them. At least there was that to be thankful for. Speaking of which, she'd been lax in giving proper thanks for her deliverance. Again.

It was hard to enunciate clearly with the mule's gait bouncing her around, but she did manage to string together a simple, heartfelt "Thank…you…Father!" by inserting one crisp syllable between each stride.

The unexpected sound of her voice after she'd been quiet for so long must have startled the old mule. It shied, pranced sideways for a few yards, then kicked out at an invisible nemesis before continuing forward.

Had Faith been riding with a saddle, or even just a bridle, she wouldn't have had trouble staying aboard. Riding bareback was another story. She was already slipping off the right side of Ben's back when his unexpected lunge pitched her forward. Instead of falling all the way to the ground, she closed her arms around his upper neck and hung on for dear life.

Straddling his mane, her face nearly between his big ears, she wondered what in the world to do next.

Ben took any decision from her by lowering his head and proceeding to shake her off like a pesky insect.

All Faith had time to do was yell "Be-e-e-e-n! Whoa!" before she landed in a heap at his feet. If he hadn't been so seasoned and wise he might have run right over her. Instead, he carefully sidestepped, stopped and waited, looking about as sorry and disconcerted as a traveling preacher who'd misplaced his only hymnbook.

Faith sat there in the dust for a moment, making a mental and physical assessment of the parts of her that hurt. Two hands weren't nearly sufficient to soothe all her bumps and bruises, not to mention wipe the dirt out of her eyes or check the scrapes she'd gotten when she'd slid to the ground.

She'd decided no bones were broken and was getting to her feet when she heard a female voice say, "Nice dismount."

"Irene?" Faith's head snapped around. Her mouth gaped. Not only had the other woman managed to follow her through the twilight-dim wilderness, she'd also picked up Faith's riding horse and brought it along. "You startled me. I didn't hear you coming."

"You're not supposed to. That's one reason our ponies aren't shod."

"You mean Indian ponies, don't you?" Faith asked, frowning slightly.

"That's what I said."

"No, you said *our* ponies. You may not realize it, but you talk like that all the time. It's as if you identify more with the Indians than you do with your own people."

Irene nodded. "I suppose I do. This was my second summer with the Cheyenne. They treated me with respect and made me a part of their tribe while I learned their ways. It's going to take me a while to get over those influences."

Faith was dusting off her doeskin skirt as she spoke. "I guess I can understand that. Right now I'm glad I traded my calico for this dress. If I'd been wearing a cloth outfit when I took that fall just now I'd probably have been torn to ribbons."

"Are you all right?"

"I think so."

"Then we'd better be going. Connell is going to wonder where we are."

"Humph. That makes two of us," Faith said, scanning the countryside with a puzzled frown. "All this land looks the same to me. I'm sure glad you showed up. I have absolutely no idea how to get back to our camp."

"It isn't too far. We'll have to pick up and move if the men from the wagon train come looking for you. I haven't seen any sign of them so far, but they may change their minds." She held out a rope. "Here. Throw a loop on your mule like you should have in the first place and let's ride."

Faith was already beside Ben, meticulously checking him for injuries. "In a minute. I'm almost done."

"You'll be *done* all right, like a roasted Christmas goose, if you don't mount up and follow me. There's not much moon tonight and the desert gets very dark once the sun sets all the way. That can work to our advantage if we're smart."

"What about Connell?"

"He could track an antelope blindfolded if he had to. Don't worry. He'll find us wherever we go."

Faith put the rope around Ben's neck and tied it off, then took the reins of her saddle horse. She was about to mount up when an odd noise caught her attention. She froze, listening. "What was that?"

"I didn't hear anything," Irene insisted. "Come on."

"Well, I did." Faith paused long enough to see if Ben had noticed, too. Not only was he acting more alert, his ears were pricked and he was staring in the same direction she thought the sound had come from. "And so did he."

"All the more reason for us to keep moving," the older woman cautioned. "You can either come with me or stay here and fuss about some will-o'-the-wisp. It's up to you."

"I'm coming, I'm coming," Faith said quickly. Keeping hold of the mule's lead rope, she climbed into the saddle, kicked her horse and fell into line behind Irene without further discussion.

Bringing up the rear, Ben snorted and blew condensation through his flared nostrils as if making his own comment.

Faith glanced back at him. She could tell he was uneasy, as was she. Whether the third member of their trio believed it or not, she and Ben both sensed that something was amiss.

Faith might have believed she'd merely been imagining things if her mule hadn't echoed her nervousness. She shivered and peered into the distant dimness, straining to sort out the sounds of the desert at night.

It was totally peaceful. Too peaceful. That wasn't how other evenings had been. Normally, birds called and insects chirped, even in the darker phases of the moon. Tonight, absolute quiet reigned.

The only sounds Faith was able to discern, no matter how hard she tried to hear, were the soft clumping of the horses' hooves and the pounding of her own heart.

Chapter Seventeen

Circling wide to pick up Faith's trail without being seen by anyone from the wagon train took Connell the better part of an hour. By the time he did find her mule's tracks they had been joined by those of a pair of Indian ponies.

He'd been hoping Irene would see what was needed and take appropriate action. Assuming those particular hoofprints didn't belong to renegade Indians, she'd done just that and was currently shepherding Faith back to their campsite. Good. He'd have had a terrible time keeping track of both of them if they'd remained separated.

Thinking of the two women at the same time pointed up many contrasts. Irene was steady. Predictable. Sensible to a fault. He might have attributed those characteristics to her maturity had he not known her when she was a mere girl. Even back then she had been the sober, rational type, wise beyond her years.

Faith, on the other hand, was anything but prudent. She viewed life as one grand adventure and conducted herself accordingly. Where another woman might have collapsed in despair or fright, Faith Beal had trudged bravely on, head held high, spirits unflagging. When they'd first met, at Fort Laramie, she'd denied the pain of her injuries until her body had rebelled and forced her to pay heed. Now that she'd mended, it was even easier for him to appreciate her fortitude. Too bad it wasn't tempered by more discretion.

Rojo's head suddenly came up, his ears swiveling forward. Since their campsite lay only a few hundred yards ahead, Connell wouldn't have worried if a shiver hadn't pricked the nape of his own neck at the same instant.

He reined in the big gelding and dismounted. The camp was dark. Because of lingering danger from the wagon train, he hadn't expected to see a fire. He did, however, think someone should have noted his approach and called to him by now. Irene would remain wary, of course, but Faith didn't know the meaning of caution. *Not* hearing her voice made him more uneasy than he would have been if she'd shouted out a greeting—or a warning.

There was no way he could sneak closer when Rojo was with him so he let go of the reins to leave the horse ground-hitched, then dropped into a crouch and started to circle the tiny encampment. Irene's horse's tracks had led straight there, so where was she? Moreover, what had become of Faith and her mule?

Before Connell had time to ask himself any more questions he heard three telltale metallic clicks. Somebody had just cocked the hammer of a revolver! He froze.

To his soul-deep relief, the sound was not immediately followed by a bullet. Instead, he heard a sharp intake of breath, then a smothered gasp.

A lone figure arose out of the darkness. His subconscious recognized Faith in time to keep him from acting on instinct and forcefully defending himself. Relieved, though still on alert, he started to straighten slowly, cautiously.

Faith uncocked her pistol, holstered it and launched herself at him with a squeal of delight. "Connell!"

Her arms were open wide, her enthusiasm overwhelming. The plainsman caught her as she barreled into him, but her momentum carried them both to the ground and temporarily knocked the wind out of him.

"Oof."

Faith didn't seem to notice. "Oh, Connell. Praise God!" she blurted. "I've been so worried!"

"Thanks. I think."

He gave her a wry smile, then asked, "Do you mind?" before clasping her waist and bodily moving her to one side. Once he'd regained his feet he gave her his hand and pulled her up, too.

Faith was blushing, flustered. "I'm so sorry. I didn't mean to knock you over. I was just so glad to see you. I've been terribly nervous, out here all alone."

Connell stiffened, fully alert and scanning the darkness beyond. "Alone? Irene isn't with you? Why not? I followed your tracks."

"She was here. She took Ben and the horses to water."

Reassured, Connell began to relax. "Then everything's okay. She wouldn't have left you if she'd thought there was any danger. How long has she been gone?"

Faith's words tumbled out like water through floodgates. "I don't know. It feels like forever. I was supposed to wait right here by the fire—only we didn't light one—and tell you not to worry, that she'll be back shortly. She swore she never gets lost. I didn't know what else to do. After she went away, I began hearing things prowling around in the dark so I got out Papa's gun. Oh, Connell! I might have shot you. I'm so glad I didn't. You shouldn't go sneaking up on me in the dark. I mean, what if I'd…oh, my."

Connell let her babble on till she'd run out of things to say, then reassured her with a soft chuckle. "Hey, you didn't shoot, so stop fretting."

"I suppose I should have, shouldn't I?"

He rolled his eyes. "Shot me? No."

"No, not *you*. I mean whatever else is out there. I know something is. I can feel it. Ben sensed it, too."

"Probably coyotes." Connell noticed she was trembling and put his arm around her shoulders for comfort. "You should never shoot at anything unless you can see it clearly and be sure it's really what you think it is." He gave her an amiable squeeze. "If you'll remember that one rule you won't blow holes in your friends by mistake."

He'd intended to raise her spirits with the silly comment. Instead, Faith stared at him for a second, then buried her face in her hands and burst into tears.

"Hey, enough of that. The scary part's over. Everybody came through safe and sound, even the dumb kid who jumped on her mule bareback and started a stampede."

Faith sniffled, wiped her damp cheeks with the backs of her hands and looked up at him wide-eyed. "I—I did?"

"You sure did."

"What happened? I was so busy trying to get away I never looked back."

"Let's just say that Ramsey Tucker was good and bamboozled by the whole thing. He rode up after I got the stampede stopped and wanted to know what I'd seen. I swore I hadn't seen one single Indian brave."

"You lied?"

"Nope. He didn't ask me about seeing any squaws. My conscience is clear." Connell's smile grew. "I knew you'd be proud of me for telling the truth."

Faith slipped one arm around his waist and leaned into him

to take full advantage of the way he was still hugging her shoulders. "I'd be proud of you no matter what. I can't believe anyone would offer to take my place the way you did when Black Kettle was so angry."

"I can't believe I did it, either. It wasn't planned."

"That doesn't matter. You did it. That's what counts. I'm so, so grateful. And I'm so sorry you were hurt."

Turning slightly to fully face him, Faith put her other arm around his waist and clung to him with a fierceness that surprised her while she choked back sobs. She hadn't meant to weep anymore, but her emotions were overwhelming.

"Hey, there's no need for that," he said, closing his arms around her and gently rubbing her upper back. "It's all over now."

"No it isn't. It'll never be over." Faith was afraid to let go, to stop drawing courage from his solid strength.

"Sure it will." Connell wished he could honestly say that her trials would soon be at an end, but it wasn't fair to lie to her, even if the truth was painful. "Look, we've come this far in one piece so we must be doing something right. Your problems will all work out for the best. And I'll stay with you till everything is settled."

"You—you will?"

"Of course I will. That's what friends do."

"We are friends, aren't we?" she asked, swiping away the last of her tears and looking up at him. "I'm sorry I've been acting so silly. I don't usually fall apart like this. When I stop to think about everything that's happened, I just can't seem to keep from crying." She managed a smile. "I don't want you to think I'm like Charity."

"Not a chance," Connell assured her. "I already know you're one of a kind."

"I am?"

"Oh, yes," he drawled, nodding. "When the Good Lord made you, I imagine He realized He'd outdone himself so He stopped right there. One Faith Beal was enough."

Silently, Connell added, *And in my case, one is probably one too many.*

Faith would have gladly stood in the man's tender embrace for hours if she hadn't felt him suddenly tense. She looked up. "What is it? What's the matter?"

"I don't know. I heard something out there."

"Maybe Irene is bringing the horses back."

"Maybe." He grasped her shoulders to set her away from him. "In which case I don't suppose she'd be all that thrilled to find us acting like a couple of Cheyennes standing under a blanket."

"We weren't!"

"No, we weren't. But it might have looked like we were, which is bad enough." He turned to scan the prairie beyond their camp. "It's a new moon so there isn't much light. You stay right here. Keep your head down."

Faith made a grab for his sleeve. "Wait! Where are you going?"

"Out there," Connell told her quietly. "Keep your papa's pistol handy while I'm gone but, for heaven's sake, don't pull the trigger unless you're positive you're not shooting at me or Irene."

"Or the horses."

That comment made him chuckle in spite of the tension in the air. "I figure you can probably tell the difference between a fella like me and a critter like Ben, especially if you think hard about it. Just remember, he's the one with the long ears."

Watching Connell disappear into the dimness of the desert

night, Faith thought about his parting remarks. His ears might be smaller, but he was every bit as stubborn as her old mule. And strong. And just as faithful.

"You're all I have left. I love you both," she whispered with soul-deep honesty. "More than anything else in the world."

Embarrassed by the admission even though no one had heard her make it, Faith blushed. She didn't know how the plainsman would feel about being compared to a mule, especially when that comparison gave equal favor to both man and beast, but she'd meant it to be the highest of compliments. There wasn't a single person on the whole of the earth that she trusted the way she trusted Connell McClain. Nor was there another mount besides Ben to whom she wanted to assign her future well-being. Now that she had him back, nobody was ever going to wrest him away from her again.

A stick broke beneath a footstep somewhere in the dark. Faith started. Crouched. Picked up her father's Colt pistol and held it at the ready.

"Don't shoot," a man's voice called. "It's us."

Breath left Faith is a whoosh of relief. "Connell. You found Irene?"

He came closer. "Yes."

"Is everything all right?" The expression on his face was muted by the night, yet Faith thought he looked disturbed, maybe even angry.

"Everything's fine. There wasn't any watering hole close by after all. We'll take the horses and Ben to find food and water at daybreak. They'll be fine until then."

He glanced at Irene, who was following with their mounts, and told her, "I left Rojo a ways out. I'll go get him. You stay here with Faith." There was a long pause in which nothing else was said before Connell added tersely, "Is that understood?"

Irene merely nodded. As soon as he'd walked away, she went to work hobbling the other horses by tying short strips of rawhide between their front legs. Trussed up that way, they could take short steps to graze yet were prevented from running off.

"I'll leave Ben for you to take care of," she said, straightening and facing Faith. "Unless you're sure he'll stick close no matter what, I'd tie him, too."

"He won't leave me," Faith assured her.

"If you say so."

"I do. I know him very well. We grew up together."

Irene made a soft sound of disgust. "Believe me, just because you've known him all your life doesn't mean he won't start to think and act differently if his circumstances change."

"Are we still talking about me and my mule?" Faith asked. "Or have we started talking about you and Connell?"

Irene retained her stoic Cheyenne expression. "If you want your mule to be here in the morning, Miss Beal, you'll take my advice and tie him."

"You didn't answer me. I've been getting the feeling that something's wrong ever since we left Black Kettle's camp. What is it? Why is Connell acting so funny?"

With a cynical laugh, Irene said, "You don't have much experience with men, do you?"

"Of course I do. I had a father. And I managed to outwit Ramsey Tucker."

"Only because Connell intervened. If he hadn't, you'd be long dead by now."

Faith had to admit she was right. "Okay. So I had help. You did, too. Ab was supposed to kill you, you know, but he went against orders and sold you, instead."

"I know."

Sadness colored the other woman's countenance, making her shoulders slump, her voice sound tremulous. It was the first time since Faith had met her that Irene had shown any sign of being downhearted.

"Then cheer up. You should be giving thanks to our Heavenly Father. We both should," Faith urged. "We were spared. There must be some good reason, some special deed we were meant to accomplish, perhaps even together." She was warming to her subject as more and more truth dawned. "Think of it. You and I were strangers until a benevolent Providence united us in the midst of all our troubles. Isn't that wonderful?"

Irene looked askance at her. "Wonderful? Do you actually believe that what's happened to you—or to me—is *good?*"

"It can be. If our faith is strong enough we can triumph over any evil. You'll see. Everything will turn out for the best. All we have to do is keep our eyes on the Good Lord and our minds open to His plans and we'll persevere."

"Life isn't that simple." Irene stared off into the distant emptiness, her vision unfocused. "And this isn't the Garden of Eden."

"I suppose not." Faith sighed. "There are times when I've thought it was beautiful enough to be, though. This country has a stark, unique beauty. Sunsets out here seem to last forever. When the sky turns all pink and orange, it takes my breath away."

At that, Irene nodded agreement. "Mine, too. In the spring, the Cheyenne and Arapaho hold a dance to honor the sun. I was traded to Black Kettle during one of those celebrations."

"That must have been awful."

"If Walks With Tree hadn't already befriended me by then it would have been worse." She smiled slightly at the memory of the kind old man. "He was very quick-witted. I suspect he realized right away that my so-called magic was a trick, but he never hinted that I might be faking."

"Because he wanted a share of your glory."

"Not entirely. Now that I've had time to think about it, I know he could have gained just as much prestige by revealing my charade. The fact that he chose not to, leads me to believe he genuinely admired me, as I did him."

"I still can't imagine having to live that way every day, among all those Indians, with none of your own people to talk to or confide in."

"Funny," Irene answered. "I'm having trouble imagining living anywhere else."

Chapter Eighteen

Faith had decided to keep Irene's confession to herself, though she had mulled it over a lot during the two days they'd rested while Ben and the horses gained strength.

By the third day, when Connell gave the order to resume their westward trek, Faith had made up her mind that his increasingly dour mood must have its roots in Irene's melancholy. It was more comforting to blame his bad disposition on the other woman than it was to entertain the notion that she, herself, might be a contributing factor.

Faith kept remembering Irene's words as their party rode toward the Sierras. It had seemed strange to hear anyone say they preferred to live with Indians rather than return to life among the settlers. Still, Faith supposed that was a natural result of a long stay in the Cheyenne camp.

In her mind, Faith likened Irene to a formerly tame riding horse that had become accustomed to living with a herd of wild mustangs. That same horse could be recaptured, and even broken to ride again. But it was never the same. No matter how well it was treated or how obedient it seemed, it always kept looking into the distance as if wishing for the freedom to rejoin its former companions.

People, of course, had sense enough to realize they couldn't do that. Irene knew where she belonged. Though she might pine for the life she'd temporarily led among the Cheyenne, she'd realize she could never go back.

Truth to tell, neither could Faith, though she had often wished she could return to Ohio and resume her life exactly as it had been before her mother's untimely death. That was an impossibility, of course. Pretty daydreams couldn't wipe away harsh reality. Right now, her only concern had to be surviving the remainder of her trek without succumbing to thirst, hunger, accident or Indian attack. Judging by the signs of failure littering the trail, success had been the exception rather than the rule for far too many preceding travelers.

Worried, she urged Ben ahead and reined him in next to Connell. "This is awful. Just look at what people had to throw away. And their poor animals. Some of their bodies are still in harness, like they're lying right where they fell." She covered her nose. "What a terrible stench."

"I told you this was going to be a hard crossing. If we hadn't let our horses rest back at the meadows, they'd be giving out by now, too."

"I can see why you didn't want to travel during the worst heat of the day." She drew the back of her wrist across her damp brow. "It's beastly out here."

Connell frowned. "You're right. You need a hat. I should have thought of that."

"I'll be fine. I'm just not used to such bright sun, that's all. I know it must be my imagination, but it feels more intense out here than it ever did back home."

"You're not imagining anything. Part of the heat comes from the reflection off the ground. With no grass or trees to break it up, it bounces back and cooks us from all sides, like venison on a spit."

Talk of the oppressive heat was making Faith a bit woozy. She did her best to keep any unsteadiness from showing but saw Connell eye her with a frown.

He held up one hand and announced, "This is far enough for now. We'll stop here and rest. Drink a little water and give some to your mule while Irene and I see to the horses. Don't let him have too much. We don't want to waste it."

"How much farther to the Carson River?"

"Far enough."

Faith swung her right leg over Ben's rump, leaned against the side of the saddle and kicked loose with the opposite foot so she could slide the rest of the way to the ground. Landing, she hid the unsteadiness of her aching legs by keeping one hand on the saddle horn and leaning on the mule for support. To her relief, Connell was concentrating on the horses and didn't appear to notice.

What she would have liked to do was pour the contents of her canteen over her head and revel in the coolness. The mere thought sent a shiver skittering along her spine. What a delicious idea—and one she would someday carry out. Now, however, was not the time to indulge a silly fantasy. Not when every drop of water could mean the difference between life and death.

She raised the canteen and put it to her parched lips. One, two, three swallows of precious liquid slipped over her tongue and down her dusty throat like quicksilver, yet they felt more like rocks when they landed in her stomach. Clearly, that was enough for now. It was Ben's turn.

The moment Faith cupped her hand to make a watering trough she realized how inefficient that method was. Ben was sure to spill most of his water the minute he thrust his big muzzle into her palm and tried to drink.

Noting that Connell had inverted his leather hat and was using it to water the horses, Faith knew she could wait her turn and do the same. She would have, too, except that Connell had assigned her only one chore and she was determined to complete it on her own.

Casting around for a suitable receptacle, she scanned nearby necessities left behind by previous travelers. Surely there would be something there in which she could offer Ben water.

Vultures circled above them, mute testimony to the seriousness of her task. Ben might be terribly thirsty before this trip was over—they all might be—but as long as Faith had water to give him he'd survive. She'd see to it.

She kept a tight hold on the mule's reins and led him toward a wagon that lay about fifty feet off the main trail. The rig looked as if its owners had merely climbed down and walked away after the axle had broken. Except for fraying of the loose flap that served as a door, the canvas covering was intact. Roofs of many other wagons were either gone or badly damaged. Therefore, Faith reasoned, this rig had been deserted recently and was more likely to contain whatever she needed.

The cautious mule balked at the odor of death all around them. Faith calmed him with her voice. "It's okay, boy. That's it. Come on."

She continued to grasp the makeshift rope reins as she stood on tiptoe to peer into the abandoned wagon. The interior was as pristine as the outside. If she didn't know better, she'd guess the family had merely stepped away briefly and would soon return. They wouldn't, of course. No one took an extended respite in the midst of a desert. Which meant that whatever they'd left behind belonged to whoever came along later and needed it.

Faith spied a deep iron pot, heavy but perfect for her needs. It banged against the back of the wagon and startled Ben as she dragged it out by its looped handle.

"Easy, boy, easy. How about some water? Would you like that?"

She carefully poured precious water into the pot and waited in the shadow of the wagon while the old mule dipped his nose and drank.

Heat shimmered off the bare ground, making even that small patch of shade nearly unbearable. Faith sagged against the tilted tailboards. How any animal—or human, for that matter—could stand this unrelenting torture for long was beyond her. It was a wonder that any survived the crossing.

Connell joined her. He was alone. "Ben okay?"

"Fine, considering."

"How about you?"

Faith huffed, then smiled. "Fine, considering."

"Good. We won't be able to rest long so make the most of it." He eyed the abandoned wagon behind her. "Did you find yourself a hat?"

"I never thought about it. I was looking for a pot to water Ben. That's as far as I got."

"I'll see what I can do," Connell said, passing her and clambering easily into the leaning wagon bed. "I'd like to find regular clothes for you and Irene, too. Time will come when it'll be a lot better if you look like city women instead of refugees from an Indian camp."

"We are refugees from an Indian camp."

"My point, exactly. Once we reach California, it'll be easier to find your father if we don't have to keep explaining who and what we are."

"When you figure out who I am, let me know, will you? I'm sure not the same person I was a few months ago."

Connell's voice was muted inside the wagon, but Faith thought she heard him mention Irene.

She peered in at him. "What?"

"I said, I think Irene feels the same way. Crossing the plains changes everyone, and the two of you have really been through some harsh trials. You're bound to have grown in the process."

"Or dropped dead," Faith said cynically. She stared at the distant purple-tinged hills. "I didn't know there was such a godforsaken place in the entire world."

"It isn't the place that's to blame," Connell explained. "Giving up is in the heart. The folks who pass through here bring their faith, or lack of it, with them. I'm just coming to understand that. Bad times can push a man either way. In my case, I guess I'd turned away from the God of the Bible long before Little Rabbit Woman was killed."

"Yet you blamed Him?"

"Exactly."

"That's foolish."

"I know that now." Connell poked his head out of the wagon and squashed a straw farmer's hat on her head, then passed her a bundle of colorful fabric. "Here. I couldn't find a bonnet so that hat'll have to do till we come across something better. Next time we camp, you and Irene can fight over which dresses you want."

"Fight? Why should we fight?"

"Beats me," he said, climbing down. "Irene's been acting about as agreeable as a badger with a toothache. That's not like her. I about fell over when I came back to camp after we'd gotten Ben. I couldn't believe she'd gone off and left you there by yourself."

"That's not my fault."

"Nope. But I never have figured you out, either, so I'm

not about to get myself between you two, no matter what else happens."

"Meaning?" Faith was scowling.

"Meaning, I'll still guide you to California, just like I promised, but you'll have to make your own peace with Miss Irene Wellman. I'd have figured she was just jealous of you if she wasn't acting like she hates everybody, me included."

This was the opportunity Faith had been waiting for, praying for. Nervous, she licked her parched lips. "Maybe... maybe she doesn't want to go back to her old life."

One eyebrow arched and Connell snorted his disbelief. "Why would you think that?"

"Because she seemed to be happy with the Cheyenne, for one thing. She did have a beau."

"Only because she thought I was dead," he argued. "Once she found out I was alive, she told Red Deer about our old arrangement."

"Arrangement?" Faith's voice was rising. "If that's all it was—or is—then I pity you both."

That said, she stomped away, leaving Connell staring after her, dumbfounded.

Little was said for the remainder of the afternoon. Conversation took energy and there was none to spare. Mouth dry, Faith licked her cracked lips and kept her head tipped so the brim of the oversize hat would offer a smidgen of shade. She knew there'd be no relief, no cool respite, until they reached the foothills of the Sierras. How soon that would be was irrelevant. The only thing that mattered was staying alive.

Too weary to pray, Faith merely closed her eyes and let the gentle rocking of Ben's walk lull her into an internal awareness of the Lord's presence. In Bible stories, many a man had been shepherded safely through the wilderness. Strong faith was the key to survival, just as Connell had said. That, and putting her complete trust in those who had been ordained to deliver her. Surely, McClain was such a man. Meeting him had been a wonderment, considering how many other travelers had been nearby when she'd been injured. The fact that he'd been the one to come to her rescue was proof enough that he was special. Heaven-sent.

Her heart swelled with gratitude—and more—taking her imagination on a flight of fancy. She pictured herself in his arms, her cheek lying against his broad chest as she listened to his heart beating rhythmically like the thudding of her own pulse in her ears, at her temples. Soft cadence. Drumming. Humming in her veins. Dulling the unrelenting assault of heat on her exhausted body and soul.

She swayed in the saddle. Flashes of light sparkled behind her closed eyelids like a night sky filled with millions of stars. At the periphery, blackness waited to envelop her, to rescue her from reality.

In the deepest parts of her mind, Faith knew she must be falling, yet her only sensation was one of floating. The desert disappeared from her consciousness, as did all her suffering and thirst. Empty, welcome blackness took its place.

When Faith came to, she was lying in the shade of a scrubby tree. Connell was bathing her face with a wet cloth and fanning her with her straw hat.

She opened her eyes and reached for his wrist to stop him. "Don't waste water."

"It's all right," he said softly. "We made it. There'll be plenty to drink from here on out."

Faith tried to sit up. He held her in place with a hand on her shoulder.

"Just lie there and rest," Connell said. "You've had a rough time of it."

"What…what happened?"

"You passed out."

"I don't remember." When she tried to moisten her lips, she realized how dry and cracked they were. "I'm so thirsty. Are you sure there's plenty to drink?"

"Positive. Irene's gone to water Ben and the horses." He cradled Faith's head, lifted it and held the canteen to her lips. "Here. Drink. Just don't overdo it or it's liable to make you sick."

She swallowed all he'd allow, then sat up and thanked him. "I don't think I'll ever quench this thirst."

"Sure you will." A relieved smile lit his face and crinkled the outer corners of his eyes. "You're looking better already. Had me worried there for a while, though. I was beginning to think you were going to quit on me."

"Never." Faith smiled as far as the cracks in her sore lips would allow. "You're stuck with me, mister."

"I'm glad to see your feisty attitude is intact, too. I kind of missed it."

"Probably not nearly as much as I did," she quipped. "I think I must have been hallucinating part of the time. I imagined I was…" A blush rose to her already reddened cheeks.

"What?"

Faith looked around to see if Irene was near before she told him. "If you must know, I was dreaming I was—we were, um—I mean, well, sort of hugging. Like back in camp after I almost shot you. Remember?"

"I remember all right. You weren't dreaming. I caught you when you started to fall and carried you till we finally found water. I didn't think you'd mind, especially since the alternative was to sling you over a saddle like a pack."

"That's what Ab did to me," Faith said. "I didn't like it one bit, thank you. Especially with sore ribs."

"How are you doing now? I haven't asked lately because you weren't favoring your side at all."

"I hardly know I was hit. Either my ribs weren't broken in the first place or I heal fast. Or both." She gave him a lopsided grin. "Of course, if these were biblical times I'd say it could also have been a miracle."

"The amazing thing is that we managed to make it this far in spite of all that's happened," Connell said, getting to his feet. "You rest. I'll go see what's keeping Irene."

"Wait! There's something you should know. Something that's been nagging at me. I can't quite put my finger on what's wrong with Irene, but I'm sure something is. I can feel it." Faith could tell by the look on his face he wasn't taking her seriously.

"Intuition?"

She shook her head soberly. "More like a sense of foreboding."

"Now you *are* imagining things." One eyebrow arched. "As a matter of fact, Irene mentioned the same notion about you. I suspect you're jealous of each other."

"Over what? You? Don't be silly. I know you're only helping me because you got stuck with the job. And I know you're the kind of honorable man who doesn't make a vow unless he intends to keep it."

She sighed, then went on, "It's not *your* motives I'm worried about, it's hers."

"You don't have to fret about Irene," he said. "She's as reliable as anyone I've ever met. I know she's been through a lot in the past year or two but you can trust her completely. I do."

"You trust her with your life?" Faith asked quietly, cautiously.

"Of course. And so can you."

Nodding, she bowed her head as he walked away, waiting until he was out of earshot before whispering, "I'm afraid I'm not so sure."

Chapter Nineteen

The trip through the high Sierras was rigorous beyond belief. By the time Faith and the others reached the western side of the range, she was in awe of any and all who had braved the difficult trek. Wrecked wagons that bespoke lost dreams and perhaps lost lives framed the steep, rutted trails and littered the canyons.

Though the sight saddened Faith it was hard for her to continue to grieve for nameless strangers when she was feeling such a sense of success. Every day for the past week she'd asked Connell, "How much longer," and every day he'd answered, "Soon."

Now that the higher elevations were behind them the weather was warm again, though not nearly as uncomfortable as it had been in the desert. When Connell called a halt and suggested the women bathe while he set up camp and prepared an evening meal, Faith was more than glad to oblige. Though she'd loved the comfort of her Cheyenne garb, she was ready for a change of clothes. And the doeskin was definitely ready for a scrubbing. The thought of lighter-weight calico over a cotton chemise and drawers absolutely thrilled her.

Irene remained silent and waited as Faith gathered up the dresses and personal items they'd procured back at the Humboldt Sink. Together, they made their way downstream from where Connell had placed their camp.

Without hesitation, Irene plunged into the waist-deep water, clothes and all.

"Isn't that cold?" Faith asked.

Irene didn't answer. Crouched down up to her neck, she was stripping off her leather garments and rinsing them in the current.

Following Irene's sensible example, Faith waded in. Icy rivulets crept inside her leather moccasins and leggings, chilling her immediately. Shivering, she gave a high-pitched "Ooh!"

"Hush," Irene warned. "Get down into the water, like this, and be quiet, before you draw every bandit and renegade Indian in the territories."

That thought sobered Faith. She ducked and scanned the brushy riverbank, imagining menace in every shadow, behind every tree. "Sorry. It's so beautiful here I forgot to be cautious."

"Women can't afford to forget," Irene told her.

Faith sobered even more. "Was it very bad?"

"What?" Irene continued to tend to her washing without looking up.

"Living with savages."

"Savages? You mean Ramsey Tucker?"

"I wasn't referring to him, but I do see what you mean. I suppose savageness or civility is all in whatever point of view a person holds, isn't it."

"You are learning," Irene said quietly.

"Do you really wish you could go back to the Cheyenne?"

Irene ducked under the running water for a moment before

surfacing and swiping a hand across her eyes. "I refuse to dwell on what cannot be."

"But what do you really want to do?"

She heaved a deep, sorrowful sigh. "If I had any choice, I'd go back to being a carefree girl in love with the young man my family befriended after his mother died. Then I'd run away with him like he wanted me to do many years ago and we'd start a new life."

"Connell?" Faith's throat tightened at the thought.

"Yes. We imagined we were in love. Maybe, in a childish way, we were. I don't know."

"Why didn't you go away with him?"

"Family obligations. I felt those came first and he had a terrible urge to see the Territories, so we were at an impasse."

"What made you change your mind and come west?"

"My parents' deaths, mostly. When my excuse was gone, I wrote to Connell at the last address I had for him, in Sacramento City. I never dreamed he'd still want me after all the time that had passed."

"It's a wonder your letter even reached him."

"I know. I was actually surprised when he answered. He told me he was lonely, and why. So was I. It seemed the most sensible thing in the world to renew our old promise to marry."

"And then you met Ramsey Tucker."

"Yes."

Again Irene ducked beneath the rippling water but not before Faith glimpsed the shimmer of unshed tears. As soon as she came up for air, Faith said, "It's not your fault. None of this is. Tucker lied to you the same way he's lied to my sister. He's very accomplished at getting his way."

"I know."

"Maybe we can procure a settlement from him, on your behalf, when we liberate Charity."

"Money, you mean? Oh, no. Not money." Faith saw Irene's eyes spark, narrow and fill with malevolence. "All I want from Ramsey Tucker is his mangy scalp. It would pleasure me greatly to lift it myself."

"You're not serious!"

Irene stared straight at her and said with unmistakable conviction, "Oh, yes, I am."

Faith knew she should quote the scripture where God said vengeance belonged to Him, but she feared that if she did, Irene's anger would focus on her as well, so she kept silent.

Irene didn't tarry long at the river. Left alone to rue her temporary timidity, Faith prayed for greater strength, wisdom and the courage to express her faith no matter whose displeasure or what obstacles she had to contend with in doing so.

Shivering, she undid her braids and let the river rinse her hair clean the way prayer had cleansed her conscience, then climbed out and followed Irene's example by donning the settlers' clothing they'd brought from the abandoned wagon.

Now that they weren't facing imminent death, Faith could think of other amenities she wished she'd had the presence of mind to pick up when she'd had the chance. Not the least of those was a hairbrush or comb.

She leaned to the side and twisted her long tresses to remove as much water as possible, then looked around for something with which to fasten her hair back. Irene had laid their Cheyenne clothing over brushy lower limbs of trees to dry before starting back up the hill toward their campsite.

Lagging behind, Faith realized she'd lost the colorful ties the young Cheyenne girl had used to hold her rolled braids in place. She was about to give up and forget about doing anything with her hair when she spied a narrow strip of beaded leather tied to a branch beside their old dresses. It was just what she needed. It was also not hers.

Faith opened her mouth to call after Irene for permission, then remembered the older woman's sensible admonition of silence. Surely, it wouldn't hurt to borrow the decorative tie. After all, if Irene had wanted to wear it herself, she'd have done so.

Without further qualm, Faith undid the knot, slid the leather thong under her hair at the nape of her neck and tied it. Having been braided until now, her hair wasn't as tangled as she'd expected, especially considering all she'd been through. She smiled, patting and smoothing the sides. Probably just as well she didn't have a mirror. Some things were best imagined rather than seen.

Besides, she thought with derision, who cared what she looked like? Certainly not Connell McClain. He had Irene. If any man was a perfect match for poor Irene Wellman, it was the plainsman.

"So why does it bother me so to see them together?" Faith muttered. She started to argue the point with herself, then stopped. It was true. She knew she should be exhibiting Christian charity and thanking the Lord that her rescuer had found his betrothed, yet she couldn't help wishing otherwise. It wasn't the right attitude to harbor. It was simply human.

Faith smiled and muttered, "Well, well. What do you know? One character flaw after another. I guess that's what I get for praying for more wisdom."

Connell had a simple meal almost ready by the time Faith returned to camp. His future bride was sitting sideways on one of the saddles while he squatted by the fire, turning a makeshift spit to finish cooking a rabbit and several small game hens.

Faith grinned. "That smells wonderful. I didn't know how hungry I was till just now." When he looked up at her, his eyes widened and his eyebrows arched, much to her delight.

She twirled to display the calico frock. "Do you like it? It's almost a perfect fit."

"I'll say." Straightening, Connell stared. "Looks like it was made for you."

"Maybe it was. I wish I had a proper ribbon to match." She touched her hair and gave Irene a quick glance as she added, "This was the best I could do. I found it down by the river. I hope you don't mind."

Before Faith could react, Irene leaped to her feet, screeched in Cheyenne and began to claw at the beaded thong, grasping handfuls of hair with it.

Confused, Faith fought off the attack as best she could. If it hadn't been for Connell's intervention she might have been seriously hurt. He held the struggling Irene at bay while Faith untangled the thong and handed it back to its owner.

"I'm sorry. I didn't think I was doing anything wrong."

"You weren't," Connell replied. Keeping Irene at arm's length, he stared down at her. "What was that all about?"

She twisted out of his grasp without answering, fisted the tangled tie and ran back toward the river where they'd left their Indian garments.

Rubbing her scalp, Faith turned to Connell. "I *told* you she was acting funny. Do you have any idea what's going on?"

"No."

In spite of his denial, Faith was certain she'd glimpsed more than concern in his expression when he'd looked at the object Irene had coveted so. Either it was of special significance by itself or it bore markings that identified it as belonging to a certain person or tribe. Possibly both, she concluded. Although their garments themselves were unique, perhaps the tie was even more so. Perhaps it had belonged to Red Deer.

Faith's breath caught. Suddenly feeling her senses prickling in warning, she stared after Irene. What if the thong had been tied to the branch for some reason other than to dry it? What if it had been placed there as a sign, a marker for someone who was following?

That thought was so bizarre she gawked at Connell, slack jawed and speechless. There was thunder in his expression, lightning in his eyes. Could he be thinking the same thing she was? Was he finally ready to listen to reason and take precautions?

Faith closed her mouth and let it twist with sarcasm. He was already certain she was insanely jealous of Irene, which wasn't far from the truth. Any accusation against Irene, coming on the heels of their tiff over the hair tie, would sound like nothing more than another foolish manifestation of female rivalry.

What could she do, short of knocking Connell over the head and forcing him to pay heed to her concerns?

The more she pondered all the strange things that had occurred since they'd liberated Irene, the more Faith was certain the other woman was up to something. It was beginning to look as though her rescuer was going to need someone to stand firm beside him, and there was only one person in a position to offer support. Her.

She made her way to where her saddle and gear were piled and strapped on her papa's Colt. The holster and enormous revolver looked incongruous atop her new dress but she didn't care. Unlike Charity, she'd decided long ago that self-preservation was far more important than fashion.

Resting a hand on the pistol grip, Faith stood straight and

faced Connell, daring him to disagree with her decision to once again travel fully armed.

Instead of the argument she'd expected, he merely nodded thoughtfully and said, "Good."

Faith watched Connell as they ate, noting his growing unease. His gaze kept darting in the direction where they'd last seen Irene as if expecting her to reappear.

Finally, Faith asked, "Do you think I should go after her and apologize?"

The plainsman shook his head. "No. She'll come back when she's ready."

"Are you sure? I don't mind going."

He got to his feet. "You stay put. Keep the fire built up. I'll go fetch her. The last thing I need is to have both of you wandering around in the hills getting into trouble."

"Do you think she's in trouble?"

"Not till I catch up to her." He sighed. "Irene's as good at wilderness survival as I am, thanks to the Cheyenne. I'd just feel better if I knew exactly where she was."

Faith huffed. "Me, too. I know you don't want to hear this, especially coming from me, but I can't help thinking she's up to something."

"What makes you say that?"

"No one big thing," Faith replied. "Just lots of odd little things that don't add up. Can you honestly say you haven't noticed?" She saw his expression close, his eyes narrow.

"We'll talk about this later," Connell said flatly. He paused beside Rojo and swung his saddle onto the horse's back. "I'm going to mount up in case she's gone farther than the river. You keep track of Ben and the other horses. Make sure they don't disappear while you're sleeping."

"Sleeping?" Faith was on her feet in a heartbeat. "Aren't you coming right back?"

"That's my plan, unless I have trouble finding Irene."

"I should come with you then."

"You'd just slow me down."

"Thanks a heap, mister. Have I slowed you down so far?" She pulled a face. "Never mind. I know I have and I'm sorry. I just don't feel right letting you go out there all alone." Without conscious thought she rested her hand on the butt of the revolver, realizing belatedly that her actions were amusing him.

"I promise to let you protect me some other time," he gibed with a cynical smile. "Right now, I want you to concentrate on looking after yourself." Finished tightening the cinch, he swung into the saddle. "And one more thing. This river feeds straight into the American. Remember that."

Faith frowned up at him, wondering why he felt the need to be so specific until he continued with, "You can find Beal's Bar by sticking to the riverbank and following it downstream. Understand?"

"I understand your directions," Faith said. "What I don't understand is why you're telling me this. Are you trying to scare me? Because if you are, it's working."

He wheeled Rojo in a tight circle while the horse pranced with eagerness. "Just stay alert. I'll be back as fast as I can. I promise."

"Wait!" Faith hurried closer and reached out to him. In an instant he'd bent down and lifted her off the ground, holding her close while she threw her arms around his neck and kissed him soundly.

Just as quickly he put her down, backed his horse away and galloped into the night.

Unsteady, Faith pressed her fingertips to her tingling lips and blinked to try to clear her head. There had been a desperate quality to Connell's goodbye kiss. A yearning that echoed all the pent-up emotion she'd been trying to deny in her own heart.

Realizing their shared feeling lifted Faith's spirits.

It also scared her silly and piled enough guilt on her heart to make it ache.

Chapter Twenty

It was nearly dawn before Faith yielded to fatigue and closed her eyes. The campfire had burned down to glowing embers by the time she stirred again. Except for Ben and the two horses the Cheyenne had given them, she was alone.

How long should she wait for Connell? she wondered. If he'd found Irene, he would have returned as he'd promised. Therefore, he must still be searching. Unless…

Breath caught in Faith's throat. Unless he'd been hurt. Or worse. The notion was so dreadful, so unacceptable, it made her heart race and her head throb.

Every instinct told her she must search for him. Logic countered by reminding her she had no idea where he'd gone. Nor did she know where *she* was. Her only clue was Connell's instruction about following the river's course to Beal's Bar. Clearly, he'd wanted her to proceed in case he didn't make it back, but how could she leave the area without knowing what had happened to him?

She stood, forlorn in the midst of the vast Sierra range, and looked toward heaven. "This isn't right. It isn't fair, Father. I can't leave him. I can't."

Yet, if she didn't go on alone, Charity and Tucker might reach the mining camp ahead of her. Then her innocent father and sister would be in terrible jeopardy. Only Faith knew the whole truth. Only she could save her family from Tucker's planned perfidy.

She had no choice but to break camp and head downriver. Heart heavy, she doused the campfire, packed their supplies aboard one of the horses and saddled Ben. It occurred to her to leave a sign or an arrow to guide Connell but she decided against it. He already knew which way she was going. There was no use giving anyone else a clue to her whereabouts.

And speaking of not leaving behind any sign, she had one important task left. Leading her mule, Faith headed toward the river to pick up her deerskin dress. It was still draped on the bush where she'd left it to dry.

Irene's Cheyenne clothing, however, was gone. So was the beaded tie that had caused such an uproar.

Praying and hoping and wishing, Faith continued to follow the river as Connell had instructed, even after she lost sight of the clear trail of Rojo's prints along the bank. Either the man had ridden his horse into the water or she'd somehow missed some trace of him on the rocky ground. Whichever it was, she was truly on her own.

Too bereft to form coherent plans and too numb to recall comforting scripture verses the way she wanted, she let Ben pick his way along while she thought of Connell and prayed randomly for his safety and well-being.

"And for his happiness," Faith added. "I do want him to be happy, God. Honest I do. I just don't understand all this. Why did I have to fall in love with him when everything is so hopeless?"

Just then, Ben blew a noisy snort and Faith thought she

heard a horse nicker a soft reply. She reined the mule in. "What is it, boy? What's wrong?"

His ears pricked, head turning slowly. Faith stood in her stirrups, straining to see into the distance. There didn't seem to be any reason for the mule's concern, yet he was growing more and more agitated. Behind her, the horses she'd been leading were equally nervous. Suddenly, one bolted, jerked the lead rope out of her hand and galloped off. The other followed.

Shouting "Whoa!" had no effect on either of them and Faith had no clue as to the equivalent Cheyenne word. She was, however, sorely tempted to use some of the colorful language she'd heard more than one so-called gentleman shout in similar circumstances.

"Well, pooh," she finally said, talking to the mule and patting his neck. "At least I've still got you."

He blew another loud snort. This time, Faith knew she heard a horse or mule reply. Urging Ben forward, she took her bearings on the river behind her and went to investigate.

In minutes, she realized her prayers had been answered. Or had they? She stifled a shout and slid from Ben's back.

Connell lay sprawled on the rocky ground, facedown. Rojo stood guard over him. There was blood on the fancy beaded rifle scabbard hanging from his saddle and a nasty-looking cut on the horse's foreleg.

Dropping to her knees beside the prostrate man, Faith touched his shoulder with trepidation. "Connell?"

To her relief, he stirred, moaned.

"Oh, thank God. You're alive!"

He sat up slowly, with effort. "What happened?"

"Don't you know?"

One hand explored his bloody forehead. "Maybe Rojo stumbled. Is he okay?"

"I think so." Faith helped the plainsman stand. "He's cut, but he seems to be putting weight on that leg. How did he fall?"

She saw Connell stiffen and reach for his pistol. It was no longer in its holster. His rifle was gone, too. All he had left was the knife he used for skinning. No wonder he was suddenly on full alert. If his horse had merely fallen, Connell wouldn't have lost both his guns. It didn't take a genius to figure he'd been assaulted and robbed.

"We have to get out of here," he said.

Faith easily adopted his attitude. "Now you're making sense. Let's go. You can ride Ben till we make sure your horse isn't badly injured."

"No. You mount up and ride. I'll follow when I can."

"In a pig's eye, mister. I came to rescue you and that's just what I intend to do."

"You *what?*"

"You heard me. I'm saving your sorry hide. Now stop arguing and get on that mule before I get really upset."

"You don't know what you're saying. It's too dangerous. Whoever knocked me out might still be around."

"Oh?" Faith cocked an eyebrow. "I thought you got that knot on your head when your horse fell." She could tell she'd bested him, at least for the present.

"Never mind how I got hurt. Just do as I tell you."

"If I'd followed your orders and stayed by the river you might still be lying in a heap with your poor horse bleeding all over you. Now, are you going to do this my way or do I have to sit myself down right here and wait for you to come to your senses?"

Muttering to himself, Connell nevertheless agreed. "All right. Mount up. I'll ride one of the other horses. Where did you leave them, anyway?"

Faith didn't think this was a good time to tell him she'd lost the spare horses so she merely smiled and said, "Give me a boost and swing on behind me. Ben can carry us for a short way and Rojo can follow till we have time to sort everything out."

To her relief, Connell went along with her plan. If she hadn't been so worried about meeting up with whoever had attacked him, she'd have spent more time fretting about how to explain her careless loss of the extra horses.

The throbbing in Connell's temple was the least of his concerns. Even if Rojo had been sound and he'd still had all his weapons, he'd have had to decide which of the two women to help first. Both of them were special to him—Irene because of their long history of friendship, and Faith Beal because she needed him and…

He paused, dismayed by the clarity of his mental ramblings. Faith was special because he not only admired and cherished her, he loved her! She was intelligent as well as the bravest, most virtuous woman he'd ever met.

What a sobering conclusion. The qualities he most admired in her were the very ones that would preclude his ever revealing his deep affection. Honor and righteousness meant everything to Faith. He knew she would never consider marrying a man who had broken his vows to another woman, even if he could bring himself to do so. Which he couldn't.

After all the trials Irene had suffered attempting to join him in California he couldn't just turn away from her. She was like a frightened, wounded animal in need of healing, of the comfort a faithful husband could offer. He'd had his chance at the lighthearted romance of youth with Little Rabbit Woman. It was time to settle down and fulfill his vow to Irene, as he'd promised so long ago.

Still riding with Faith, Connell rested a tender gaze on her shoulders. Ever since he'd foolishly given in and mounted Ben behind her, he'd had to fight the tendency to wrap his arms around her and pull her back against his chest.

He could still taste the sweet kiss they'd shared when they'd last parted. It had been so spontaneous, so right for that moment, he hadn't stopped to think about what he was doing until after the fact. Now, he was beginning to worry that he might have altered the way Faith viewed their relationship. If so, he had some serious atoning to do.

He lightly touched her arm. "Faith?"

"Yes?"

"This is far enough. We'll be safe here. Stop and let me down so I can check Rojo."

She reined in the mule. As soon as Connell swung a leg over and jumped to the ground, Faith dismounted beside him.

"We need to talk," she said quietly.

"That's what I was about to suggest."

"Really?" He'd already started to walk away so she dogged his steps. "You figured it out?"

"Figured what out?"

"About the other horses. I tried to hold on to them but they spooked and ran away. There was no way Ben could catch Indian ponies running scared so I let them go."

"You what?"

"I let them go. What did you expect me to do, go galloping all over the mountains after them and get myself good and lost?"

"No. I expected you to hang on to them."

"I tried to. I don't know what scared them but something sure did. They took off like they'd been shot."

Connell's gaze narrowed.

"Well, they did," she insisted, hands fisted on her hips. "I'm glad I was riding Ben instead of one of them."

"So am I." He glanced past her to scan the hills. "All right. What's done is done. It's obvious I can't leave you alone under the present circumstances so I'll escort you the rest of the way to Beal's Bar. It shouldn't be far. Once you're there, your father can look out for you."

"What about Irene?" Faith saw his jaw muscles knot.

"That decision's been made for me. I can't track her far on foot and I won't ride Rojo till I'm sure he's okay. I'll pick up a spare horse when I drop you off."

"Drop me off? Just like that? I thought you were going to stay and help me get even with Tucker."

"That's all changed. I have to find Irene."

"I know you do. I just thought…" Faith's voice trailed off. "Oh, never mind." She didn't like sounding petulant so she added, "Do whatever you feel you must. I understand. I just wish you could be there to see Tucker taken down a peg. I thought Irene wanted to be in on it, too."

Suddenly, Faith brightened. "I know! Maybe after you find her you can *both* come to Beal's Bar."

Before she finished speaking Connell was shaking his head slowly, soberly. "No, Faith. As soon as Irene and I are back together I'm taking her to my ranch near Sacramento City. She deserves a home of her own and the life I promised her years ago."

"Of course." Though Faith turned quickly away, she feared Connell had glimpsed the tears she was fighting to subdue. When she felt his gentle touch on her arm once again and heard the pathos in his voice, she was certain.

"I'm so sorry," he said. "All I wanted was to rescue you, to do you good. I never meant to cause pain. Please don't cry."

"I'm not crying," Faith insisted. "I just got something in my eye, that's all."

Connell turned her to face him, his hands softly caressing

her upper arms through the sleeves of her calico. "If things had been different, I…"

She reached up and placed her fingertips on his lips to silence him. "Don't. Don't say nice things. I can't bear hearing them." Blinking back emotion, she was about to go on when the nearby snap of a dried branch made her gasp and hold her breath.

Connell instinctively reached for his missing pistol, then drew his knife, instead, and placed himself staunchly between Faith and the noise.

Less than fifteen feet away, an Indian woman stepped into the clearing. She was chuckling and shaking her head. "It's a good thing for you two that I'm not hunting scalps."

Together, Faith and Connell shouted, "Irene!"

He started toward her. "Where have you been?"

"Following you two," Irene said. "I spotted our Cheyenne horses grazing back a ways and brought them along." She eyed Connell's forehead. "What happened to you?"

It surprised Faith when his reply was gruff, his attitude off-putting. "Never mind. Where have you been?"

"Out here, same as you. Only it looks like I've been a lot more careful." She pointed back the way she'd come. "I also came across your Hawken rifle. I left it with the horses, over there a ways, when I followed the sound of your voices."

"And the packs? The supplies?"

"All there," Irene said.

"Then go get them. I need medicine to treat Rojo's cut before we go any farther."

The last thing Faith wanted was to interfere, so she volunteered to fetch the horses, assuming he'd be glad to get rid of her. With a bright "I'll do it," she took a step in the direction Irene had indicated. To her surprise, Connell stopped her.

"No. Stay right where you are. She'll bring the horses." He glared at his Cheyenne-garbed betrothed. "Won't you?"

"Of course," Irene answered flatly.

Faith's gaze bounced back and forth between her two companions as she tried to decipher the tacit undercurrent. Something more was going on than that which was evident and whatever it was had made Connell irate and wary. Irene's mood was more difficult to label. Her closed yet cautious expression reminded Faith of the Cheyenne.

That was it! Even in settler's clothing, Irene Wellman had carried herself with the proud aura of a Cheyenne. And now that she was once again dressed as one, she wore her off-putting attitude like a badge of honor.

"Stay here with Rojo," Connell told Faith. "Having Ben nearby will help settle him so he doesn't move around too much and open up that cut again. I'll go with Irene and bring back the horses." He started to leave, then paused. "And don't get careless. Keep your pistol handy."

"You are coming back this time? For sure?"

"For sure," Connell said.

She watched him stride purposefully after the already disappearing Irene and heard him shout, "Slow down. I don't want you out of my sight. Understand?"

Irene's answer was faint but Faith did manage to hear Connell say angrily, "What in blazes is going on?"

That, Faith agreed, was a very good question.

Chapter Twenty-One

Faith had hoped that her companions would have settled their personal differences before they returned with the horses. Instead, they had apparently argued to the point where they were no longer on speaking terms.

Tired of their childishness, Faith stroked Ben's velvety nose and talked aside to him. "Can you believe it? Look at them. Grown folks acting like spoiled brats. And they're fixing to get married. Imagine that."

The old mule lowered his head and nudged her gently. Faith smiled. "Sorry, old boy. I'm fresh out of apples. You'll have to wait till we get to Papa's and see what treats he's got for you."

She looked to Connell and raised her voice. "How far are we from Beal's Bar, anyway?"

"My guess is about half a day," he replied.

"Is that all? Well, what are we waiting for?"

"I don't want to push Rojo. We can make camp here, rest up, and still have plenty of time to get there ahead of Charity and Tucker."

"You're sure?"

"Positive. Even with our side trips—" he glanced daggers at Irene "—we're ahead of schedule."

"I could ride on ahead," Faith suggested.

Connell was adamant. "Not alone."

"Why not? It's sure not very enjoyable keeping company with you two. Besides, if I hadn't followed Ben's instincts and left the riverbank, I'd be by myself right now anyway."

"But you're not, are you? I'd think even you would have figured out that the Good Lord intends for me to keep looking after you."

"Oh really?" Faith fisted her hands on her hips. "And I get no credit for rescuing you? Seems to me you're the one with the short memory, mister. Besides, I thought you were anxious to get rid of me."

"I never said that."

"You most certainly did. You told me you were going to drop me at my father's, then turn right around and take Irene home to your ranch."

Irene had been listening quietly. Now, she spoke. "No."

Connell whirled. "What do you mean, no?"

"I'm not going anywhere with you, or anyone else, until I've seen Tucker get what's coming to him."

Faith recalled what Irene had said about taking justice into her own hands. The memory made her shiver. Yes, she wanted to see justice done, but she didn't want to be a party to another murder. Standing over her own grave and knowing it contained the body of the man who had planned her demise had made her painfully aware of the heinous consequences of such an act.

Being a Christian meant she believed she'd go to be with the Lord when she died, would greet her mother and other loved ones again in heaven, but it didn't mean she was eager to depart immediately! Or that she was willing to send another human being on his way to eternity.

There had been a time when, consumed with irrational anger, she'd wished for the chance to end Ramsey Tucker's life with her own hands. That time had passed. There was no goal more important than rescuing Charity and making her see the folly of her ways. Once that was accomplished, the problem of Tucker should solve itself, unless Irene interfered and killed him before Charity realized what kind of man he really was.

Now that Irene was again garbed as a Cheyenne, Faith found the woman's countenance threatening. In order to muster the courage to speak her mind, she had to keep reminding herself that as a Christian she was clad in the whole armor of the Lord.

"Irene wants to kill Tucker," Faith announced. "We mustn't allow that. He needs to be unmasked and properly punished by the law so my sister can see him for what he is, a thief, liar and murderer. Behaving like him will only undermine our position of truth."

Connell nodded. "I agree. However, if the wagon boss manages to talk his way out of this mess, he'll be free to repeat his crimes against other innocent women. We can't allow that either."

"Of course not." Pacing, Faith pressed her fingertips to her throbbing temples and took a deep, settling breath before she continued. "I just want you to promise—both of you—that you'll work with me, not against me. I know my father will help us, too."

"Assuming we locate him," Connell said. "If not, once Charity and Tucker are away from the protection of the men on the train, we may have to kidnap her for her own good."

"I don't object to doing whatever is necessary to rescue my sister," Faith said, "but it's my fervent hope that we can best Ramsey Tucker at the same time."

"In other words," Connell drawled, smiling, "you want the impossible."

She returned his smile. "Why not? This whole trip west has been one improbable event after another."

"One disaster after another, you mean."

Faith shook her head. "No. The tornado that killed my mother was a true disaster, but even that's been used for good. Think about it. If Charity and I hadn't been forced to travel west when we did, you and I might not have met at Fort Laramie and you'd have had no reason to join Tucker's party and travel with us. If you hadn't, you might never have met Ab and Stuart and finally located Irene. See? It all works together, just like the Good Book says."

"Ha!" Irene huffed in disgust. "That's easy for you to say. You weren't married to a heinous man like Tucker and sold into slavery. If God is so good, why did I have to suffer all that?"

"I don't know," Faith said with evident empathy. "But I have thought about your situation and come to one important conclusion. You need a man like Connell, a man who understands Indian culture and is comfortable with you, just as you are. Just as you want to be."

Her gaze traveled over the older woman's outfit, pausing at the toes of her moccasins before returning to her dark, sad eyes. "He'll be a good husband for you. I know he will." If emotion hadn't choked off her words she'd have added, *Please, be a good wife to him.*

She turned away to hide her gathering tears as she thought, *The kind of good wife I would be, if he were free to love me the way I love him.*

Rising at dawn, Faith was dressed, mounted and ready to travel as soon as the others were. Though they were about to enter a populated area, Irene had chosen to continue dressing like a Cheyenne, Faith noted. All the more reason for the woman to fit comfortably into the life that awaited her. Faith's mind was convinced Connell and Irene belonged together. It was her stubborn heart that kept arguing the point.

Looking for distraction, she urged Ben ahead of Irene's horse and trotted along beside Connell. Seeing such a big man mounted on the scruffy Indian pony instead of his magnificent canelo made her smile.

Grinning, she said, "Hello down there, mister. How much farther?"

He gave her a taciturn look. "Maybe an hour. Maybe less."

"How can you be so sure? We don't have a map."

"I know where the Feather River joins the American. Your father's camp is supposed to be just south of there. As soon as we hit the river there'll be plenty of men to ask, which reminds me," Connell said. "I don't think you should identify yourself unless you have to."

"That's exactly what I was thinking," she said, smiling. "If we can get to Papa without the whole camp finding out who I am, maybe we can keep my survival a secret and catch Tucker unaware." It pleased her to see appreciation in Connell's expression.

"Smart girl."

Girl? I'm a woman, she wanted to screech. *Grown and madly in love with you, you big idiot.*

Instead of uttering such a revealing retort she merely said, "Thank you," nudged Ben in his sides and rode on.

Faith was about fifty yards ahead of the others when she heard Connell and Irene start to argue.

"What happened to the dress I got you?" he asked. To which Irene replied, "I like this one. It's better suited for riding."

"Fine. So tell me again where you found my rifle."

"I already told you. On the trail."

"What were you doing behind me?"

"Who said I was?"

"I do."

"Okay, so maybe I was on my way back to camp."

"That still doesn't explain how you managed to catch the horses Faith lost."

"They're Cheyenne. They came right to me. Probably recognized me."

"Who else is supposed to recognize you?" Connell demanded. "And who knocked me off my horse? Was it you?"

"Don't be ridiculous," Irene said flatly. "Rojo stumbled and you fell, that's all."

"And my rifle? Did it fall, too?"

"I suppose so."

"Then maybe you'd like to explain how you managed to locate it? Faith and I looked all over. It wasn't anywhere near the place where she found me. Am I supposed to believe some stray coyote dragged it off like a dog with a bone?"

"How should I know? Maybe you were groggy and wandered around after you were hurt. Maybe, maybe…"

Faith couldn't quite hear the rest of Irene's excuse. She didn't have to. It had been plain for some time that the other woman wasn't being totally forthcoming. What that might mean, however, was yet to be seen. Living as a captive had left poor Irene as wary as a rabbit in a snare, which could mean she was merely being cautious and circumspect out of habit, not necessarily dishonest by choice.

If I could talk to her alone, woman to woman, maybe I could get closer to the truth, Faith reasoned.

Given their current traveling arrangements, however, she

couldn't imagine an opportunity to do that until after they'd arrived at Beal's Bar, and by that time, it might be unnecessary. By then, Connell might have spirited his bride away to their new life, negating any reasonable cause for concern.

But I'll still care about him, Faith told herself. *No matter where he goes or what he does, I'll care for the rest of my life.*

Nothing in the newspapers back home in Ohio or in her father's few letters had prepared Faith for the perilous final approach to the mining camp. Beal's Bar lay at the bottom of a barely accessible canyon. If she hadn't been aboard Ben and trusted his sure-footed gait she doubted she'd have had the nerve to attempt the steep, narrow trail. Yes, she trusted in God's protection—but she also knew it was wrong to test Him by behaving foolishly when she knew better.

Connell led the way, entering the trail after a brief conversation with a scruffy miner who had just come up from the valley. Trembling, Faith was glad she was last in line during the descent. Showing fear was unfitting, especially since neither of the others seemed at all nervous.

As they neared the river at the end of their precarious trek, Faith relaxed enough to appreciate the beauty of the sparkling water that snaked through the gorge. It rippled over and around rocks in a random pattern that made it look like quicksilver seeking a path through scattered mountains of glistening gravel.

In the midst of it all, atop a rough rise that looked low and insignificant enough to be inundated at any moment, lay the makeshift buildings of Beal's Bar. There were tents, wooden structures, and various cobbled-up combinations of both. The largest edifice was almost completely canvas-covered, roof and all. Someone had painted "Majestic Hotel" across the front, an arguable conclusion if she'd ever seen one.

Wide-eyed, Faith scanned the motley group of men that had begun to gather at their approach. Most of the miners were dressed similarly in flannel shirts, pantaloons with the legs tucked into boots, and black felt hats with wide brims that shaded the only parts of their faces that weren't covered in whiskers.

Where shade and beards left off, dirt took over. Considering that the town was situated practically in a riverbed, their lack of attention to personal hygiene seemed strange to her until she peered into some of their eyes. In spite of all the shouted greetings, whistles and grins, she recognized the same hopelessness she'd felt while crossing the desert. If this was truly the land of milk and honey, someone had failed to convince these poor folks.

Connell stopped his horse and waited for her to ride parallel before he said, "Stay close. Most miners aren't used to having decent women in camp. I'm not sure how rowdy they'll get."

"Nonsense." Faith rested her hand on the butt of the Colt. "I can take care of myself. All I intend to do is ask directions."

"All right. You and Irene wait here while I go make some discreet inquiries."

Before Faith could object, he dismounted and strode through the crowd into the makeshift hotel. Not about to take orders when her own father was involved, she started to follow, then thought better of it. There were other mules around but none as big and impressive as her Ben. It wasn't wise to leave him unattended.

Instead, she spoke to the nearest miner, a bearded derelict in tattered clothing whose skin was as weathered as the cracked leather of his boots.

"Excuse me, sir, we're looking for Mr. Emory Beal," Faith said. "Do you know where I might find him?"

"Mebbe." He spit into the dirt. "What's it worth to ya, pretty lady? A little dance, mebbe?"

She drew herself up, back straight, chin jutting proudly. "I'm certain Mr. Beal will reward you for your information if he feels remuneration is called for."

"Re—what?" The man guffawed. "Well, aren't you a puffed-up little prairie chicken. All right. If'n you're not interested in staying in town and keepin' us company, how's about her? She ain't bad lookin'—fer an Injun."

A quick glance at Irene told Faith her companion was thinking about eliminating that miner's need for future haircuts. Permanently.

"I'd mind my manners if I were you, sir," she warned, smiling slightly. "My Cheyenne friend has a short temper. Now, are you going to give us directions or not?"

He spit again, pointing. "It's that way. The cabin on the rise at the end of this here trail. But ol' Emory can't give ya what me and some o' these other boys can, lady. My claim's rich. Beal's diggin's played out months ago. I hear he's nigh busted. Wouldn't surprise me to see him hightailing it up to the Feather to try his luck there, if he ain't left already."

Others in the crowd were nodding agreement. Faith looked to Irene, then at the hotel door, then back to Irene. "I don't see any reason to sit here and stew, do you?"

"None. If we can find the cabin, so can he."

"Right. Then let's go."

Wheeling Ben, Faith led the way up the canyon in search of the father she hadn't seen in well over a year.

Chapter Twenty-Two

Connell dashed out of the so-called hotel in time to see Faith and Irene riding off without him. He cursed under his breath. If it wasn't one of them causing him grief, it was the other. And now both. No telling what they'd said or done while he was inside. Probably given the whole situation away, he thought, disgusted.

He'd left them so he could quietly inquire about the overall circumstances in town, including whether or not anyone had seen Faith's fool sister. Thankfully, nobody had, which was the first good news Connell had heard in some time. Next stop was the Beal cabin.

He swung onto the Indian pony, grabbed Rojo's lead rope and rode off amid jeers, laughing and calls of "Lose something, mister?" and "Hey! Where's your women?"

The long, narrow valley left few choices of travel. Connell knew approximately where the Beal cabin lay, thanks to the bartender in the hotel. Judging by the direction Faith and Irene had headed, they'd found out, too. All he needed to do was follow them, the quicker the better, and hope he got there before they made any more stupid moves. If Emory Beal was half as impulsive as his eldest daughter, he was liable to grab a shotgun, blow a hole in Tucker without considering the consequences, and hang for murder instead of the other way around. That was not the kind of retribution Connell had in mind.

Emory was coming out of the one-room cabin as Faith and Irene rode up. Hardly able to contain her excitement, Faith grinned, waiting for him to realize who she was. Seconds ticked by. Emory was apparently so concerned about the presence of an Indian woman he wasn't paying heed to anything else, including the once-familiar mule.

Little wonder he didn't know her, Faith decided, fidgeting. Her face was half-hidden by the brim of her borrowed hat and although she was wearing a calico dress, she'd had no boots or shoes so she'd kept the moccasins the Cheyenne had given her. Besides, unless her sad letter had reached him, Emory thought she and Charity were still back in Ohio—with Mama.

Sobering, Faith slid to the ground beside Ben and threw the reins over his head. When she said, "Papa!" there was such pathos in her voice, her father's jaw dropped.

He stepped forward. "Faith?"

"Yes, Papa!" She flung herself into his arms, clinging like the child she once was.

He was weeping with her. Faith leaned away to wipe her cheeks. "You didn't get my letter?"

"There's been no mail from home for months." He looked past his daughter to the other rider. "Who's that? And where's Mama and your sister?"

"It's a long story, Papa," Faith said. She kept an arm around him as she turned toward the cabin door. "I think we'd better go inside to talk."

He resisted, staring at her with evident dread. "No. Tell me right now. Where's your mama?"

Pausing, Faith took a deep breath and prayed silently for strength, for the right words. There was no way to soften the blow. Nor was there any way for her to escape being the messenger of tragedy.

"Mama's gone to Glory," she said simply. "There was a tornado. The whole house collapsed. There's nothing you could have done, even if you'd been there."

She watched as his shock and disbelief were replaced with soul-deep sadness. Anger would come later. It had for her. And then she'd finally stopped blaming God and had moved on with her life, just as Connell had after his own losses.

Pulled back into the present by thoughts of the plainsman, she glanced down the slope and saw him approaching, tall in the saddle, leading his prize canelo because of its injury.

"The Good Lord has watched out for me," Faith told her father. She pointed. "That's Connell McClain. We owe him my life."

"Charity, too?"

"I pray so," Faith said.

She waited while Connell and Irene dismounted, then made formal introductions. Emory didn't question the way Irene was dressed or hesitate to greet the rough plainsman, yet he did seem befuddled, in a fog. Faith kept hold of his thin arm while he showed everyone to the corral at the rear of his cabin. As soon as they saw to the needs of Ben and the horses, he invited the party into his home, made them welcome and offered to share a meal while he listened in awe to their tales of the harrowing journey.

Hearing her own words, Faith was struck anew by the awesomeness of her deliverance. It was getting a lot easier to see how God had worked for her good than it had been at the time she was going through the trials. How simple life would be if only she knew exactly what her heavenly Father wanted her to do next.

By the time Faith had finished telling her story and had shared her candid opinion of Charity's dilemma, all she wanted to do was bury her head in a soft pillow and sleep for days. She also wanted to give her father a chance to be alone with his grief, yet she knew there was no time for either. Her sister might arrive any day. There were preparations to make. Plans to agree upon.

"Ramsey Tucker wants your gold, Papa," she said. "The men in town told me your claim's played out. Is that true?"

Emory nodded slowly. "Yes."

"Then what are we going to do?"

"I'd give everything I have to see you and your sister safe and well and happy," he answered. "But since I have nothing of value to offer, we'll just have to make Charity's husband understand."

"It's not that simple," Faith explained. "Tucker doesn't take kindly to bad news. He probably won't believe you're penniless no matter what we tell him."

"I'm not. Not exactly," he said. "I'd saved out a few nice nuggets to show your mama." Eyes misty, he went to a tin sitting in plain sight on a shelf beside his bed, opened it and removed a yellowed white handkerchief.

He handed the small bundle to Faith. "They're yours, now, Faith. Yours and Charity's. I never want to see another fleck of color. Never. It's all been for nothing."

"Oh, Papa, don't say that. You did what you thought was right. I know you wanted to make a better life for all of us. That's not wrong. It just didn't work out the way you'd expected. Mama knew you loved us. That's why she made me promise to come west and find you."

"It's a wonder you did. Many's the man who disappears for good in the diggin's," Emory said, sighing.

Irene had been silent during most of the conversation. Now, she spoke up. "Where Tucker is concerned, it's mostly his women who are never heard from again. How can you all just sit there, talking about that man as if he were less than evil?"

"It's not like that." Faith sought to placate her. "We have to prove his character to Charity as well as make him pay for his crimes." She scowled a warning at Irene. "And I don't mean take the law into our own hands."

"Why not? The minute Ramsey Tucker sees you and me he's going to know his evil doings have been exposed. Then what? We can't let him walk away with your sister, even if she won't believe us. She's a witness. Once she puts two and two together, she'll be in terrible danger."

Holding the handkerchief containing the gold nuggets, Faith fingered their hardness through the fabric. "Maybe we could trade?" A smile lifted the corners of her mouth. "Suppose Papa offered to trade Tucker his valuable mining claim in exchange for his daughter's freedom? We all know he'd accept. And that would certainly show Charity her husband's true colors, wouldn't it?"

Connell laughed. "It sure would. I like the way your mind works, Little Dove Woman."

"And then what?" Irene demanded.

Faith had a ready answer for that question, too. The whole plan was suddenly coming together brilliantly in spite of her weariness. "Papa can keep our presence secret while he deals with Tucker. Nobody in town knows who we are so we'll be safe enough. I don't think the Good Lord will mind a temporary falsehood in order to right a wrong."

"You? Lie?" Connell chuckled. "It's okay with me, if you think your conscience can stand it."

"I'll live," Faith retorted cynically. "While we get things ready here, you backtrack up the canyon and see if you can spot Tucker coming so we won't get caught unawares."

"I might be persuaded to do that for you." Connell glanced at Irene. "If my future bride doesn't mind waiting a bit to see her new home."

His innocent words tore into Faith's heart and left it bleeding, empty. She averted her gaze rather than chance seeing anyone's unspoken query into the reason for her pain. She thought she'd die when her father said, "You know, there's a traveling preacher due here in a few days. He could marry you. We might even be able to come up with a regular dress for the lady from the Kentucky gal down at the Majestic. I know I've seen her wear a pretty one."

Faith wanted to scream. To wail. To jump to her feet and confess her love for Connell in spite of Irene's presence. She opened her mouth, but all that came out was a croak any frog would have been proud of.

Irene, however, had no trouble stating firmly, "No."

"No?" Connell looked puzzled.

"No." Standing proud, Irene addressed everyone, Faith included. "You all seem to forget. I'm already married to Ramsey Tucker. Until that problem is resolved, one way or another, I'm not free to marry anyone else."

Faith breathed a relieved sigh. In all her mental ramblings regarding Irene and Connell, she'd never once thought of the problem that Irene's marriage to Tucker was still binding. He didn't think of it that way, of course, because he believed Irene was dead. They all knew better. And the proof was standing right there in front of her, very much alive.

Truth dawned. She gasped. "That's right! Charity *can't* be legally married to him. Isn't that wonderful?"

"For you, maybe," Connell said flatly. "But it sure puts a serious crimp in my future plans."

Faith watched her father closely for the next several weeks. Some days he seemed almost normal. Other times, no matter how he tried to hide it, she could tell he was dismally unhappy. She understood how he felt. Every time she thought of Connell she experienced a jolt of awareness, a sense of abiding love that warmed her all the way to her soul. Those blissful thoughts were always spoiled by an imaginary picture of him standing beside Irene, reciting wedding vows.

Except for an occasional foray out to check on Ben and the horses, Faith had kept to the cabin. Her father had explained to his friends that his wife's cousin and her traveling companion were visiting and no one had doubted the story. In the Territories and those few states west of the Mississippi, men didn't ask questions, nor did they welcome being queried about their own past lives. It was a place to start again. To take a new name, if necessary, and leave behind the failures of the past.

Seated by the small stove in one corner of the room, lost in thought, Faith was suddenly overcome by the realization that nothing could ever be as she remembered it. In a vague way she'd sensed that truth when she'd first set eyes on her father and his simple cabin. It wasn't only that their family home in Ohio had been leveled by disaster, it was knowing that none of them could go back to the kind of life they'd once shared.

They'd all changed. Grown. Faith especially. She'd been forced into taking charge and as a result had found a fortitude within herself she'd never dreamed existed. The carefree child she'd been such a short time ago was merely a fond, distant memory.

And now?

Faith sighed. Her duty, once all was said and done, was to her father, just as Irene's had been when she'd chosen to take responsibility for her elderly parents rather than marry Connell and accompany him to the wilderness. Funny how history repeated itself, wasn't it?

The sound of an approaching horse and Ben's answering bray drew her from her reverie. She jumped to her feet to greet Connell with a grin as he burst through the door.

"They're coming!" he shouted. "About ten minutes out. Is everything set?"

"Yes." Faith hurried to the tin box. "I have the nuggets right here. Papa's been spreading the word he's made another big strike. We're as ready as we'll ever be."

"Good." Connell scanned the room. "Where's Irene? Is she okay?"

"She's fine. She's gone down to the river with my father. He's showing her how to find gold with a Long Tom." *And I'm fine, too, thanks. Real tickled to see you,* Faith added, deriding herself for being so excited that Connell was finally back in Beal's Bar.

"Well, don't just stand there. Let's go. We have to warn the others and plant those nuggets."

"Right." Faith followed him out the door. "I'll go saddle Ben."

"There's no time for that," Connell said. "Take my hand. We'll ride double."

"You're sure Rojo is well enough to carry the extra weight?"

Chuckling, the plainsman grabbed her arm and swung her up behind him in one fluid motion. "Don't worry. He's all healed up. Hardly even a scar. Besides, even a lame horse wouldn't feel the little bit you weigh."

"I'm so glad he's okay."

"Me, too. In case I didn't remember to thank you, we owe you a lot for coming to our rescue."

"You didn't remember," Faith said, adjusting her skirt as best she could while the horse pranced and shifted beneath her. "But you're quite welcome."

"Good."

He wheeled the big gelding, pointed his nose down the slope toward the river, and kicked him into action.

Straddling the apron of the saddle behind him, Faith knew if she was to keep her seat she had no choice but to wrap both arms around Connell and hang on for dear life. She couldn't help smiling. There was nothing like necessity to overcome inhibitions, was there?

All her good intentions, all her promises of self-control, fled the moment she touched him. Arms around his waist, Faith pressed herself against him, held tight and closed her eyes.

Their trip was over in moments, but she nevertheless thanked the Lord for giving her that one last chance to be so near the plainsman, to innocently lay her cheek against his warm, broad back and dream of what could never be.

Moving quickly in spite of her whirling emotions, Faith dismounted, helped Emory place the nuggets in the narrow, wooden race of the Long Tom, then stood back. By shading her eyes with her hand, she was able to watch Charity and her villainous husband descending the steep trail toward the river.

"They'll be here soon. Time for the rest of us to hide," Faith said, giving her father a peck on the cheek. "Will you be okay, Papa?"

Emory nodded. He hadn't taken his eyes off the nuggets

since they'd laid them in the shallow, sandy water. His white-knuckled grip on the lever that kept the sluice from rocking gave Faith pause. Though he'd claimed gold had no effect on him anymore, clearly he was deluding himself. Then again, those few nuggets were the only bait they had for their trap. Losing them would be catastrophic.

"Remember, Papa, Charity thinks I'm dead," Faith reminded him. "You can't let on otherwise until Tucker has made his move or we'll lose our advantage."

Emory agreed. "When she finds out you're alive she'll be so happy I know she'll forgive us for holding back. A few more hours and we can tell her everything."

"I hope it's that quick."

Connell tapped her arm to get her attention. "It'll be even quicker if you and Irene don't skedaddle. Take Rojo and hide him behind the cabin with Ben. I'll stay close to your father, just in case." He eyed Emory's fisted hand. "The way he's shaking, it'll be a wonder if he lasts long enough to convince Tucker he's found the mother lode."

Faith couldn't argue with that. Emory's complexion had grown so ashen she'd been thinking the same thing. "All right. Since you've shaved your beard off he may not recognize you anyway, especially without your horse."

"True." Drawing his fingers slowly over his jaw, Connell smiled at her. "I wondered when you were going to notice the change in me. Were you surprised?"

Surprised? More like thrilled, Faith thought. The urge to caress his bare cheek had been so strong the first time she'd seen his handsome face sans whiskers, she'd barely managed to control her desire. Only the presence of Irene had stopped her from making a fool of herself.

"You'll do," Faith said, trying to sound uninterested. She'd have been convinced she'd succeeded in misleading him if Connell's roaring laughter hadn't continued to echo up the valley from the sandbar long after she and Irene had reached the cabin.

Chapter Twenty-Three

Real windows were a luxury few dwellings in Beal's Bar enjoyed. The two-story Majestic Hotel had three genuine glass panes which, according to Emory, had been packed in from Marysville at the exorbitant cost of forty cents a pound!

Emory's cabin had one small window in the front, beside the door, which was covered with thin cotton cloth in the summer and blanketed securely come winter. It was easy for Faith and Irene to stay out of sight by simply remaining with the horses and Ben. Conversation inside the cabin echoed up the stovepipe like a megaphone, much to Faith's surprise and delight.

The sound of her sister's voice brought tears of relief to her eyes. Charity had survived! And she was mere feet away, on the other side of the wall. Unfortunately, so was Ramsey Tucker.

"My wife and I thank you for your hospitality," Tucker said. "I'm glad to see you're doing so well. Naturally, since her poor sister met with such a sad end, Charity has been beside herself."

"Of course." There was a choked sound to Emory's voice. Faith hoped Tucker would assume the telltale emotion was due to something other than perfidy.

"Charity was never strong like her sister," Emory said. "I can see she's in need of nursing to get her strength back."

Faith heard the younger woman begin to sob inconsolably. She chanced a peek inside by lifting a lower corner of the fabric-covered window opening and saw Charity in their father's tender embrace, her pale blond curls a stark contrast against his dark vest. Ramsey Tucker stood back, his lips curled in a sneer, watching the family tableau unfold.

"If you'll make me a partner in your mine I might consider letting her stay here with you—until she's well, I mean," Tucker said smoothly.

With an arm around her shoulders, Emory gently led his younger daughter aside before he asked, "Would you like that, Charity? Would you like to stay with your papa?"

Nodding, she burst into another wave of loud weeping.

As her father turned back to the wagon boss, Faith saw fire in his gaze. *Not yet, Papa,* she thought, praying he'd be able to hold his tongue and control his temper. *Wait till we finish carrying out our plan.*

As if in answer to her thoughts, Emory schooled his features. "I haven't been well, myself," he said. "It's dark and dank down here in this narrow valley and winter's coming. I need to recuperate where the sun shines and there's no more cold water soaking my boots. There are times, standing in that icy creek all day long, when my bones ache and I think my poor feet have frozen clean off." He smiled slightly. "I wonder…no, never mind. It's silly."

Tucker rose to the bait. "What?"

"It was just an old man's folly," Emory said. "For a minute there I thought of asking you to take over the mine for me while Charity and I moved to Sacramento City."

"You going to make me a partner, like I asked?"

"No. That wouldn't be fair to you, doing all the hard work

while I sat back and got rich." He reached into his vest pocket and withdrew the handkerchief in which he'd wrapped his supposed new find, then handed it to Tucker. "You saw me take these out of the Long Tom when you rode up so you know my claim is a good one. Would you be interested in purchasing the mine?"

"The whole thing? No partners?"

As planned, Emory vacillated. "On second thought, I don't know. I've worked awfully hard here." He looked to his red-eyed, travel-weary daughter. "And I wouldn't want to come between you and your wife."

With that, Charity began to howl like a coyote caught in the steel jaws of a fur trapper's snare.

Tucker guffawed. "Me and the wife aren't gettin' along that well, as you can see. I only married her so she could stay with the train after she was left alone. You want her back, old man, she's yours. I give her to ya. Consider it payment for your claim."

Emory snorted and shook his head. "Nice try, mister, but as much as I love my girl she's not payment enough for a claim as rich as mine." He named an exorbitant price.

"I'll give you half that and not a penny more," Tucker said flatly. Faith held her breath. Behind her, she heard Irene's sharp intake of breath. It was almost over.

"I'll think on it," Emory said. "You got that much money with you?"

"I can get it."

"Sorry. We can't wait for you to ride all the way to a bank and I won't take scrip," Emory said. "Winter's comin'. Pretty soon the trail up the pass will be too icy for horse or mule. Guess we'll just have to leave my claim for the winter and hope it's okay till spring."

Muttering a curse, Ramsey Tucker said, "Wait here, old

man. I'll be right back with your money." He started for the door, then paused and wheeled around, hands balled into fists. "And shut up that squawlin' woman, will ya, or I'll shut her up myself."

Outside, Faith sensed her mule's unrest and calmed him with a hand on his neck. She stroked his velvety nose. "Easy, Ben. Easy. He's not coming after you. I won't let him hurt you ever again. I promise."

Irene was ministering to the canelo, as well. Faith smiled. Any woman who'd make the effort to soothe a helpless animal was okay with her, even if she was a rival for Connell's affection. Given some of the other choices the plainsman could have made in his travels, Irene would make a fine wife. She was probably a lot like Little Rabbit Woman, his late Arapaho mate, which was all the more reason to be happy for him.

Faith made a wry face. Think it often enough and she just might start to believe it. Eventually.

Emory sat Charity in his only real chair, a rocker where he'd whiled away many an hour of loneliness, and patted her hand. "Stay right here, girl. And stop crying. Your daddy's fixin' to make everything up to you. But you've got to trust me, you hear?"

She nodded. "I'm so sorry."

"Nothin' to be sorry for." Having no handkerchief, he handed her the corner of her apron. "Dry your eyes and watch. You're about to see a comeuppance the likes of which you've never dreamed."

"But Papa—"

"Hush." He straightened, shielding her with his body as Ramsey Tucker returned carrying a small poke.

He slammed it on the table with a vengeance. "There. It's gold coin. Count it if you want."

"There's no need. I trust you," Emory said.

"Good. Then I'll be having the deed to all this, including your claim. Put it in writing. You may be the trusting sort, but I'm not."

"We should both sign," Emory said. "So there's no misunderstanding."

"Fine with me. I can read, so no trickery."

"You're buying my cabin and my diggings, is that correct?"

"And all your tools. Be sure to spell it out. I don't want any questions after you leave."

"Of course." Emory took out the stub of a pencil and wet it with his lips while he opened a small notebook. "Let's see now, the date is around October twenty-ninth, I think. That's close, anyway. We just heard California became a state, so I know for sure it's late October."

"Fine, fine. Get on with it."

Emory's hand was shaking. He finished writing, tore the paper from the book and handed it to Tucker. "That look right to you?"

Tucker read it and shoved it back at him. "Sign."

"You, too. Here. I made a copy."

"All right, all right. Whatever you say." Grinning, he signed and immediately spit on the dirt floor. "Since this is my house now, take your useless daughter and get out."

"In a minute," Emory said. "First, there's some folks I'd like you to meet."

"I got no truck with any of your friends. Gather up your clothes and skedaddle."

Passing the table, Emory pocketed the poke Tucker had given him, took Charity's hand and led her to the door. When he opened it, Connell was waiting.

Tucker gaped. "What in blazes…?"

"I believe you already know Mr. McClain," Emory said.

Connell entered, glaring at Tucker, then stepped back to clear a path for the women.

Faith was first. She came into the room, head lowered, her hat brim shading her face and hiding her features. When she raised her eyes and looked straight at the wagon boss, there was vindication and triumph in her expression.

Before she could speak, however, her sister gave a high-pitched shriek and fainted dead away. If Connell hadn't been expecting such a reaction and stationed himself close by, she'd have hit the floor. As it was, he managed to catch her before any damage was done.

He looked to Faith with a grin. "I seem to be good at keeping the Beal women from keeling over, don't I?"

"That, you do."

Tucker had recovered his self-control enough to say, "She's no Beal, she's a Tucker, like it or not."

"Oh, I don't know about that," Faith drawled. "It seems to me you have one too many wives, Captain."

On cue, Irene stepped through the door. There was no smile on her face. Her spine was stiff, her gait halting. Hate sizzled in her dark eyes.

The astonished look on Tucker's face was so comical Faith had to giggle. "That's right," she said. "Your dear wife, Irene, is alive and well. Isn't that wonderful? You know what that means? It means my sister can't possibly be your legal wife. You were still married when you forced her to wed, you, you…"

Words failed her. She'd expected Tucker to show some redeeming emotion: remorse, fear, maybe even relief at seeing that another of his wives had survived. Instead, he began to grin maliciously.

"You can't prove a thing," he boasted. "I don't care what

that crazy woman says. Every man in the company knew Indians took her, just like they took you. If she survived, so be it. I was never legally married to her, either. I have a wife waiting for me back in Missouri, the stupid cow. Now, all of you, get out of my house!"

Faith wanted to pummel him with her fists, to wipe the smug grin off his ugly face. Judging by the look Irene was still giving him, she wanted to do much worse.

That was all it took to convince Faith that a strategic retreat was in order. Taking the older woman's arm, she tried to urge her toward the door.

Irene balked. Faith felt the muscles of her arm bunch beneath her touch just before she jerked free.

A knife blade flashed.

Faith wasn't braced well enough to stop Irene's attack. The woman raised the knife over her head, gave a guttural scream and lunged at Tucker.

Though he defended himself, a red slash appeared on his cheek. Blood trickled down his face. With a howl he flung himself at Irene and they landed in a heap on the hard-packed dirt floor, barely missing the small table.

Tucker had one meaty fist clamped on her wrist, stilling the knife. With the other he began to batter her mercilessly.

In two strides Connell was beside them. He passed the unconscious Charity to Emory.

Everyone was shouting, Faith the loudest. She leaped atop Tucker, hoping to slow his assault on Irene.

She might as well have been a flea on a dog's back for all the attention he paid her. Nevertheless, she resisted when Connell tried to pull her off.

"Get out of the way," he ordered.

It took several seconds for his command to register with Faith. In those moments, a cut opened on Irene's temple.

Frantic, Faith filled her fist with the wagon boss's hair and yanked. Irene was like family. She couldn't step back and let him do her any more damage.

Gripping Faith around the waist, Connell lifted her, kicking and screeching, off the pile of struggling humanity. He grabbed the captain's shirt collar and jerked him away from Irene, who scrambled to the side, stunned.

Faith hurried to her, steadying her and keeping her from rejoining the fray. Clearly she was in no condition to continue her fight. Tucker was twice her weight and mean as a rattler. Enraged, there was no telling what he might do.

Obviously concerned for Charity, Emory had carried her out the door. Faith tugged Irene and followed. They stumbled around to the rear of the cabin where Emory placed Charity on the ground by the corral.

"What about Connell?" Faith shouted.

"I'm going back to fetch my Colt and help him," her father answered. "You stay here."

"No. I'm going with you!"

Before her father could argue, Ramsey Tucker appeared, armed with a pickax. Empty-handed, Faith placed herself between him and the other women, praying Connell was hot on his trail.

Her breath caught. Her heart sped. Where was Connell? Could he be hurt? Maybe even mortally wounded? That thought tore her apart, made her knees weak and her head swim.

Fighting to maintain an air of defiance and fortitude, she prayed silently, fervently, for deliverance. After all they had been through together, was their quest going to end like this, with their entire party slaughtered by the madman they had vowed to destroy? It was unthinkable!

Suddenly, the tall, robust figure of a stranger appeared. He was clad in deerskin breeches and naked to the waist. In one hand he carried a lance. In the other was a shield decorated with eagle feathers and familiar images. Faith couldn't decide who frightened her more—Tucker or the Cheyenne brave.

Irene pushed past. She threw herself at the Cheyenne, shielding him. The arm he encircled her with was striped with wounds in a geometric pattern that could only have been self-inflicted. Faith had seen similar scars while in the Indian camp but never the fresh wounds of the blood sacrifice.

Her heart broke for the couple. It didn't take a genius to deduce that this must be Red Deer, Irene's betrothed. Had he followed them all the way to California? He must have. No wonder Faith had kept sensing an unseen menace! All those times Irene had disappeared into the night finally made sense.

Confusion in Tucker's expression gave Faith hope. While he was distracted, perhaps someone could disarm him. But who? Why didn't one of the men act? Connell would have.

Her glance darted to the now silent cabin. For all she knew, dear Connell could be lying dead inside, a victim of Tucker's malice. Her heart wrenched with actual physical pain.

No one moved. Red Deer seemed content to shield Irene. Emory was in place to defend Charity. That left only Faith.

She lowered her head like a billy goat and plowed into Tucker, blindsiding him and hoping against hope that her efforts would be enough to snap the others out of their apparent stupor and bring them to her aid.

The attack caused Tucker to drop his weapon. It also staggered Faith. Reeling, she fell back, barely cognizant of her vulnerable position.

With a guttural roar he went for her. Backing away, she tripped. When he lunged, she rolled beneath the rails of the corral where Ben and the horses were shuffling nervously.

Tucker followed without hesitation.

Screeching for help, Faith tried to regain her feet but her skirt tangled around her legs and she floundered in the dust. Eyes wide, she saw stout hooves stomping the ground beside her, barely missing her head.

In a heartbeat, Tucker was towering over her. Though he was now weaponless, his grimace declared his deadly plans more clearly than any words.

Helpless, Faith closed her eyes and raised her arms to shield her face. She was beyond prayer, beyond hope.

Above her, Ben snorted. Just when she thought the mule might come to her aid he wheeled, apparently fleeing. Tears stung Faith's eyes. Her heart broke. Even Ben, her staunchest ally, was forsaking her in the face of the captain's wrath.

Time stood still. Tucker loomed. Irene screamed something in an unknown tongue.

Faith peeked between her folded arms. An animal snorted. Hooves flew above her. Ben! He hadn't deserted the fight. He'd simply turned to aim his kick!

The force of the mule's hooves lifted Ramsey Tucker off the ground and sent him flying into the rough-cut rails of the corral. He hit with a crack that sounded as if the wood had split. His back and neck arched unnaturally.

Faith rolled out of the way as Ben charged. His lip was curled, his teeth bared, his long ears laid back against his lowered head.

As Tucker made his final slide to the ground, the mule bowed his neck, stiffened his legs and came down on the body with both front feet. Hard.

Faith could tell that the last assault was unnecessary. Tucker had died the moment his back had snapped. It was over.

She struggled to her feet just as Connell rounded the corner of the cabin. A more blessed sight Faith had never seen.

Though he was holding his side and walking unsteadily, he was alive. That was enough for her.

She glanced at Irene and Red Deer. Their decision was plain. They were a couple. There was no question about it.

Connell saw it, too. Nodding, he passed them by and went straight to Faith. "Are you all right?"

She caressed his cheek and nodded. "Yes. You?"

"I've been better," he said. "I saw what happened. Guess old Ben finally got even for all the abuse."

"Yes." Soberly, Faith considered her loyal mule. "They remember cruelty, sometimes for years. Ben was always gentle with me but the captain was a different story. I know it's not a very Christian attitude, but I think he got exactly what he deserved."

"They say the Lord works in mysterious ways."

Agreeing, Faith glanced at Irene. Red Deer had assumed a defensive stance, clearly ready to do battle for his chosen wife if need be.

Connell shook his head and managed a smile. "She's all yours," he said. "I release her from her promise to marry me."

Irene evidently translated, because as soon as she'd finished speaking the Cheyenne eased his stiff posture.

"Where will they go," Faith asked Connell. "She can't go back to Black Kettle, can she?"

"No, but the Arapaho will take her in again because she once belonged to them. Even if she were Cheyenne they'd go to live with her mother's tribe instead of staying with Black Kettle's band."

"So, Red Deer will be safe, too?"

"Yes." Connell chuckled. "I owe him for one of the knots on my head but I'll forgive him—as a wedding present to Irene."

"He is the one who was following us, who knocked you off Rojo, isn't he?"

"I'm sure of it."

"You're not angry?" Faith remained close to him, sighing when he slipped his arm around her waist.

"How can I be?" Connell said softly. "He brought you and me together and solved Irene's problems, too. What more could I ask?"

Faith gazed up at him. "Together? Us?"

"If you'll have me," Connell said. "The Sacramento Valley is lush and rich, good for cattle and farming. And I'll build you a new house if you don't like the one I already have."

"What about my family?"

Connell looked to Emory, who was still in the process of reviving Charity. "May I have the honor of marrying your daughter, sir?"

"This one or that one?" Emory jested.

"This one. Definitely this one." Connell gave Faith a light squeeze and winced. "As soon as my ribs heal a bit. Right now, I think I'd better sit down."

Epilogue

The traveling preacher stood in the rear of the Majestic, Bible in hand, while the miners crowded around.

Faith had managed to piece together a presentable frock from some calico Connell had found for her and was radiant. He stood beside her in his buckskins, beaming from ear to ear, while the preacher made them man and wife.

A raucous cheer went up as the ceremony concluded. The prospectors had come from all walks of life, all parts of the country, yet were united in a celebration of joy not often seen in the gold camps.

"I wish Irene could have stayed long enough to be a part of this," Faith told her new husband, "but I understand why she and Red Deer felt they should go. I hope they're as happy as I am."

"I'm sure they are," Connell said. "And so is your sister. We'll be lucky to get her to come to Sacramento City with us after all the attention she's getting from these lonesome miners."

"Papa will see that she behaves herself. He's anxious to leave here as soon as possible. It's a wonder the winter weather has delayed as long as it has."

"I know. Are you packed and ready to travel?"

Faith nodded, her eyes filling with admiration, thankfulness and unshed tears. "Yes. And this time I'm not a bit afraid."

"Because Tucker's dead?"

"No," she said, sliding her hand through the crook of her husband's arm. "Because you're here. I can face anything with you as my guide."

Connell patted her hand and chuckled. "Just as long as you don't confront any more chiefs like Black Kettle and scare me to death, I'll be content."

Faith giggled behind her free hand. "Do you really think I'm a legend?"

"If you aren't already on account of Ab's or Walks With Tree's tall tales, you soon will be," he said with conviction. "By the time Irene—Singing Sun Woman—and Red Deer have told our whole story over and over in the camps it'll be common knowledge that Little Dove Woman is a force to be feared and admired."

"Just so long as my husband feels the same way," she teased, giggling nervously. "I think I'm more afraid of disappointing you than I was of any wild Indian. I just hope I can be…"

"Kiss her!" someone yelled. A chorus of similar suggestions swelled.

Connell smiled as he bent to do as the crowd wanted. An instant before their lips met he whispered, "I believe I've finally figured out how to stop you from talking out of turn."

"Well, it beats a spear in the side," was all Faith managed to say before he silenced her with a kiss.

She slipped her arms around his neck and kissed him back. After all they'd been through, she guessed she could allow him to think he had the upper hand. At least for a little while.

Dear Reader,

I love the history of the American West. My personal library contains many pioneer journals and research books, yet no matter how many times I read them I am always amazed at the fortitude of these hardy souls. Their lives were more amazing than fiction and their faith was often beyond measure. It takes a special kind of person to leave the familiar behind and travel into new and unknown lands. They displayed courage that seems beyond us in this modern world.

They also relied on their Christian faith, deeply and irrevocably, because they had trusted God in many ways for most of their lives and already knew He was faithful. If you find yourself in a situation that seems hopeless, remember these brave souls and do what they did—turn to God with all your heart and He will be there for you.

I love to hear from readers, by e-mail at VAL@ValerieHansen.com or at P.O. Box 13, Glencoe, AR 72539. I'll do my best to answer as soon as I can, and www.ValerieHansen.com will take you to my Internet site.

Blessings,

Valerie Hansen

QUESTIONS FOR DISCUSSION

1. In the 1850s, was it normal for two unmarried sisters to try to cross the plains in a covered wagon without having a man along to help them? Why or why not? How are things different today?

2. Were Faith and Charity wise to join the first wagon train available and trust the wagon boss without asking for references? Would that kind of thing have been feasible or would they have been laughed at?

3. Did you know that not every traveler used oxen to pull a Conestoga wagon? Have you ever thought about how complicated it would be to spend months surviving such a harrowing trip?

4. Plains Indians had widely varied customs, which was a surprise to me when I began researching to write this book. Were you also surprised to hear that the Cheyenne and Arapaho were so different?

5. At this time in history it was common for nearly everyone to profess their Christian faith even if they were nowhere near a church. Now that we have more churches and virtually instant communication, do you think it's a better atmosphere for our faith or not?

6. Connell McClain had promised to marry Irene many years before. Did you admire him for trying to keep that vow or were you surprised that he was so faithful and determined?

7. Life among the Indians was very different from Faith's experiences in Ohio. Did you notice that Indian society was governed by the same kinds of strict laws settlers lived by? Was Faith right in going against those customs while in their camps, or should she have tried harder to keep their rules?

8. The California gold-mining camps were very primitive and life there was hard, yet people kept trying to get rich quickly no matter what sacrifices they had to make. Do you think it was greed that drove them, or were they being realistic? Was it a hope for a better future or a form of gambling with their lives?

9. In the era of this story it was considered morally wrong for Irene to fall in love with the Cheyenne brave. Have things changed in our lifetime?

10. Faith is a strong-willed woman who perseveres no matter what the circumstances. In the end she finds the happiness she's been wanting, while Charity is left emotionally devastated by her terrible marriage to Ramsey Tucker. Do you think there is still hope for Charity in spite of all that has happened?